I Will Find You

By

Tony Drury

City Fiction

ISBN: 978-1-910040-36-2

ALSO BY TONY DRURY

The DCI Sarah Rudd series
Megan's Game
The Deal
Cholesterol
A Flash of Lightning
The Lady Who Turned

The early career of Sarah Rudd
On Scene and Dealing
Journey to the Crown

The Novella Nostalgia Series
Lunch with Harry
Twelve Troubled Jurors
Forever on Thursdays
The Man Who Hated
A Search for The Truth

CHAPTER ONE

The Pyrenees National Park. Thursday: evening

Jack and Gabrielle smiled at each other as they finished their last ever glasses of champagne: the bottle that Jack had taken from the luxury apartment would never be paid for but that did not matter anymore. They had been together for twenty-two years and his wife continued to stir his emotions as, an hour earlier, they had sat together writing letters which they had left in their hotel room. Their marriage, despite expensive medical help, had remained barren but the words Gabrielle had written to her nephew Oliver were beautifully crafted.

They had spent the last two days walking the forested mountains situated between the French and Spanish borders. Their favourite gorge was the Cirque de Gavarine which was said to be nature's version of a cathedral due to the amphitheatre of dark mountainous granite which enclosed the valley. At around a thousand feet was a footbridge swaying in the autumnal evening winds above the Grande Cascade, the highest waterfall in Europe, which was rushing down into the valley where there were isolated chalets, illuminated and curtained, as their residents prepared to rest for the night before starting the next day's ascents.

For Jack and Gabrielle Glover there was to be no tomorrow. They had known before they left England what was going to happen but, as they moved towards the centre of the footbridge, they were fighting the greatest of human emotions: the will to live. The wind was cold and the wooden slats were treacherous, but that did not matter. They closed in together and he held her in his arms, relishing the aroma of her scent and kissing her for one last moment together as she quietly sobbed.

She looked into his eyes and, once again, asked the question but she already knew the answer because they had exhausted every possible avenue to overcome the forces against them. He knew she had to ask as he slowly shook his head from side to side. He smiled for one last time as he gazed at the most beautiful woman he had ever known in his whole life.

They moved towards the safety ropes, climbed over, wrapped their arms around each other and jumped into the abyss below. Almost immediately they were torn apart by the velocity of their fall as his heavier body landed first. Seconds later, Gabrielle splashed into the raging torrent of water, the bones in her body shattering on impact resulting in her instantaneous death.

Jack lingered on for around eight seconds, electrical impulses coursing through his brain, as he vaguely saw the face of a man, a London-based banker, who was the reason that their lives had become pointless.

But the banker, a mega-rich collector of fine art, gold and selected currencies, all safely stored in offshore deposit boxes around the globe, had made an error when he had failed to realise to whom Jack's wife Gabrielle was connected. It was, perhaps, the first serious misjudgement he had made during twenty-three years working in the financial sector of the City of London. He was later to discover the consequences of his mistake in a cave at Archangelos, one of the Dodecanese Islands in the Aegean Sea, where he was to experience indescribable pain.

But for now, back in the waters of the Grande Cascade in the Pyrenees National Park, Jack Glover sensed several final flashes of consciousness which swirled around his exhausted brain, his hand hovering in the water as he searched for his wife. Perhaps, in that final moment of life, he imagined justice being dispensed.

Five Months Later
Delamount Security, Knightsbridge,
West London.
Monday: morning

Ex-Detective Chief Inspector Sarah Rudd started the day by standing under a hot shower, drying herself vigorously, putting arnica oil on her bruised arm, selecting her favourite business outfit and, while sipping Continental coffee, messaging her partner Max, who was alone in his flat several miles away, asking him to give her some space. Their altercation the previous evening, fuelled by a second bottle of wine, was a consequence of Max's belief that he was staying the night and Sarah's sudden change of mood.

Her request to Max was now proving challenging because they were sitting in the meeting room at the offices of Delamount Security where they were both establishing themselves as effective operatives. Sarah was avoiding eye contact but could not miss the hand-written note which read, 'Please Sarah, let's talk', which he slid in front of her. As he looked across, trying to spot signs of a reconciliation, the door opened and the atmosphere immediately changed.

Norman Delamount slammed his papers down on the table. His grey hair seemed greyer and white streaks were beginning to show, adding to the frown on his forehead which resembled the rippling sand in an estuary as the tide goes out. Sarah gasped as she realised that his white shirt was creased.

Despite the late winter chill, the office window was open and the noise of the West London motorway-bound traffic made small talk difficult to hear. Sarah re-read Max's note and suffered a spasm of guilt as she reflected on her perplexing mood swings: she would speak to Max later and in private. Three other staff members present in the meeting remained silent and concentrated on their cups of coffee. Heidi, who was obsessed with cleansing her skin, finished sipping her mug of hot water, stood up and went over to close the window, ignoring the two visitors.

Max realised that Norman Delamount seemed absorbed in reading a file and so he turned his attention to the cold-water aquarium situated to the left of the window but out of range of direct sunlight. The gift, from a client, had been delivered following the successful release of a schoolboy kidnapped in Southeast Asia. Delamount Security had located the hideout and negotiated the payment of the ransom. The international businesswoman, in addition to paying a substantial fee, expressed her gratitude to her friend, Norman, by sending him some Paradise fish from the Korean Peninsula. They would survive provided the room temperature was above ten degrees centigrade.

The company chairman, Norman Delamount, closed the file and looked around the room. The attendees realised that their boss was ready to commence the meeting because he was hammering on the table and causing Heidi's re-filled mug of hot water to spill over her notes. She knew the contents because, as the marketing manager, she had first raised the issue of changing the company name and was fortunate to survive the volcanic reaction from the chairman. Heidi had stood her ground, arranged a secret survey of staff opinion and ensured that a majority agreed that a change of name was desirable: 'Delamount Security' had served its purpose but, with Norman's decision to reduce to a three-day week at the end of the summer, a fresh start was welcomed. Heidi had recruited Sarah and, together, they approached Norman in his office at the end of a working day. Words and phrases such as 'the target market paradox', 'search engine optimisation' and 'global penetration' made little impact on the chairman but 'increased revenue projections', together with several refills of his favourite malt whisky, seemed to strike home. The chairman had long realised the sense of Heidi's proposal but had decided to exact the rewards of female adulation before wilting and agreeing that Heidi should commission professionals to suggest possible rebranding options.

The two members of the marketing agency selected for the purpose, who were now present at the meeting, did not do that: one was blinking rather a lot as the managing partner prepared to address the management team. Sarah's initial impression was positive because the presenter seemed sensitive to the ambiance of the room and she thought his appearance was empathic; she knew that Max thought it was a waste of time and money. Norman's two partners had already decided to go with the flow. Heidi was desperate to know what names the agency was going to suggest.

The surprise answer was just one name – and it

worked! The agency leader referred to the whiteboard with its hidden message and started with a succinct summary of the brief, their research, the rationale and the process. Sarah nodded in recognition of their professionalism as the suggested company name was revealed. All present stared at the classic wording: 'Soteria Cosmic Group'. The logo was designed around the 'S' and the 'C' and the first of the two presenters said that the inevitable development would be into SC Group. The theory was that the full name gave the business a pedigree. The younger agency member overcame her inhibitions and explained that Soteria was a Greek goddess of safety and salvation which gave gender balance and promoted function. The second word, 'Cosmic', was simply because many of their competitors were trying to cash in on the public understanding of 'cyber' as it related to global crime.

Sarah was ticking boxes: she and Heidi responded positively to a suggestion of gender balance. Max eyed Heidi and remained perplexed that a woman who changed the colour of her hair on a weekly basis and went on climate change marches could be so effective in her work. The two Delamount partners wanted to be on a plane flying to their next assignments.

"I have to say that 'Soteria Cosmic Group' works for me," concluded Sarah.

"Cosmic, the cosmos, the universe; cool," agreed Heidi.

The lead partner of the agency repeated the suggestion that after a year or so 'Soteria Cosmic Group' would most likely become SC Group.

"Why not the logo with 'Soteria Cosmic' in words beneath it?" asked Norman.

"Cut the crap. It's SC Group," suggested ex-DCI Max Hemmings.

Everyone who was present in the meeting stared at 'Mad Max', as he had been known during his illustrious police career.

Five minutes later, SC Group was agreed. The planning and promotion would require a month's further commitment by the agency but, for them all, SC Group was born. Sarah looked at the chairman and sensed that something was wrong. After shaking as many hands as possible, the agency personnel left and Norman quickly moved on to review several business matters.

The fee earned from the rescue of the schoolboy was almost the last of the good news stories in recent SC Group business history. The quarter's profits were down and the failure to protect a visiting South American businessman, who had been shot down and wounded in Pall Mall, was seriously embarrassing.

Norman was asked by one of his partners if a review had been carried out of the security arrangements. Max listened carefully as it was suggested that the gunmen seemed to be well informed on where and when the departure from the hotel was to take place. Norman's response discouraged further discussion and the meeting broke up shortly afterwards. He instructed Sarah to follow him into his office.

*

Norman closed the door, slumped down in his desk chair, lifted the telephone receiver to tell his personal assistant, Daisy, that he would not be taking any calls for the next hour. He waved his hand in the air and so Sarah sat down. There were none of the usual courtesies; no coffee and no water.

"Was your man paying attention in the meeting?" he snapped.

"Max is not my man, Norman, and he misses nothing."

"The South American incident was a complete mess," he continued.

"Max was not involved. You make the decisions but he would never have allowed it to happen." She paused. "Max has his faults, Norman, but he's the best security officer I've ever met. The Metropolitan Police was disappointed when he joined Delamount Security – or should I say SC Group?"

"But, of course, you are biased," suggested her boss.

"I'll ignore that cheap shot, Norman." Sarah brushed her hand through her hair. "Let me tell you this: Max once saved my life on the streets of London."

Norman Delamount stood up, picked up a file, went around his desk and sat on a chair opposite his colleague who turned to face him. He was dribbling imperceptibly at the edge of his mouth but there was enough spittle to cause Sarah to blink.

"Have you read the newspaper reports about the bankers' fraud?" he asked.

She hadn't, but she had listened to the radio report of a heart-rending story which made even a battle-hardened former Detective Chief Inspector gasp. She hated the greed of the banks which is why she had always voted for the Labour Party.

"They deserve their forty-seven years in prison,"

she responded. "It's a pity we've given up hanging criminals."

Norman opened the file and handed her a press cutting. It was the story of a couple who had built up a property letting agency, hit cash flow problems and were told by their bank that they must deal with a third-party advisory partnership. They ended up losing everything including their home and, despite cashing in their pensions, they finally ran out of money. They had to catch a bus to the airport because their car had been repossessed but they managed to buy plane tickets using the remaining credit card available to them. After travelling to the Pyrenees National Park, they jumped off a mountain footbridge and committed suicide, together.

Sarah studied the cutting. She recalled the radio report and she stared at the woman.

"She was attractive," she said. "What a waste of two lives! At least the bastard bankers are in prison for a long time."

Norman returned to his desk, went into the file, took out a photograph and handed it to Sarah.

"This is Graham de Lille Rutherford. He managed to avoid the investigations. He was the real ring leader."

"So, where is he?" asked Sarah as she studied the handsome individual.

"He's gone to ground." Norman wiped his eyes. "You said the woman was attractive," he continued.

"Yes," said Sarah. "A rather lovely face." She smiled. "I think there's a bit of you in her, Norman," she observed.

"Her name is Gabrielle," said Norman. "She was my daughter."

He broke down and sank back into his chair. Sarah stood up and locked the door of his office. She went over to his desk and took the phone off its cradle; she handed him a glass of water.

"I had an affair," he said. "Gabrielle was born but I managed to hide her from my family." He sobbed into his handkerchief. "She grew up in London with her mother who died when she was seventeen. We met every so often, sometimes with her husband Jack, who I liked. Last summer we lunched on our own and she told me that she and Jack needed financial help. She didn't say too much but she seemed unusually distracted."

"What did you do?" asked Sarah.

"I gave them three hundred and fifty thousand pounds," he said. "I thought I was doing the right thing by insisting the funds went into their company account. Gabrielle argued with me but I thought that I knew best because I could not take the chance that they might squander the money." He hit the desk with a heavy fist. "I was stupid."

"Did you know the whole story at that time?" said Sarah.

"I should have asked more questions but Gabrielle's pain was destroying me."

"What happened to the money?" she asked.

"My agents have traced almost the whole amount to de Lille's Caribbean bank account."

Sarah looked at his photograph for several intense minutes.

"He looks a charmer," she said.

"They always are," said Norman.

"Where do we go from here?" asked Sarah.

His eyes glistened. He stood up and walked over

to the window of his fourth-floor office overlooking Hyde Park.

"Find him for me, Sarah. Here's my file." He straightened his jacket and picked up the phone to tell Daisy he would now take calls. He started to tidy his desk. "Only you. I only want you to work on this. You can leave your Jack Reacher lookalike here."

Sarah could not help smiling at his suggestion that Max resembled the literary American ex-army mercenary.

"And then what?" she asked.

"Get the evidence we need," he said. "I want to see Graham de Lille Rutherford behind bars and I want to throw away the key."

"Is that a promise, Norman?" asked Sarah. "No nasty remedy?"

"You're right," he said, "and yes, I had thought about it. But we'll play by the rules."

She watched as Norman resumed looking at the photograph of the fraudster. He put it back into the file and handed it over. She tucked it under her arm, quietly unlocked the door and started to leave the office. He called her back and asked her opinion about the rebranding of his security company. Sarah turned and smiled.

"Soteria," she chuckled. "I've always wanted to be a Greek Goddess of salvation."

Norman was standing erect and she noticed that the creases seem to have fallen out of his shirt.

"SC Group is right, Norman, no worries."

She went down the stairs and entered her own room. This was the territory that Sarah Rudd best understood. Her job was to find enough evidence on de Lille Rutherford to allow her former colleagues in the Metropolitan Police to secure a conviction and put him away for a long time.

She read a text message, replied in order to decline Max's offer to take her for lunch, went into the park, sat down to munch a tuna and tomato granary roll and to think about Graham de Lille Rutherford. She reviewed his photograph now embedded in her mind and concentrated on his eyes. As some horse riders trotted past, she looked down at a text message.

'*PLEASE, Sarah. Is it me?!! xxx*'.

"No, Max," she said to herself, "it's not you."

But, for the time being, she could not cope with his ongoing and frustrated passion for her. Her whole focus was on understanding a London-based banker called Graham de Lille Rutherford.

*

Max disappeared for several days to visit his mother in her retirement home, Sarah met up with her daughter Susie when they went to a Zara Larsson concert at Wembley. While Sarah enjoyed the music, she read the programme notes and hoped that the Swedish feminist would not have too great an influence on her daughter. The following Sunday, a visit to a wine bar, a chat and news about Zack, the latest suitor, banished any such thoughts.

Sarah threw herself into researching Graham de Lille Rutherford, starting with his photograph and staring into his eyes. She banished all previous knowledge because it was essential that she began with a clean sheet. By the end of the first week there was a fairly complete fact file containing personal and business information. This was supplemented by press cuttings and the transcript of the trial at the Old Bailey of the three bankers: de Lille was never mentioned but she could smell him behind the steering wheel.

She met a former colleague who was now a Detective Superintendent with the Metropolitan Police. Over coffee and nutritious blueberry muffins, a chance remark was the first occasion on which she became aware of rumours concerning de Lille Rutherford's possible paedophile activities. The shutters came down and Sarah realised that her friend was not willing to divulge any further information, leaving her to secure the evidence she would need to expose that heinous crime. She knew that Norman had the connections to secure a conviction if she could only pull all the pieces together. She realised that her progress was beginning to falter, until, while walking around the park, an idea came into her mind. It proved to be smart thinking and a few days later she had the information she needed. She turned her attention to establishing which of his global hideaways de Lille was using.

Late one night she closed her folder and finished drinking a can of diet fruit juice. She left the office and, on reaching the reception area, nodded to her friend on security duties. As she walked back to her flat in a Kensington side street, she was muttering, "Wherever you are, Mr de Lille Rutherford, we are going to lock you away. You can't hide from us."

Sarah stepped aside to avoid a late-night reveller who was stumbling her way home and who staggered into a garden where she was violently sick. The former police officer followed her and encouraged the troubled woman to remain doubled over as she urged her to clear it all out. She used her scarf to wipe the woman's face clean of vomit and, after a few moments, she led the distressed drinker back to her bedsit.

Parrot Cay, Turks and Caicos Islands.
Saturday: afternoon

Zeander, a resident of the Islands, was semi-naked and slumbering, face down on the sun lounger, as Graham de Lille Rutherford moved the parasol so that her skin was protected from the early afternoon rays and then gave her buttocks a pat. He returned to his seat and sighed as his thoughts moved ahead to when he would be the guest speaker at The Westingham Society, a London-based Conservative think tank named in honour of an economics professor who, in the early twentieth century, wrote at length about wealth creation and distribution. He was barely remembered but his work was used by several modern political strategists. In the post-Brexit period, de Lille realised that the Conservative Party was returning to its 'One Nation' roots.

De Lille was demonstrating one of his strengths: hard work. He had researched the term 'One Nation' and realised that it was, at times, used politically and in the media by individuals who did not really understand the message its creator, the Conservative Prime Minister Benjamin Disraeli, was trying to express. In his second term of office in the late nineteenth century, Disraeli wanted to extend the appeal of his party to working people, so much so that it was nicknamed 'paternalism'.

De Lille recalled his hours of political study but

was distracted as Zeander stirred and turned over, leaving her lover to gasp at her body. He returned to more academic matters and repeated to himself the explanation of 'One Nation' politics: 'The advocating of the preservation of the established institutions and traditional principles within a political democracy with the combining of social and economic programmes to benefit the ordinary person'. He had memorised this statement and spent a week, night after night, writing it down until he knew that if he was ever challenged, he could repeat the words without hesitation.

Zeander rolled off the sun-bed, stood up, allowed the sun to warm her skin and then dived into the swimming pool. De Lille watched her with mesmeric fascination, smiled to himself, lay back and reflected on when he had secured control of The Westingham Society, a move which accelerated his ambition to develop greater political influence.

The chief executive of the society, Martin Balcombe, had tried, several years earlier, when working for Graham de Lille Rutherford as an investment manager at his finance house, to defraud his boss, albeit on a minor scale. Upon the discovery of the offence, de Lille had scared Martin Balcombe witless and then suggested that if he, de Lille, agreed to leave the personnel file detailing the crime in a safe deposit box, he would allow Martin Balcombe to continue working under his 'control'. Both sides saw the sense in this arrangement and, two years later, when the position of chief executive of The Westingham Society think tank became vacant, de Lille used his political connections to secure the job for his 'associate'. Based in prestigious Mayfair premises, it housed a staff of five and held ongoing political events; there were two meeting rooms available to its members.

Martin Balcombe settled in quickly and was soon reporting back to de Lille on political and financial information secretly recorded in the meeting rooms. It was he who gave de Lille the lowdown on a member of the House of Commons who had, allegedly, assaulted a research worker during a weekend conference and was trying to prevent possible adverse publicity. De Lille used the information to contact the MP involved and suggest that he could keep the situation out of the newspapers. In return, he expected regular briefings on the workings of the Committee for Tackling Modern Slavery and People Trafficking on which the flirtatious MP sat. The MP assumed he wanted to know more of what the Chairman –the Prime Minister –was undertaking, but he was way off the mark. De Lille was interested in any security data the committee had on the organised crime groups which could have a possible commercial value. The research worker involved in the original allegation of a sexual assault proved more resolute in pursuing her determination for the politician to be exposed. One night she was knocked off her bike by a speeding truck while cycling across Waterloo Bridge, over the river Thames, and was hospitalised for several months.

Back on the tropical islands, De Lille's thoughts returned to the afternoon heat as he focused on the sight of Zeander, who had now returned to the lounger, sighing aloud and reaching into her bag to find a packet of cigarettes. As she put one to her mouth, she found that Graham had his lighter ready for her as she held his hand steady before blowing smoke into the air. He nodded to the waiter who came over and took the order for a Pina Colada and, for himself, a glass of wine which arrived within minutes. He waved the waiter away and allowed his thoughts to return to London and the personal triumph which lay ahead for Graham de Lille Rutherford in the coming week at The Westingham Society.

He returned to Zeander's contours and watched as she lay back and enjoyed the cigarette in between sipping her cocktail. He sighed and decided he had enough time for more immediate pleasures before the car came to collect him for the start of his journey back to London Heathrow airport. The pilot of his Cessna Citation CJ4 private Jetstream plane had texted him to confirm the departure time booked with the flight authorities.

A Private Office, Curzon Street, Mayfair.
Saturday: 6.00pm

Lord Simon Mallington was one of Graham de Lille Rutherford's most important political contacts. The landowning peer of the realm was sitting at his desk sipping at his brandy and continuing to resist the temptation of the unlit cigar in the ashtray. He was intent on replying carefully to his transatlantic friend.

"De Lille Rutherford is impressing a lot of us," he said, and then he held the receiver away from his ear. "Hold your horses, George," he interrupted, "we are satisfied there is no possible reflection on the Conservative Friends of Washington." He picked up the cigar and, with one hand, lit it, blowing the toxic chemicals into the air as he listened to the American voice speaking rather quickly. He replied with his trademark calm reassurance.

"He seems to be escaping any connection with the banking case. He's shrewd," continued the peer. "The Serious Fraud Office know it's him but they cannot put a finger on his direct involvement." He once again held the earpiece away from his head before returning to their conversation as he put his extinguished cigar in a bowl.

"George," he pleaded, "please slow down." He nodded. "Yes, there's a dividend on its way and I assure you that de Lille always pays." He smiled before changing the discussion. "What are you doing about your President's re-election chances?" he asked, laughing as he listened to the response.

"George. Must go. Yvette and I are going to the Opera tonight. Rossini: Semiramide. The Queen of Babylon kills her husband, chooses her young lover and then gets murdered." He listened to the comments from across the ocean. "To be honest, I go to watch the crumpet." He paused. "De Lille is speaking to our think tank on Wednesday. I'm having it streamed to you." He again listened to the response. "My pleasure, George, and I promise that you'll enjoy it."

He held on to the phone, realising that his transatlantic associate was continuing to talk, as he made his interruption.

"Thank you, George," he said. "I'm pleased you like having him in the CFW."

The call ended and Lord Mallington decided to re-light his cigar. He blew the smoke into the air, picked up the file, made a note of their conversation, re-read the latest confidential report and put it back into his private cabinet under 'd' for Graham de Lille Rutherford. He reflected on the conversation that had just taken place and the way in which the Conservative Friends of Washington was becoming an increasingly significant political asset.

But now it was time for some Rossini magic.

*

It was a dream that was recurring – not every night but, for ex-Detective Chief Inspector Sarah Rudd, too often for comfort.

"*Max! Make me a promise.*"

Sarah was thrashing around in her bed, her nightwear soaked with perspiration.

"*Never leave me. Please, Max.*"

The body of Dr Martin Redding, her intended murderer, had been mangled by a Mercedes truck and there was mayhem at the central London Holborn traffic lights. She was in the arms of former police officer Max Hemmings; he had saved her life with his warning shout and now she was clinging to him and making her request that he never leaves her.

Sarah's eyes opened, she grabbed at a bedside bottle of water, drank rather greedily and then, sitting up, she removed her lingerie and wrapped the bed sheets around her. The recollection of those final moments of danger and the growing closeness between her and Max made her feel a little naughty. She was divorcing her husband, Nick, and her beloved daughter, Susie, who stayed with her in London at weekends, confided that her father had a girlfriend. Sarah's son, Marcus, was focused on his studies and the possibility of advancing his passion for the sport of judo. He never understood why his mother broke up what seemed to him to be a strong marriage. His school friends were sometimes with a single parent and told of rows, affairs and money problems.

Although Sarah and Nick seemed to have everything, the statistics were against them: they showed that non-police marriages had a high rate of breakdown and divorce. Nick tried to understand the workload and dangers his wife faced as a senior police officer but he had his own career challenges.

In her heart of hearts, Sarah knew the truth. Nick had been a good husband and they had worked well together in the early days when establishing a home and introducing Marcus and Susie into the world. They shared the geriatric burden of ageing parents and their joint incomes enabled a house move and holidays abroad. The truth was that Sarah found her husband rather one-dimensional.

Max came along and exploded her frustrations but, being Sarah, it was not that straightforward. The pending divorce, the move to London, the job with SC Group, a growing professional relationship with Norman Delamount, her flat in Kensington and the weekends with Susie aggregated into a sensational new beginning. But she kept Max at bay, encouraging him to stay on some evenings, when the passion flowed, only for Max to find that the next night he was told to go home, back to his bachelor flat.

Sarah was sitting up in bed, trying to rationalise her moods and wondering whether it was time to allow Max more into her world. Which is when she turned on the television to watch the early morning news from the Middle East only to find herself staring with utter horror at what she was seeing.

She cried out, "No, please stop," as the soldier lashed out at the orphan refugee.

CHAPTER TWO

Queen Street, Mayfair, London. The Westingham Society.
Tuesday: 7.30pm

The Westingham Society was filled to overflowing – which came as no surprise to Graham de Lille Rutherford, as that is what he had instructed the Chief Executive, Martin Balcombe, to organise. There were four invited members of the national press and a regional reporter.

Martin Balcombe rose to address the gathering of the loyal Conservative Thatcherite clan and judged his introduction carefully with a mix of humble sincerity and a build-up to the main event as he invited the guest speaker to come to the lectern.

Graham de Lille Rutherford felt immaculate in his thousand-pound suit which had been flown in by his Kowloon-based tailor. He had been to the gym for training sessions with his personal coach and revelled in the intensity of his methods. The applause he was now receiving well rewarded his hard work and meticulous preparation.

He started by saying nothing, simply staring at the mobile equipment by his side. He imperceptibly raised his right hand and a picture of Margaret Thatcher appeared on the screen, causing the audience to stand up and cheer.

"A question," he said. "It is the only question I will be asking tonight." He smiled and several of the elderly ladies felt faint. "What …?" He stopped. His wife Isobel realised that she was feeling stimulated by his aura.

"What," he repeated, "are the most important words Margaret Thatcher ever said?"

A person at the back of the room, on cue (because de Lille had placed him there), yelled out:

"No, no, no!"

The room erupted with audience applause and de Lille chuckled.

"Thank you, sir," he said. "Not the right answer, but a good one." He paused to keep his timing on track. "We are exiting the European Union". The room exploded. "And, by the way, just to let you know that we are taking good care of David." More applause followed.

"We now have a Prime Minister who has given us back our future as a world power."

Almost all the Conservatives at The Westingham Society stood up and cheered:

De Lille waited until they sat down.

"Your final chance," he said. "What did Maggie say that we should never forget?"

He raised his right hand and some words appeared on the screen:

The problem with socialism is that they eventually run out of other people's money.'

There was some muffled laughter and an intake of breath.

"That single sentence," he continued, "is, for me, the most important truism that Mrs Thatcher ever spoke." He paused. "It is why she was one of the greatest Prime Ministers the world has ever seen."

This time the applause lasted four minutes and de Lille rode with it waiting for the guests to settled down before he continued to speak.

"I will say, without any hesitation, that our Prime

Minister, Terence Barrington, is doing a fantastic job. The Conservative Party has returned the United Kingdom to its people and we are back in control."

More applause followed and de Lille used the time to reflect on his lunchtime conversation with the number two in the European Monetary Fund and their shared view that the global financial collapse was about one year away. He sipped some water, raised his right hand and his photograph appeared on the screen. He was sitting at his desk and behind him was a photograph of Winston Churchill.

"I am going to talk about myself," he announced. "I'm going to tell you why I am a Conservative." He paused. "But I will need the agreement of another person." He raised his right hand and his picture was replaced by that of an attractive woman who was wearing a dark blue business suit. There was a gasp from several of the male guests and nods of approval from the women.

"This is Isobel," he said. "She is the most important person in my life." He paused and raised his right hand resulting in the picture being replaced by one of a family group.

"The little hooligan on the left is our son, Nicholas, and our beautiful daughter on the right is called Emily."

There followed a mixture of beams, groans and applause.

"Isobel is here tonight and I am going to ask her to stand up."

She was, by prior agreement, sitting in the third row and, on cue, she rose to her feet, turned around, waved, smiled and sat down. She was wearing a light blue dress. As more clapping of hands followed, the screen was turned off.

"My message tonight," he continued, "for your consideration, is that Maggie was right and it is inconceivable that the British people can ever again be allowed to elect a Labour government. But," he was carefully raising his voice, "for the Tory dynasty to continue, we have to clarify our message."

The members of the press were now stirring from their boredom and beginning to show some interest in Graham de Lille Rutherford, whose personal wealth was occasionally being mentioned in political circles.

"Conservatism is simple," he continued. "It is the belief in the wealth creation process and the fair distribution of the wealth that is created." He was now underway. "Most people do not want to be entrepreneurs. Their wish is to go to work, earn a fair wage and look after their families. These people are the backbone of this country." He hesitated, by design, and hit the lectern with his fist. "This only works if a small sector is creating the wealth and this means our bankers, our industrialists, our business leaders." He sipped some water. "These people want to earn big money and I say "Let them!" and we should incentivise them by reducing corporate and personal taxes, reduce inheritance tax and give them every encouragement possible. It is their empires that will create the wealth."

The reaction was slightly muted as the members of the audience absorbed his political agenda. Graham knew the importance of timing and gave them only a few moments of respite.

"What are we seeing in America?" he asked. "President Merryweather is igniting a wealth creating tornado." He paused and wiped his brow. "I ask you, corporation tax down to twenty-one per cent is simply brilliant. The Dow Jones stock prices are at their highest ever."

A woman stood up and Martin Balcombe prepared to restrain her.

"Are you prepared to condone that bastard's attitude to women?" she shouted. "He's a sexual predator."

Graham de Lille Rutherford smiled and waited while the questioner sat down.

"Madam," he said. "I applaud your spirit and I congratulate you on the point you are making." He then fiddled with the controls and showed again the family photograph. "You have already seen that I place the highest value on family life and I'll be absolutely honest with you. I wish that President Merryweather, whatever the truth, would stop attracting these lurid headlines. I shudder when I think that several women might have been abused." He paused and waited for the moment to strike.

"But, madam, we must concentrate on the majority and President Merryweather is making America more prosperous. He's sorting out the health care fiasco created by the previous regime." He paused. "Madam, if we have to live with the odd indiscretion, then I'll live with it, with the greatest of reluctance, if it means the majority of the American people are benefitting from his policies."

The lady in question nodded as she received a special de Lille smile.

"Let's talk about creating wealth in our country."

He paused and raised his right hand. A name appeared on the screen: 'Robin Pargetter: Wilton,

Wilton and Ashurst.'

"Perhaps only a few of you know Robin. Stand up please, Robin."

A bespectacled man in his fifties, sitting towards the back of the room, rose, nodded modestly and sat down again.

"Thank you, Robin," said de Lille. "Robin is one of the most brilliant tax accountants I have ever met. He and I have put together these statistics." He raised his right hand and a new slide was projected onto the screen.

"Please don't worry if you can't read all the figures because we are handing out a printout now for you all to read." Heads were bowed as the guests looked at the paper handed to them.

"What this analysis does is to explain to you how much money Isobel and I paid in tax to Her Majesty's Revenue and Customs last year. Robin has signed this statement off to confirm it is correct."

He allowed his audience to digest the contents of the fiscal analysis.

"What this shows you is that Isobel and I, from our salaries and dividends, earned four hundred and twenty-one thousand pounds last year and we paid a total of one hundred and sixty-four thousand pounds in the various taxes shown on your sheet." He paused. "That is nearly 40%". He stood erect. "And that is the money that I and the country's wealth creators generate that funds the benefits system and the NHS." He waited because he knew that the NHS was always a vote winner. "On top of that we pay our rates on the house, VAT on goods and services we buy and I employ forty-two people in my global finance house."

He allowed a few moments to pass.

"But there is more, as some of you know, because seven years ago, Isobel and I decided that we wanted to put more back into society. We agreed to allocate ten per cent of our net income to a good cause. One thing led to another and..." he raised his right hand and the screen was lit with the picture of an Edwardian house in Ealing, West London, "...this is Hope House. It is the charity that we spend much of our time running. Without the support of some City friends it would not be possible. We are currently caring for sixteen immigrant boys and girls between the ages of eight and fourteen most of whom have been abandoned by their parents. We've had our failures, of course, but so far we have succeeded in helping over twenty youngsters gain a start in life."

The applause rang out as Isobel smiled at those around her.

"Ladies and gentleman. That is why I am a Conservative. I create wealth, we pay our taxes and Isobel and I help disadvantaged children. Who needs Labour?" he yelled.

The applause was long and genuine. The wines and canapés that followed were well received and de Lille's publicist was busy arranging personal interviews with the journalists.

Isobel was taken home by their driver because de Lille told her he needed to return to his office to chair a conference call with their Japanese office. In fact, he drove himself, in her car, to Hope House. The night carer let him in and an assistant met him outside the bedrooms. She opened a door.

"Uncle Graham is here to see you, Chaudra," she said. "Just remember what I have taught you. Do exactly what Uncle Graham tells you to do." She turned back to her boss.

"It was her tenth birthday, yesterday, we think," she said.

The door was closed and she returned to her room, opening the envelope he had given her. She would send most of the money back to her family in Afghanistan. Later, as she closed her eyes, after her fifteen-hour shift, she thought that she heard a youthful moan.

De Lille reduced the lighting in the room to one lamp by the side of the bed.

"Hello, Chaudra," he said. "I've bought you some sweets."

Kensington, West London.
Tuesday: evening

"Max, she looked straight at me. She was pleading."

Sarah closed the one open window in the lounge of her flat and finished wrapping a nightgown around herself.

"I have not slept for three nights," she continued.

The background music was probably from a Lloyd-Webber musical and an empty bottle of Pino Grigio was lying on the carpet.

"She reminded you of Susie," he suggested.

"Yes," said Sarah. She wiped her brooding eyes. "A few years ago, that was her –exactly the same look."

Max leaned across and held her hand.

"Once more, take me through it," he asked.

"It was a news report from Turkey, on the Syrian border. They were following a group of refugees who were desperately trying to escape. A crowd of men, women and children were fighting to get on a truck. This girl, perhaps seven, maybe eight, was almost aboard when a soldier lashed her across her back." Sarah paused and swallowed. "She clung on to the side and it was obvious she was screaming. She was whacked again with a stick and, as she fell back, she turned to her left and looked into the camera. She stared straight at me, pleading for my help."

Max poured a vodka, added ice and handed the glass to Sarah. She drank it rather greedily.

"Of course she wasn't," said Max. "This is emotional mumbo-jumbo."

"She knew I was watching," said Sarah.

Max was wrestling with his personal conundrum. He and Sarah were progressing towards to an improved relationship. The obvious fulfilment she was generating from the task Norman had given her was resulting in Sarah Rudd at her tantalising best. This was the building block for their future together and then, out of the blue, Sarah sees a child on television being brutalised. There was no logic to her thought process. He was determined not to let go of what they were achieving together and decided to argue her out of it.

"You'll never track her down," said Max. "It's simply impossible."

Sarah held out her glass and offered a cryptic smile.

"But I have found her," she said.

Max knocked over the bottle of vodka as Sarah continued with her news.

"I've spoken to the news producers and they were wonderful. I had a Skype call last night with their reporter who is now back in Ankara. He watched the clip with me and he remembered it quite well. He told me that it happened at the Bab al-Salameh border crossing camp where the Syrian refugees try to get into Turkey."

"How long ago was this?" asked Max.

"Last weekend," replied Sarah.

"She's long gone," said Max. "She's probably dead."

"She's alive," retorted Sarah.

"How do you know that?" asked Max

"I...I just know she's alive."

"And you're planning to go to Turkey, find her and bring her back to the UK."

"Yes," said Sarah. She handed Max a photograph.

"That's her?" he asked.

"Courtesy of the News programme," she grinned.

"Don't believe you," said Max. "You've broken about three protocols and several laws."

"You recall the terrorist attack on London Bridge?"

Max held up his hand.

"Of course. Khuram Butt and two others drove a van over London Bridge and onto the pavement killing six people and knocking a Frenchman into the Thames."

"Eight," said Sarah. "They killed eight people."

He poured himself a large scotch and replenished her vodka.

"You're getting a taxi," she said.

"As I walked here, we'll agree on that," he laughed. "I'm lost. What has this Jihadist Butt to do..."

"A favour was done on the evening, giving the News producers an advantage."

"By whom?" he asked.

"Someone close to the counter-terrorism command," she said. "I happen to be friendly with that person. We were on a Hendon officer's course together."

"And you and he became involved," angered Max.

"Unlikely. Sareem and I became friends and we've kept in touch. She's now a sergeant." Sarah put her hand over her near-empty glass. "She's maintained the relationship and she called in the favour."

Max mulled over this latest revelation.

"What has our boss to say about this mad idea you have concocted?" he asked.

Sarah sighed and reflected on her emotional assault on Norman Delamount.

"Norman says that SC Group will survive without me for four weeks. That's the unpaid leave he's agreed." She put down the empty glass. "He's paying me, anyway, with a bonus. The banking case is almost closed and he's rather pleased with me."

"There are some loose ends," said Max.

"He said you'd deal with those." She smiled. "It's his favourite one-liner: 'We'll unleash Jack Reacher.'" She snorted. "He's not a patch on you, Max," she said. She stood up and untightened the cord on her dressing gown.

"I've a present for you." She smiled.

Max looked at the temptation in front of him. He could never fully fathom her moods. He was hurting with pent-up desire and reasoned that this was his only opportunity before she left for the Middle East on her bloody rescue mission.

She went over to the sideboard and picked up a package.

"De Lille. It's all in here. I've managed to infiltrate

Hope House. The immigration people now know about it." She paused and wiped her eyes. "I've told Norman you'll be able to close de Lille down and finish him."

"Thanks," he said. He looked, bemused, at his companion.

"I fly out tomorrow morning," she said. "Seven forty-five," she added. "I'll get a tube train and I'll be no bother." She looked at her lover. "I'm sorry, Max, but I need to go to bed."

He moaned inwardly and sighed.

"I'll take you to the airport," he said. "Have you told your family?"

"Susie knows," she said, as she sat down. "She thinks it's fantastic. She wanted to come."

"And Nick?" he asked.

"The divorce papers are in process and so it's almost over. Marcus is siding with his father but I understand that."

"Which leaves us," said Max.

Sarah stood up and stretched out her legs, knowing the affect it had on Max – but she did not care. She needed the reassurance that she still attracted him.

"Us," she said.

"You are proposing to travel to one of the most dangerous places in the world on a hopeless search for a girl you do not know, who has long gone and who won't want to go with you anyway."

"Her eyes said something different," she said, quietly.

Max approached and took her in his arms.

Do you recall what you said to me at Holborn?" he asked.

"You mean when you saved my life?"

"Almost," said Max. "Martin Redding killed himself but, if he had not fallen under the truck, I would have killed him."

"And you are going to remind me that I said, "Never leave me, please, Max", said Sarah.

"It has crossed my mind. Yes," said Max.

"I still mean it," she continued. "I have to go, Max. She was begging me to help her."

"Sarah," said Max, "in your career as a police officer you never failed, did you?"

"There was the odd blemish," she laughed. "The man with the keys."

"You'll fail this time, Sarah, and you'll get hurt."

"She was pleading for me to help her, Max."

"No, she wasn't. Your emotions are shredded by the banking case. Let's go away together," he begged.

"She was pleading, Max."

"So am I," he said. "Please don't catch that plane in the morning. It's a ludicrous search that will end in disaster."

Sarah stepped back and looked at the man of whom she was not completely sure but who she was now going to take into her bed.

"I will find her," she said as her gown fell open.

*

Parrot Cay, Turks and Caicos Islands.
Thursday: morning

Her name, Zeander, was pronounced with a 'ch' sound rather than 'Z'. She was washing her feet in the early morning seawater. She had discarded her silk robe and seemed impervious to the slightly chilly winds, content to rely on the two pieces of her silky bikini to protect her. She had a full figure and her tanned skin simply endorsed her allure, as did her blonde, short cropped hair. The Parrot Cay resort was proving an ideal retreat for her and her companion. Graham de Lille Rutherford had his office in Providenciales, which was forty minutes away, and vast wealth deposited with the local banks. His mansion, about two miles along the coast, was being rebuilt.

Since the United Kingdom Government returned the British Overseas Territory to home rule in 2012, the economy first stabilised and then expanded as the tourists returned. The financial services sector accounted for nearly fifteen per cent of its earnings and was the reason the British financier was there. He had no intention of paying any more tax – over and above the token income tax on his UK earnings –of any sort, to anybody.

Despite the tranquillity of the moment, Zeander was a challenge because he was in love with his wife, Isobel, and was feeling more contented as their lives together flourished. But he also adored being with Zeander who was the male dream. She was committed, loyal and relished every aspect of their relationship. On their second night together, she had told the banker there was nothing she would not do for him.

He looked at Zeander's body as she bent over to pick up a shell. They had last made love at two o'clock in the morning and he was surprised at the reaction she provoked in him just a few hours later. He was still remembering her performance on the boat the previous afternoon when her understanding of the island folklore was utterly seductive.

They wandered back to the hotel and had breakfast together. He then called a cab and sent her off to the shops, giving her a thousand dollars as he told her he wanted to be alone. She happily skipped away having whispered in his ear what would be happening to him on her return.

He ordered a large pink gin and settled down besides the swimming pool. This, in itself, was unusual because de Lille tried to maintain a disciplined regime and was careful over his alcoholic intake. This particular morning, he needed to understand why his contact had decided to use Delamount Security to protect his South American agent: they were a division two player in their field, but he had been persuaded they were pushing for promotion. He picked at the bowl of fruits. He would not let this issue interrupt the good life.

He knew that he could not afford for Isobel to find out about Zeander and he had their London maid sworn to message him if his wife made any move to fly out. But he was not prepared to part with his concubine. He was in the middle of an Arabic-based financial operation which would earn him vast sums of commission and a possible peerage. His publicist had leaked the amount of his contribution to the Conservative Party to the 'Financial Times'. He was secretly financing a senior Labour peer who was willing to take money from anybody and any source, whatever the credentials. At the pinnacle of his armoury was the growing relevance of the London-based Conservative Friends of Washington, whose tentacles led directly to the President of the United States of America and de Lille's mentor, Lord Simon

Mallington.

De Lille was playing for high stakes: this was his adrenalin. He watched as a teenage girl dived into the water as he marvelled at her physical maturity. His mobile buzzed and he read the text message.

'Phone me: secure line. SM'.

He strolled back to his room and made the call, simply listening and not saying a word.

"Sarah Rudd at SC Group has broken your cover. We're trying to neutralise the threat."

He put the phone down and frowned as he pondered the possible implications.

"A woman, threatening me!" cried the misogynist. "Surely I deserve better?"

He returned to the pool side and was disappointed to find that the teenage girl had disappeared. He wondered when Zeander would be back as he decided what to do about Sarah Rudd. He made an international call on his mobile phone, removed the SIM card and threw the console into the bin.

SC Group, Knightsbridge, West London.
Saturday: lunchtime

In the four hours Max had spent analysing the file left for him by Sarah, he had amassed an understanding of the fraud perpetrated by de Lille's finance house. It was a partnership involving three former executives from one of the United Kingdom's major financial institutions. There was a secret document which they had all signed, de Lille appearing nowhere except he pulled all the strings.

Following the global financial crash in 2008, Britain's main banks were having problems both with trading conditions and with the financial regulators.

De Lille, who was making a good living by investing capital in struggling businesses and then selling the assets for personal gain, realised that there was a golden opportunity.

At the heart of his scheme were bankers' bonuses. The executives of the top five biggest banks were obsessed with their annual pay-outs to fund their lavish lifestyles. The recession hit hard and so when de Lille approached one bank and offered to take off their books many of their troublesome business customers, the board of directors jumped at the idea. There were several who had doubts and wanted to know more but they were quickly talked down and one was forced into early retirement.

The scheme devised by de Lille was straightforward. The bank would introduce struggling business customers to de Lille's company. It would be done with great charm and positivity, and the customers, who might have their house and personal assets on the line, would be given little option. The banking facility was restructured with loans made by de Lille's company using convertible instruments which contained a right, under certain circumstances, to covert the loans into shares at low prices. It was so simple but the reality was that it, potentially, gave de Lille ownership of the companies.

The main ruses were turnover and profit targets imposed on the owners. The business people were usually so desperate that they would agree to anything and, often, could not afford proper legal advice. The bank was well pleased because the account was removed from the 'delinquent list' and the bank's balance sheet strengthened which pleased the financial regulators. The money that was introduced by way of loans to the individual companies was immediately taken out again under the cover of 'performance payments' to de Lille's company.

In reality it was totally fraudulent but was driven by greedy bankers focusing on their annual bonus payments and de Lille's henchmen soaking riches from hard-working and desperate business owners. The financial regulators had no idea it was happening and the irony was that they gave de Lille's company their regulatory authority to act as finance officers.

The three ex-bankers would go in and extract every last ounce of financial assets, and they often threatened with punitive 'legal' letters which included indicating the daily amount of interest accruing. These were designed to scare the living daylights out of the owners and this was often exactly what they often did. De Lille's officers were free to sell company assets and take the money out in fees and dividends.

They became increasingly avaricious as their personal wealth increased: the home on the islands of Greece, the charter flights to avoid airport congestion, the boats and their bikinied staff, the private schooling for their children; there was no end to what they could have.

This was possible because, by now, the business owners inevitably missed the agreed targets and this triggered the conversion of the loans into shares. De Lille made certain they held enough loans to ensure the next part of the fraud. The company would be placed into receivership. The bank and de Lille's company would turn out to be the main 'preferred' creditors: the ordinary creditors, as so often was the case, were destined to receive nothing.

The receiver immediately called on the original

owners to pay up on their guarantees and the lawyers they used were relentless. Often, the owners would have to sell their homes and other assets and, on occasion, de Lille managed to reach their pension pots. Some fought back and several faced periods in hospital following road accidents. In one case a home went up in flames and De Lille grabbed the insurance proceeds. Several faced endgame and suffered ill health; three committed suicide.

Every time a national newspaper tried to report on the situation it would receive a court injunction and although several fought back, they then found telephone calls were being made from Westminster to the editor. The police were overwhelmed and most forces gave up investigating although some observers questioned whether they had ever really tried.

Max picked up a separate section headed 'Jack and Gabrielle Glover' and, as he read the contents, he began to shake with anger. He was staring at a letter received by Norman Delamount in early September the previous year which read as follows:

My beloved Dad,

When you read this, Jack and I will no longer be with you. We have lost our home, our car, our savings and our pensions. As I write this to you, we have received another letter from the lawyers saying that we are to be sued for misappropriation of company funds.

We do not have children of our own which has made our decision easier and, apart from my darling Jack, you are the only other person I will miss apart from Zeebie, my cat. We blame ourselves. They said they were bankers and we assumed that meant they were professionals of integrity but they were very nasty people; virtually all of them. If Jack has a fault – and, in truth, he doesn't – he was too ready to grasp at any perceived answer to our situation, such was the depth of the depression. I thought we had a Bank of England to ensure the standards of our banks.

De Lille was incredibly smart, he sucked me in and Jack followed. His three henchmen were sniffer dogs.

I'm not sure it will help but there was an incident with de Lille which you will not like and for which I hang my head in shame. It occurred on the day when we were to sign the agreement which triggered the loans and our assumed salvation. I had worn a flowery dress and, it is true, I was flaunting it just a wee bit. Jack never stopped telling me I was lustful. At one point, Jack and the three assassins were in the boardroom and I found that de Lille had followed me into the canteen. It was a Saturday and there were no other staff on the premises.

Almost without realising, I found that he had pinned me up against a wall. He lifted up my dress so I slapped his face. He laughed and said that the next few minutes would determine whether he gave his agreement for the signing of the papers. He wanted sex as payment for our future, so I thought. He was cool and I can recall it as though it was a few minutes ago. He said, with a smile,

"It's so simple, Gabrielle. I love your name. You will lower your knickers and I will fuck you. Then we can go and watch the signing of the papers."

That is what happened. Later that evening I lay in the bath and spent an hour trying to rid myself of him. Jack wanted to celebrate with a champagne dinner.

I never saw de Lille again.

I'm so sorry, Dad. I wanted you to be proud of me.

Your loving daughter,
Gabrielle x

Max climbed some stairs and went into Norman's office where he poured himself a large scotch to which he added some water. He returned to his desk and read the remaining section marked 'Hope House'. Across the front of the section was the word 'CARE' written in red letters.

He began to turn the pages. "Who the hell is DS Rita Hemsworth?" he wondered. He came across a copy of her warrant card. It was Sarah. "What have you been doing?" Max exclaimed to himself but it soon became self-evident. Sarah had gained entry into Hope House by posing as a Metropolitan police officer. Her file had been immaculately prepared and the interview notes with the matron gave little away but when Sarah had gained access into the rooms, she managed to take photographs of several of the distressed children.

It progressed ever downwards in that she had found a room which was clearly dedicated to filming children being abused. Her notes confirmed that there was a sample of the depravity in her desk. Max knew where it would be and so he temporarily closed the file, entered her room, found the DVD and went to the TV where he started to watch it. After a few minutes, he dashed to the toilets where he retched.

He returned to his desk and read Sarah's closing notes. She said there was enough evidence to pass the file to the Metropolitan police and end Mr de Lille's reign.

Max sat back in his chair and realised he was not alone.

"Makes unpleasant reading," said Norman Delamount.

Max turned and looked at his boss.

"Frankly, Norman, it could not be worse. The scene in the film where the two girls were abused..."

"I've watched it all, Max," said Norman. "Unfortunately, you're wrong."

Max held up his glass and Norman nodded in agreement. They went into his office where he poured two generous measures and indicated that Max should sit down.

"I'm wrong?" questioned Max. "Can it be worse than what I've seen today?"

"This is about Graham de Lille Rutherford," said Norman.

"There's enough for the Met," said Max.

"Except that the star witness might not be available," he said.

"Sarah? You've heard from her?" exclaimed Max.

"No. We've not heard from her. She has landed. That's all we know."

"But..."

"We've heard something else." He drank some scotch. "It's not good, Max."

"I need to know," he said.

"Yes, you do. De Lille has put a contract on Sarah's life. The IRA has taken it."

"Hell!" said Max. "But with your connections, surely?"

"There's only one way to terminate it and you know exactly what that is."

Max stood up and walked round the room.

"How good is your information?" asked Max.

"De Lille is paying a million euros in order to commission the best killer. I will get some information from time to time but the only thing I know for certain is the gunman's name."

"If I mention a name, you have the option of shaking your head," said Max.

Norman remained grim-faced.

"Michael Duggan," said Max.

Slowly, Norman nodded his head.

"I was worried you'd nod your head," said Max.

"Killing him won't stop the contract," said Norman. "There will be others if he fails."

Max walked slowly round the room. He looked out at the traffic and the carefree walkers in Hyde Park.

"We both know there's only one route to saving Sarah's life," he said.

Norman looked at his associate. He was beginning to buy into this man and Jack Reacher was history. Mad Max was starting to become a player in SC Group.

"Stop the man who gave the contract," said Norman. "I've briefed my pal at the Met and our file is being delivered tomorrow." He paused. "It will take time and de Lille has an army of lawyers ready at all times." He coughed. "He's managed to engineer a hold over several judges," he added. He looked at Max. "There is another way."

"Yes," he said. "I know that."

"Money's no problem," said Norman.

Max stared at him.

"This is not about money, Norman," he snapped. "This is about the woman I love."

"So, go and eliminate de Lille," said Norman. He hesitated but then put his hand on Max's sleeve.

"As fast as you can," he added.

"That won't stop Michael Duggan," said Max.

"It's the necessary first step to doing so," he said.

+ + +

CHAPTER THREE

Hope House, Ealing, West London.
Sunday: afternoon

Earlier that morning, Isobel de Lille Rutherford had sat her children around the kitchen table and showed them a map of the Middle East. She explained that their father was away on a business trip and so she had prepared an outline of the various countries and had coloured in one of them. She had wrapped up a packet of sweets which was the prize for whoever of the two could first identify the territory.

Breakfast was over and it was Emily's turn to go first. She thought long and hard.

"Iran," she announced and then groaned as Isobel shook her head.

Nicholas grabbed the chart and stared at the prize.

"Iraq," he triumphed, only to watch his mother indicate a wrong answer.

Emily knew that this was her chance to win the prize and so she looked closely at the map.

"Afghanistan," she announced and cried out triumphantly as she was handed the packet of sweets.

By the time the afternoon came, and they boarded the car to drive to the orphanage, all the sweets had been eaten. They arrived at Hope House and entered the Edwardian building. Isobel watched with some amusement as Nicholas and Emily rushed toward the group of orphans and abandoned immigrants who were playing together in the recreational room. She liked the exposure this gave to her children in understanding the modern multi-racial world.

Isobel left them to play together and walked

45

around the building with the matron who was attentive and directed her to the west-facing section. They entered one of the bedrooms, Isobel threw back the blankets, checked the mattress and told the Afghan woman how pleased she was with the cleanliness of the premises and said she would like to inspect the kitchens.

At around four in the afternoon she drove Emily and Nicholas back to their home in Mayfair. She was pleased with the visit to Hope House.

"Who did you play with?" she asked her son.

"Surante," replied Nicholas, as he watched the traffic through the car window.

"And where's he from?" she continued.

"He doesn't know," replied her son.

"Mummy," said Emily. "I played with Chaudra. She's from Iraq."

"That's nice, darling," said her mother as she concentrated on driving in the late afternoon congestion.

"Yes, she told me she was feeling sore."

"She must tell the matron," replied her mother.

"She's done that. She's had some cream rubbed on her."

"That's good, darling. Now please let me drive."

"Mummy," said Emily. "Why would a man put his thing in Chaudra's bottom?"

*

The Syria/Turkey Border, Bab al-Salameh.
Tuesday: afternoon

Sarah Rudd's flight to Turkey had been delayed; immigration at Ankara airport was a shambles, with officials questioning the validity of her visa; and the internal flight to Gaziantep involved an older, single-engine plane, a scary landing and two guards who stole her phone and her money – apart from the dollars hidden inside her clothing. She discovered that the driver meeting her at the airport had disappeared. Allowing for Eastern European time differences, it was fourteen hours before she reached the Turkish/Syrian border.

Bab al-Salameh, 'The Gate of Peace', had developed a grid system combining rows of huts and tents, and abandoned cars were everywhere housing even more refugees. As the early evening light started to fade, Sarah focused on a tower and decided to walk in a straight line towards it. She then moved a few paces to her right and made the return journey, finding that her progress was tortuously slow and that there was suspicion and mistrust everywhere. The Syrian occupants often refused to even look at the photograph she tried to show them but Sarah persisted, up and down, until she could travel no further. She lay on top of a heap of refuse sacks and snatched some furtive sleep. Early the next morning, as the sun's rays hit her skin, she stood up, took in some refreshment, and then continued her search for the girl in the photograph, hour after hour.

She could not prevent her eyes filling with tears of despair as she watched the wasting body of a boy scrabbling in the dirt for food. She knew it was not her priority, and he would almost certainly die, but she finally grabbed the little refugee from out of the polluted gutter and hugged him as he coughed up some blood. She laid him down on a blanket she was carrying with her, took off all his clothes and washed his body using the water from her personal flask. As her hands passed over his sores, she felt him shudder with pain. He looked up at her and smiled as she took out her pyjamas and dressed him in them. She searched for, and found, a pair of scissors which she used to remove the surplus material. Sarah made one legging into a comfort sheet which she thrust into his hands. She then looked around at the camp housing many thousands of Syrian refugees who had fled from the war-torn district of Aleppo.

Throughout her illustrious career as a highly decorated police officer, ex-Detective Chief Inspector Sarah Rudd had used a special skill which, more than once, had fuelled tensions with her senior officers and yet which resulted in several remarkable achievements. When she had saved the lives of the Royal Couple in an attempted shooting in The Mall, she had received the Queen's Gallantry Medal. One of her proudest moments had been preventing a train travelling to London carrying four hundred commuters being bombed by extremists. And, against all the odds, she had found her daughter, Susie, at the point where the kidnapper was about to kill her.

That was her final act as a police officer and of her marriage to school teacher, Nick, because she had fallen for Detective Chief Inspector Max Hemmings. He had also left the police force and joined the newly-named SC Group in London. He did not have to work too hard to persuade Sarah to join him; it was the opportunity she believed could open up a new life for her. She never imagined that she would find herself in a refugee camp on the Syrian-Turkish border grappling with the humanitarian disaster confronting the world.

The special skill which Sarah possessed was two-fold: understanding processes and being prepared to challenge authority. She picked the boy up in her arms and was pleased to see that he was gripping the comfort sheet with all his fragile strength. She had already identified the medical centre and reached its entrance within minutes ignoring the queue which was inching forwards, hour after hour, as the sun and blasts of dust and sand took their toll. The people waited because there was no alternative: they occasionally received small bowls of food and water bottles from the Red Cross workers.

Sarah checked that the boy was secure in her arms, marched to the front, past the makeshift reception desk, ignored the cries of protest from both those at the head of the queue and the staff, and barged into a curtained-off area. Three white coated practitioners were hovering over an old woman.

"Get out," ordered a tall official in perfect English.

"I'm staying," replied Sarah.

"You're out of order," said the nurse.

"What are her chances?" asked Sarah.

"If you want to know, they are not good. She has typhoid," said the medical orderly.

"Amongst other things," added the doctor.

"Then let's save this boy and give him his life back," ordered Sarah.

"There's a system," said the doctor. "Please get out."

"Did you ever see the film *A Bridge Too Far*?" asked Sarah.

"For heaven's sake," cried the doctor. "I admire your spirit but you must adhere to the system."

"It was the story of the Allies' attempt to shorten

the Second World War by capturing the bridge at Arnhem."

"And they failed," snapped the doctor.

"James Caan was an American officer who had promised a scared soldier that he would look after him. The boy was shot and Caan took him to the medical centre where a harassed surgeon refused to treat him."

"If I recall," said the doctor, "he was dying."

"Caan took out his revolver and threatened to shoot the doctor," continued Sarah.

"What happened?" asked the nurse.

"The doctor saved the soldier's life," she said.

"But you don't have a gun," said the doctor.

She looked him straight in his eyes.

"I promise you," she said, "I will find one within a few minutes."

The doctor whispered some instructions, the elderly patient was laid on the floor and he came across to Sarah and took the boy off her. She watched as they carefully laid him on the table and undressed him. The medical orderly turned him over and they examined his bottom, a fluid bottle was linked up to his pitifully thin right arm and the doctor gave him an injection. He was continuously listening to his lungs. Finally, the boy was wrapped in a white cover and the nurse carried him away to the congested ward: the orderly went with her carrying the fluid intake apparatus. The doctor came over to Sarah.

"He has pleurisy," he said. "Two hours later would have been too late."

Sarah turned and began to leave but the doctor went after her.

"If I remember the film," he said, "after it was all

over the doctor asked James Caan if he would have used the revolver on him?"

Sarah remained grim-faced.

"If you ask me the same question," she said, "you'll get the same answer."

As she exited the area, she noticed that the medical orderly had returned and was lifting the body of the elderly woman off the ground to take it to the mortuary.

SC Group, Knightsbridge, West London.
Tuesday: early evening

Max needed to call in at the offices of SC Group. He was weary and he had things to do before he left and, yet again, he felt frustrated that Sarah would not live with him.

The offices, near to Harrods Department Store, housed on average twenty people and included a twenty-four hours manned call centre linking with the around nineteen operatives worldwide. Norman Delamount retained his own office on the top of four floors and operated between that and the boardroom. There were three other members of staff on the floor including Daisy Maitland, his personal assistant, who arranged his diary and social arrangements. The other two personnel were the original founders of the company who had sold out to Norman ten years earlier. One now looked after their American interests and the other, the rest of the world. They were more often than not travelling abroad.

Some sixth sense had told Max not to email his plans to Norman. He decided to use a Word document, which was printed off and deleted, and which gave details including his flight timings, his hotel and the initial moves to track down Graham de Lille Rutherford. The final section concerned Sarah and a request that, should anything happen to him, his outstanding pay should go to her. The last sentence contained a heartfelt thanks to Norman for giving him the chance of a lifetime and his determination to 'sort out' the evil banker and then he would go after Michael Duggan. Originally there was a reference to his daughter, Gabrielle, but that was deleted after further thought.

The envelope in his hand was marked 'strictly personal'. Max exited the lift, assumed that the floor was deserted, opened the door into Norman's office whereupon he found Daisy Maitland, Norman's personal assistant, sitting in the chair usually occupied by the company chairman. Although she immediately tried to cover it up, she was viewing a page of his computer. Max was impressed by her instant reaction as Daisy behaved as though nothing was amiss and closed down the screen.

"Ah, Max," she said, "so that's where the boss is tonight. He never tells me anything."

They had, from the beginning of his time at SC Group, struck up an easy-going relationship, due in part to the infrequency of their contact except when Max was required in the boardroom.

"Something important?" he asked.

"I need to know where Mr Delamount is tomorrow morning," she said.

"But surely that's on your computer," said Max.

"Should be," quipped Daisy, "but the chairman has a habit of putting things in and not telling me." She swivelled round in the chair and revealed an expanse of tanned legs.

"Rumour has it you're on your own at the moment," she said. "If you're hungry, I'm available to be escorted for dinner."

"Interesting," said Max. "Daisy, can I please ask you a question?"

"I suggest the Hilton, Galvin's restaurant," she said. "It's on the twenty-eighth floor so if I am not enjoying myself, I can jump out of the window."

"That's certainly a challenge," conceded Max. "The question I wanted to ask you is if you know what a clue is?"

"A clue?" exclaimed Daisy. "Not a clue," she laughed.

"I used to be a detective," said Max. "I spent most of my time trying to solve crimes. On occasions I knew who the bad guy was but I needed clues to secure a conviction. Perhaps we'll call it evidence."

"I'm getting bored, Max," said Daisy. "I'm somebody who needs constant stimulation."

"I'm sure you do," said Max. "What I'm trying to say is that I often detected the criminal and then had to gather the evidence."

"I'm now seriously bored," she said, standing up to return to her office.

"Sit down," ordered Max, and Daisy did just that.

"It has crossed my mind that information is leaving SC Group. The episode where we failed to look after the South American businessman worried me."

"Am I the bad guy?" laughed Daisy.

"I'll need clues before I know the answer to your question," said Max.

"Yes, you will. Goodnight Max," she said.

"I think I can see a clue," said Max.

She laughed again.

"And I think you're past your sell-by date," she snapped.

"What's that in front of you, Daisy?" said Max.

She looked down and went bright red in the face.

"It wouldn't be the password to the Chairman's security files, would it?" suggested Max.

"Mr Delamount wouldn't mind me accessing his files," she said.

"Who's paying you?" asked Max.

"Fuck off," she retorted.

"It wouldn't be Graham de Lille Rutherford, would it, by any chance?"

Daisy stared at her adversary.

"Max, you're out of your depth. I can have you removed with one phone call," she said.

"I think you need to know something," said Max. "I'm not a very nice person."

"I've often wondered what Sarah sees in you. Mind you, she's desperate, so that's probably the answer."

"What's his hold on you?" said Max.

"Fuck off. I'm going home."

"My guess is pornographic photographs. Earned a bit of money when you were desperate, did you?"

She didn't notice, but Max was slowly circling behind her, reaching out and then grabbing her arm. As he pulled up her sleeve, he saw the injection scars in the crook of her elbow which revealed a tale of blackmail.

"I'm almost off it," she said.

"How did you get involved with de Lille Rutherford?" asked Max.

Daisy seemed to simply give in. She sighed and

slumped back into the chair.

"I had a boyfriend; a doctor. He said I was bipolar and suggested diazepam could help. That's Valium to you."

Max chose not to tell her that he knew more about drugs than she would ever know.

"Go on," he said.

"I became dependent and started to build up debts. Doctor wonderful introduced me to a personal banker and then he disappeared and I found myself in front of Graham de Lille Rutherford. When he realised where I worked, he offered me drugs for information."

She paused and wiped her mouth.

"Max. I'm working hard to get off it and I'm making some progress. I just want to disappear and start again."

"Do you have access to de Lille Rutherford?" he asked.

Daisy laughed.

"Life is never straightforward, is it?" she said. "I used to go to his offices and I built up a rapport with a member of his team; she's called Thelma. I then discovered I'm bisexual."

"You do have some access," he said.

"She talks," revealed Daisy.

Max closed their conversation and suggested they went for a drink together. Half a bottle of red wine later, he and Daisy were agreeing a deal. She readily understood that Max did not want to tell Norman Delamount about this situation because he suspected Norman's low state of morale: the death of Gabrielle, and the file produced by Sarah, might make him vulnerable to further setbacks. He proposed that he would retain Daisy's confidence if she could provide him with information about de Lille's movements. It was a high-risk strategy but Mad Max took high risks.

"You are saying that I'll have to carry on sleeping with Thelma," said Daisy.

"Is that a problem?" asked Max.

"Oh no," she laughed. "Perk of the job."

"I'm going to obtain a new phone for you," said Max. "I want you to use it purely for contacting me, nothing else."

"Got it," she said, and then she looked at Max.

"Sorry what I said about Sarah. I'm sure she's not desperate."

"I wish she was," said Max, as he poured them both another glass of wine.

*

The Syria/Turkey Border, Bab al-Salameh.
Wednesday: early morning

Sarah Rudd stopped in her tracks, wiped the sweat away from her eyes and was annoyed that her clothes were already wet with perspiration because the sun seemed never to stop blazing down from the skies. She decided to return to a tent where she had spoken to three women and where a number of children were hiding within the rear flap of the canvas covering. She focused on the more senior occupant. Sarah had shown her the girl's photograph and questioned her as much as she dare because she knew, instinctively, that she was hiding something. Throughout her career Sarah had been successful at determining when a suspect was lying; it was her experience that the fifth sign was the clincher. The first was an excessive adjusting of clothing, the second, undue swallowing and the third was when the person put their hands to their face. By themselves, these indications were not conclusive but when the individual put their lips together the evidence would be mounting. But Sarah knew that the fifth sign was rarely wrong. She thought back to her text books: "Lying requires more cognitive energy." The suspect tended to have to concentrate more when they were fabricating the truth so exerting excessive mental energy; as a result, they blinked less.

She stared at the woman: her eyes were motionless. She grabbed her by the arm and pulled her out into the fresh air.

"Please," she pleaded. "You know where she is, don't you?"

Slowly, almost imperceptibly, a hand was raised and a finger pointed behind them towards a hut with a red cross sign on the door. Sarah muttered her gratitude and rushed to the door which she pushed open. The only occupant, a nurse, was half asleep. She looked at the photograph and smiled as she held up a hand and told Sarah to sit down. A few minutes later she reappeared holding a blonde child who she handed to her.

As Sarah muttered "Hello", the girl smiled.

"Do you know her name?" she asked the nurse.

"Najwa," she replied. "That's all we know about her."

Hope House, Ealing, West London.
Wednesday: afternoon

Detective Inspector Georgina Morris sighed and wiped her hand across her deeply creased forehead.

She looked at her colleague Detective Constable Benson and then at Isobel de Lille Rutherford.

"There is nothing we can find," she said. "Absolutely nothing."

Isobel's nightmare was deepening and her solicitor was on his way to advise her. She was reflecting on recent events – her husband was still away on business despite her desperate messages to him asking that he return home.

Twenty-four hours earlier she had returned to Hope House, challenged the matron and then tried to discuss with Chaudra, mainly through an interpreter, what she had told her daughter. Chaudra spoke little English, and it was only when she gestured to her bottom that Isobel began to realise what might have happened. She knew that the centre was advised by a local doctor and so she wrapped Chaudra in a blanket and took her down to the surgery. She insisted on seeing Dr Martin Manning and had to wait only a few minutes before the doctor came out and, in a rather irate tone of voice, said that he would fit them in during the afternoon.

"You'll see us now," said Isobel, and marched towards the consulting room carrying Chaudra in her arms. Inside, with the door secure, she undressed the orphan and placed her on the examination table.

"Please look at her bottom," she instructed.

Dr Manning examined the redness.

"Bit sore," he said. "I'll prescribe you some antiseptic cream."

"Can you explain the infection," said Isobel.

"You're over-reacting," replied the general practitioner. "The children in Hope House have nearly all come with histories of poor nutrition.

They're vulnerable to this type of infection."

"Has there been sexual interference?" she asked.

Dr Manning laughed.

"I must move on," he said. "I've a busy surgery."

"You'll examine her again," said Isobel.

Dr Manning shrugged his shoulders, washed his hands and looked again at Chaudra's injury. The child was lying completely still.

"An infection," repeated the doctor.

Isobel walked out of the room and went to reception where a harassed, middle-aged woman looked at her.

"I want your senior partner in that room, now," she said.

One thing that Isobel had learnt in her time with her husband was that presence was everything. The receptionist never flinched as she lifted a telephone and whispered into it. Within two minutes another doctor appeared.

"I'm Dr Henderson," he said to Isobel. "I gather there's a problem."

She did not reply. She walked back to the consultation room followed by the senior partner who did not hesitate as he went straight over to Chaudra and looked at her injury. He saw that Dr Manning was sitting on a chair with his head in his hands.

Dr Henderson called for a nurse and instructed her to make the child more comfortable, at the same time asking Isobel to sit down on the other side of the room. She realised that he was preparing to administer an injection.

Events moved quickly. Chaudra was taken to hospital and the police arrived within fifteen minutes.

An hour later, they, together with officials from the council's care unit, raided Hope House. Of the thirteen children found on the premises (one was missing) three were taken to hospital for further examination and ten were taken into care. Chaudra sank into a coma but was later to recover and also went into care.

Dr Manning started to talk and the truth slowly came out. He had an ex-wife and massive gambling debts and was financing his way by covering up the state of affairs at Hope House. All but two of the children had come into the United Kingdom illegally and four of the six staff were unregistered immigrants. The matron was petrified of two men who regularly visited the home and she pleaded with the authorities that she was innocent.

It took the police little time to uncover the facts. There was no CCTV cover, the only equipment being in the room where the films were made, where they discovered boxes of pornographic material. They were later to trace two men who were regular visitors who both refused to talk and there was little evidence that they could uncover. None of the staff were able to provide much information.

DI Morris looked at Isobel de Lille Rutherford. Her solicitor was sitting at her side.

"Your husband is away," said the police officer.

"He's on a business trip and I can't reach him at the moment," said Isobel.

"You and he ran this home?" asked DI Morris.

"No. Graham set it up. I came in occasionally just to check it over."

"Mrs de Lille Rutherford, I'll come straight to the point." She paused to look at her notes. "We've more work ahead but we have found a lot of paperwork and checked the official records."

"Yes, I would expect you to do that," said Isobel.

"We can find no trace of your husband, Graham de Lille Rutherford."

"Rubbish," said Isobel. "He told a Conservative Group all about it a week ago."

"Everything is in your name, Mrs de Lille Rutherford," said DI Morris. She handed her a contract. Her solicitor immediately examined it.

"The property is owned by you alone," said the police officer. "The application to the council for the licence is in your name." She handed Isobel several bank statements. "The bank details are in your name," she continued.

"Graham asked me to sign some papers but he always said they were for tax purposes," she said.

"I wish to speak to my client," said the solicitor.

"Down at the station," said DI Morris. She asked Isobel to stand up.

"Isobel de Lille Rutherford, I am arresting you on suspicion of running an illegal children's home, on allowing the abuse of children and benefitting from financial fraud." She paused. "You do not have to say anything but it may harm your defence if you do not mention when questioned something you later rely on in court. Anything you do say may be given in evidence."

The accused put her head in her hands as the truth slowly began to dawn on her.

+ + +

CHAPTER FOUR

The Syria/Turkey Border, Bab al-Salameh.
Thursday: afternoon

The reality of her situation first came into her consciousness during the flight from Ankara to Gaziantep. The plane was a bone-shaker, no-one on the flight would talk to her, and, when she arrived at the derelict airport buildings, her money and phone were confiscated by customs officials. Then she discovered that there was nobody to meet her. As she entered the last part of her fourteen-hour journey to Bab al-Salameh, sitting in the back of a filthy animal carrier, Sarah realised that her rescue odyssey of a little girl, who she did not know, was romantic insanity.

But now she had found her. She took out the photograph provided by the news reporter: it was her.

She left the Red Cross hut, with Najwa at her side, during the early afternoon. They had been provided with water and bowls of fruit which were essential as it took her two hours to locate the medical centre where, during the previous day, she had saved the life of the young refugee. There was a long queue of sick people waiting for their turn to see the doctor but, again, Sarah ignored the rights of these individuals and barged straight in to the entrance area where she found the doctor sitting at a table with a cup of coffee and a cigarette in his mouth. He looked up and showed no surprise.

"Don't tell me that you have found a gun," he said, as he exhaled smoke into the air.

"Please," said Sarah. She pushed Najwa towards

the doctor. "Have a look at her."

He ignored the wails of protest from the waiting patients and called for the nurse who took the girl into a cubicle. They re-emerged sixteen minutes later and Najwa ran up to Sarah and put her arms around her. The doctor smiled.

"She's undernourished, she has some sores that need treating and we've put two stitches in a laceration on her back." He handed Sarah a tube of cream. "Keep her clean and put this on when there is any sign of dryness." He held out a capsule. "These are antibiotics; two a day and make sure she finishes the whole course." He smiled. "If you are not going to shoot me, I need to get back to my patients," he said.

Sarah stood up, went over, clutched his hand, and smiled as he nodded and then disappeared behind the canvas separation. The nurse tidied up and prepared to join the doctor – who suddenly reappeared.

"I should have told you," he said. "Your little girl is intact in that she has not been interfered with in any way, as far as we can tell." He hesitated. "None of my business but is she yours?" he asked.

"I found her," said Sarah. "It's a bit of a crazy story," she admitted. The doctor nodded and smiled. "I know nothing about her," she sighed. The nurse whispered to the medical practitioner who disappeared and she looked at Sarah.

"Just give me a few minutes with her," she said. She handed Najwa a candy bar and they went together into the inner area. Sarah sat alone for twenty minutes and, in that time, another four adults and a child were taken into the hospital area. She was puzzled that none ever seem to come out.

She realised that she had been dozing when she felt her hand being squeezed. The nurse was looking down, suggested they talked together and led them into a cubicle where Najwa was sitting on a bed.

"There is not much I can tell you," said the nurse. "We think she is around eight years old and the doctor has told you that physically she is able to survive but she needs to gain some strength. She speaks Arabic and is probably a Muslim." She found another candy bar and handed it to a grateful Najwa.

"There are two clues to her background and she is almost certainly Lebanese." She wiped the candy-induced spittle from Najwa's mouth. "Strange, because mostly it's Syrian refugees trying to escape into Lebanon but Najwa seems to have been going the other way."

"You said there are two clues?" asked Sarah.

"The first is her name: Najwa. Have you ever heard of a singer called Najwa Karam?"

Sarah shook her head as the nurse took out her mobile phone and started to play some vocal music. Najwa immediately smiled and jumped down from the bed and made an attempt to dance.

"Najwa Karam is about fifty-odd now. She's a Lebanese singer who has sold millions worldwide." The nurse laughed. "There is a reality TV series 'Arabs' Got Talent' and she's been a judge."

"And the second clue?" said Sarah.

"You probably know that until the Second World War, Lebanon was owned by the French. Even now more than half the children are taught French at school as their second language."

"French!" said Sarah.

"Yes. Najwa speaks French." The nurse smiled.

"Do you speak French?" she asked.

Sarah looked crestfallen.

"Un peu," she replied. "Un petit bloody peu." She looked at the nurse and took Najwa in her arms.

"She's around eight years old, probably from Lebanon, probably a Muslim and she speaks French. And she has no paperwork."

"That's about it," replied the medic.

"Has she mentioned her mother and father?" asked Sarah.

"My own French is limited," replied the nurse "but I have gained the impression that she has been alone for some time."

They were walking together down the avenue of derelict huts and shacks which were home to many thousands of refugees and they were ignored as the inhabitants maintained their daily search for food. They were passing a hut-style home fronted by an old woman who was sitting in the entrance and whose eyes met with Sarah, who stopped. Somehow, they understood each other and before long Sarah and Najwa were resting in the rear of the interior. When the little girl had been undressed, she was washed from top to bottom, dried and some carefully measured antiseptic cream applied to her sores. She struggled to swallow a tablet but finally gulped it down to earn a hug from her guardian. The old woman washed her clothes and hung them out to dry which, in the afternoon sun, did not take too long. She provided Sarah with slices of bread, some meat and fruit.

Najwa smiled as Sarah picked her up.

"Je m'appelle Sarah."

Najwa giggled and gave a smile which, over the weeks ahead, Sarah was to come to treasure. She did not respond to the French that Sarah had spoken.

Time drifted on and finally Najwa went to sleep on the sacking that had been provided for them. Sarah lay down, stretched out her tired limbs, and completed a mental list for the morning: first, to find a phone and contact Max; second, to speak to the border officials to ascertain how she could obtain the papers needed to take Najwa out of Syria and into Turkey. Once they reached Ankara, they could board a flight back to London. Slowly she succumbed to a deep sleep and nothing was going to wake her.

Sarah smelt him first and then opened her eyes. He had already pulled her clothes up and was forcing himself between her legs. He was vile and heavy and was snorting, his teeth were disfigured and, in several cases, missing. He had scars around one of his eyes and there was spittle coming out of his mouth and falling onto Sarah's face.

Her police training came into play as she rapidly completed a risk assessment. She sensed he was alone and was relying on his weight to subdue his victim and his intentions were rather obvious. He had her arms pinned to the ground and she could feel his manhood pressing against her. There were several ways to counter the attack but Sarah knew that once she made a move everything could, and almost certainly would, become more difficult as he would use physical intimidation to further his desires. She wondered about biting his face, probably his nose, but decided that was too high risk. Her best hope was her knickers.

She waited for the moment to arrive. She knew that the two most vulnerable areas of a man are his eyes and the inside of his thighs. The first requires quite considerable use of force albeit it might be possible to temporarily hinder an assailant by putting one's fingers into the corner of the sockets. There is a misconception that the second most lethal target area is a man's testicles. If the defender gets it right the resulting agony will paralyse a seven-foot giant but it is possible to achieve little more than to push the testes up inside the upper part of the scrotum. One testicle is larger than the other and the smaller testes can disappear out of the clutch of the aggressor during a frenzied assault.

Ex-DCI Sarah Rudd knew this all too well, having attended many personal assault situations. She knew that the most potent area of weakness was the flabby skin and body fat on the inside of the man's upper thighs. The wait continued as the assailant was readying himself to pull her knickers aside so he could enter her. He was probably right-handed and so she would have to pounce with her left: she felt her nails and this added to her confidence. He was now enlarged to capacity and, sure enough, he released his grip, thrust his right hand upwards and grabbed at her knickers which he almost ripped off her body. She felt his manhood getting obscenely close to her.

She pounced and grabbed at the inside of his right leg. The target area was flabby and, almost immediately, her nails were deeply embedded into his flesh. He screamed out and fought to release her grip but she was not having it, holding on and on and, when he released her right arm, she reached the inner thigh of his left leg within a nano-second. She squeezed and applied even more pressure resulting in a frantic attempt to free himself and leaving him screaming out for help.

Her timing was excellent. She let go and the assailant rolled off her, putting his own hands on the inside of his thighs. This allowed the final part of the defence to be enacted as Sarah stood up and kicked the attacker between his legs. His testicles were full of sperm and her foot crushed them against the bone, causing him to pass out as his body began to shake. She looked at the doorway and realised that the old woman was watching them.

Sarah grabbed Najwa, who was now fully awake, located her bag and staggered out of the hut. They then ran, turning left and then right down the avenues, aware of shadows and realising they were completely lost. The headlights of the oncoming vehicle caused them to stop and, as the driver pulled alongside, he lowered the window. He could have been the twin brother of the assailant except he had all his teeth.

"Dollars," he said, rubbing his fingers together.

If Mad Max had been present, he would have received a special Sarah hug. At Heathrow airport on the Sunday of her departure, he had insisted that she allow him to buy her three hundred pounds in US dollars. With the fall in the value of the pound, and the miserly rates of exchange offered by the currency desks, he had given her three hundred and sixty-five dollars. She now had them underneath the flap at the bottom of her bag.

"Dollars," the driver repeated.

She extracted the money from her secret store and held up two twenty-dollar notes.

"Over the border," she shouted.

"Not enough," he screamed. His scrambled accent suggested a background of Manchester or perhaps Romania.

"It's plenty," yelled Sarah.

"More," said the voice.

"No," said Sarah.

"Give me!" he screamed, as he looked into his rear-view mirror.

"How can I trust you?" she said.

"You can always wait for the next bus," he said.

She thrust the two notes into his hand and ran to the rear of the vehicle, picking up Najwa and throwing her on to the hard surface. She leaped up, pulled up the wooden flap and slid the bolts into their metal retainers. As they bounced along, she looked at her fingernails which had flesh and blood under most of them and so she pulled out a cloth and tried to wipe them clean.

After about thirty minutes, the lorry stopped and the lights were dimmed. The driver appeared at the back.

"We wait, no sound," he instructed. "Stay still and be quiet."

An hour later they realised that the vehicle was slowly moving forwards. The lights were now extinguished and they could see little, but could hear several dogs barking. On the horizon the start of the next day was showing as the driver appeared at the back and lowered the flap.

"Get out," he ordered.

"Where are we?" asked Sarah.

"Turkey," he snapped, and then he was gone. They watched the truck disappear.

Sarah wrapped her arms around Najwa.

"Ma cherie, nous sommes seules," she whispered, as the rain began to wash over them.

The orphan child was shaking with the early morning cold as Sarah gripped her, tightly.

Mayfair, London
Friday: early afternoon

Lord Mallington sipped his brandy and smiled at his guest. There were only a few of the seats in the private members' club lounge which were occupied and he was satisfied that their conversation was taking place in relative privacy.

"Yes," he said, "I have spoken to your father and he said that his hip operation needs re-doing. Anyway, he has outlined your circumstances, but I would rather hear the whole of the story from your lips."

Isobel de Lille Rutherford held on to her glass and tried hard to relax.

"Thank you, Lord Mallington," she replied. "I understand that you and my father met through his work at Lloyds Insurance Brokers but, before I do that, can you please tell me how you know my husband."

The peer smiled.

"Of course, my dear," he said. "Graham is a valued member of the Conservative Friends of Washington." He waved at the attentive waiter who quickly served a further glass of brandy. "The CFW, as we call it, is a loose association of those of us who believe that the most important international ally we have is America." He sipped his drink. "I'm on the committee."

"What does my husband contribute?" she asked.

The story unfolded with the peer's well-practised fluency.

"He's an awfully nice chap, knows a few people, is our type of Tory and he's rather popular with the members." He rubbed his fingers together. "Made a jolly helpful donation last year." He put his hand on her knee. "Time to tell me everything."

Isobel removed the hand.

"I'd like a cup of Earl Grey tea, please," she said. Her father had suggested that the peer was a possible route to extracting herself from the nightmare she was living.

The waiter quickly responded to the peer's instruction and Isobel was soon sipping her refreshment. Once she began, the words flowed as she re-lived the exposure of events at Hope House.

Her companion interrupted only twice, wanting to know who was advising her legally, an answer which satisfied him, and how could she not have understood the forms she had signed? Isobel had been spending sleepless nights asking herself the same question. She admitted that she was totally in thrall to her husband.

The peer nodded his head as he moved nearer to his guest.

Isobel shuddered with a growing sense of concern but she knew that, for the sake of her children, she had to see this meeting through to its conclusion.

"My father thought that you might be able to advise me, Lord Mallington," she said.

He smiled because he already knew the whole story and had instigated several moves that would assist Isobel.

"When we're alone, it's Simon," he said. "It's possible that I might know someone," he enthused.

"We'll need to go through everything in great detail." He put his hand back on her knee and squeezed. "Why don't I reserve a room here for us so we can talk it through over dinner?"

Isobel brushed away his hand and stood up.

"I am most grateful to you, but I must go."

He laughed.

"Sit down, Mrs de Lille Rutherford." He grinned. "A chap has to try and you are a beauty."

Isobel looked down at him.

"Can we agree that is the last personal remark you'll make?" she said.

"Do I get a peck on the cheek at the end?" he laughed.

Isobel found that, perhaps irrationally, she was laughing with him and then she leant down and pecked him on his cheek. He looked at her.

"Now I can die happy," he said.

He ordered two glasses of brandy and watched as Isobel sank back into the comfort of the chair as he explained that he knew more about her circumstances that he had let on.

"This is what I suggest is going to happen," he said. "Hope House is now closed and will be sold. We have files on every one of the children who has passed through and we are ensuring that each is being taken care of properly. The workers, apart from two who have disappeared, have been placed in alternative employment. We are still short of finding one of the children but we will." He paused. "We have made a donation to a local social services charity."

"Who are "we", Simon?" asked Isobel.

"Your husband has some influential friends," he said.

"What about the Hope House doctor?"

"Dr Henderson was focused on covering things up and so Dr Manning is now with another practice." He frowned. "There's a charity I know that helps doctors who find themselves in financial difficulties: I've made an introduction."

"The police?" she continued. "DI Morris is seriously scary."

"This must be confidential, Isobel," he answered, as he went to put his hand on her leg. "Whoops," he laughed. "Yellow card."

Isobel linked her fingers through his.

"I bet you were a very naughty man in your day, Lord Mallington," she laughed.

He seemed to drift away as she triggered the memories.

"Right. The police. It helps that the Assistant Chief Constable is in my lodge. I'm the Worshipful Master this year."

Isobel did not understand Masonic rules but knew enough not to ask further questions.

"You will be called to a meeting with Detective Inspector Morris at which your solicitor will be present. There will another officer attending but he will say nothing. The DI will be rather aggressive but that does not matter because, at the end of the meeting, you'll be told that the police will be taking no further action."

Isobel was fighting hard to hold back her emotion.

"You will do something for me, Isobel." He smiled. "Hah," he laughed, "that had you worried." He was now talking more professionally. "You will receive a call from a man called Roland Shaw of a London legal firm whose name I can never remember and who I want you to meet. He will ask you to sign three forms, the first of which sells Hope House, the second hands over the authority on the bank account and the third…" he hesitated, "…put indelicately, says Graham de Lille Rutherford is an abuser who attacked you and the children."

"Do I have to?" she asked. "That's my husband you're talking about," she said.

He took her by the hand.

"Do you have any idea what he really did in that home?" he asked. "A bit of child abuse was just the start. Do you want to hear what happened when he had two of the teenage girls tied together?"

Now Isobel's tears began to flow. Lord Mallington sat back and watched her suffer her personal pain. He knew that he had to proceed to the next revelation as he took two photographs out of his pocket and handed one of them to her.

"Her name is Zeander and this photograph was taken in the Caribbean and I guess that you know nothing about her."

Isobel looked at the suntanned, nearly naked native beauty and shook her head.

The peer handed the second photograph to her.

Isobel studied the damaged female body and put a hand to her mouth.

"Oh, my God," she cried.

"Your husband likes whipping young girls, which Zeander was not prepared to accept and so she found him a local teenager who was paid three dollars. This is what he did to her."

"I need to use the facilities," said Isobel. She returned after a little time.

"I will sign the forms but I have questions that

need answers," she said.

"You must have, my dear, so please feel free to talk to Roland Shaw. You can trust him completely."

"Can you email me the name of his firm, Simon, please."

"Consider it done," he said.

Isobel realised that he was staring at the photograph of Zeander.

Parrot Cay, Turks and Caicos Islands
Friday: evening

Graham de Lille Rutherford was becoming increasingly desperate. He had spent the day at his home two miles along the coast from Parrot Cay. The workmen had gone, the renovations were half completed and there was rubble everywhere. The cab firm was refusing to answer his calls and he found that his car had been vandalised.

He had spent two days trying to locate Zeander. He had to walk into Providenciales where he discovered that all his bank accounts were frozen and that none of the senior bank officials were available to him for the day. His also found that his credit cards were blocked and so he went to his solicitors but was unable to gain entry as they were closed for the afternoon. Zeander had disappeared, nobody would say anything, her hairdresser asked him to leave their premises and the managers of three dress shops all proved unfriendly.

Later that afternoon, when back at his derelict mansion, he received a visit from a Government official who told him there was an investigation into his financial affairs and he must present himself at the offices of the Internal Security department on

Monday morning at 9.00am. He was told that failure to appear would be taken seriously and he was forced to surrender his passport. He had three phones, all of which were shut down.

At around midnight, a passing couple reported seeing a man digging up the back of his garden.

Providenciales International Airport, Turks and Caicos Islands
Saturday: 2.00am

Mad Max Hemmings sighed with relief when the single engine plane landed and he was still alive. He struggled through customs and stared back at the official who finally stamped his passport. He was able to find a cab to the capital and booked in at the only hotel he could locate where he unpacked his few belongings and went to bed.

His morale was high because he anticipated catching up with Graham de Lille Rutherford the next day. He checked his phone which needed recharging and the little battery that was left showed that the three incoming messages were all from London. He was worried about Sarah but he decided that she would find her way home.

The following day, after a fruitless search, Max Hemmings of SC Group discovered that Graham de Lille Rutherford had fled the island and no-one knew of his whereabouts and so he decided to have an hour on the beach and smothered himself with suntan lotion. The text messages from Daisy Maitland started coming in early in the afternoon. By the time Max returned to his hotel room he knew that the offices of de Lille's finance house in London had been taken over by a group of new, unfamiliar officials. Daisy told him that the atmosphere was described as 'tense' but Thelma had been told that she would be staying with the firm.

The offices of Hannings & Richards, Lincoln's Inn Fields, London
Saturday: 11.00am

Isobel de Lille Rutherford shuddered a little as the late winter winds blew across the legal centre south of Holborn Tube Station in central London. Her parents were installed at home, much to the amusement of her children Nicholas and Emily. The traffic was moving free of the weekday congestion and she could see that few of the offices in Lincoln's Inn Fields were occupied. She had used the underground journey to prepare for her meeting with Roland Shaw.

She reached New Square and found the number which was clearly marked as she looked at the name plate: Hannings & Richards. She pressed for reception and within moments found herself in front of a rather impeccably dressed man.

"Mrs de Lille Rutherford," he said. "Your time-keeping is immaculate."

They entered a passageway and he explained that there were a few staff upstairs but they would be using an office off the reception area. He took her coat and indicated where the facilities were to be found. They entered an immaculately furnished room at the centre of which was an oak table and a set of six chairs.

"I've percolated some coffee for us," he said.

Isobel put down her case, sat down and relished the warmth of the refreshment. He pushed a plate of chocolate biscuits towards her but she declined the offer.

He sat down and looked at the file in front of him.

"I'm Roland Shaw," he said, "and we have been brought together by Lord Mallington."

"You're a barrister," said Isobel. She knew that was not the case but had decided to generate some early brownie points.

"You flatter me," he said. "Wish I was, 'cos they all earn more than me," he laughed. "No, I'm a solicitor, a specialist in the law of corporate finance." He finished his biscuit. "That's dealing with the rules and regulations covering UK and international companies."

Isobel wondered whether to explain to him how to bake a cake.

He took out three forms and spread them on the table.

"I think Lord Mallington told you that I will be asking you to sign these."

"That is correct, Mr Shaw."

"Any chance we can make it Roland?" he asked.

"Definitely, Roland," she said. "But I'm not signing the forms."

He raised his eyebrows.

"That is absolutely your right, Isobel," he said, and smiled. "I am allowed to call you Isobel?" he laughed.

"It's my name," she said.

"Do you want me to explain the forms to you?" he asked.

"That's thoughtful of you, but no thanks," she said. "Can you please hand them to me?"

She took them from him, opened up the leather case she had brought with her, put them carefully inside and closed the retaining lock.

"So," said Roland, "a rather long way to come for a cup of coffee."

"We haven't started yet," said Isobel. She checked her mobile telephone to ensure there was no message from her children and then she asked for some water which he provided.

"I've read your biography on the website, Roland. It's impressive."

"You knew I was not a barrister," he said.

"You're an expert on banking matters," continued Isobel.

"You flatter me, again," he said.

"What did my husband do that seems to be at the heart of his prosecution?"

Roland Shaw looked at the woman sitting across the table and frowned.

"Lord Mallington said I could totally trust you," she added.

"Why are you here, Isobel?" he asked. "We could have posted the forms to you."

"I'm with my lawyer on Monday so having them today is rather helpful. She'll be advising me."

"And who is she?" he asked.

"None of your business," said Isobel.

"Absolutely the right response. I apologise for being nosey."

"What did Graham do?" she repeated. "I know you know."

"Isobel," he replied. "Let's get the rules right. Lord Mallington has asked me to see you and I had expected you were going to sign the forms that he and I believe are in your best interests. That, however, can now be the judgement of your solicitor. We will, of course, answer any questions she has."

"You are involved, Roland. Your name wasn't picked from a telephone directory." She wiped her mouth. "I want to understand what Graham did in what I understand to be a banking fraud."

"Why?" he asked. "What benefit is there going through the whole sordid business?"

"The benefit accrues to me and I'm his wife." She hesitated. "I accept I'm heading for a divorce but I have the right to understand what he did."

Roland Shaw stood up, walked over to the window and watched the gardeners clearing the seasonal debris off the lawns.

"What he did, Isobel, is mastermind one of the most devious and repugnant frauds ever seen in the banking world."

"Is that your judgement?" she asked.

"It's the verdict of the jury at the trial of his associates; it's the opinion of the press and the regulatory bodies; and, if you are asking, it is one of the worst cases of financial fraud that this firm can recall."

"And everyone else is an angel, I suppose," she snapped.

"You really do want to understand what happened, don't you?" he said.

"I'll overlook your patronising style," she said. "Yes, I do and I think you can tell me."

"There's a bottle of wine in the fridge," he said.

"Nice idea," she replied.

"I've no peanuts," he said and they smiled together. The wine was poured and Roland Shaw kicked off.

"In the late nineteen-nineties and early two thousands, your husband built up what he called

Rutherford Finance House. It was, in fact, a bank and that was helpful because banking licences are difficult to obtain. Unlike what you and I think of as a bank – an operation that takes care of people's money and lends it to those who need money – Graham ran his as a private equity business. He took in deposits but his speciality was investing in businesses and undertaking what is called asset stripping."

He topped up his wine but observed that she had placed a hand over her glass.

"Are you warm enough?" he asked.

"I'm comfortable, Roland," she replied.

"He and his team were good at what they did. It was legitimate and considered by some to be socially responsible. Essentially they took money out of weak businesses and put it to better use in growth enterprises." He smiled. "He was clever because he attracted some senior figures in the City as non-executive directors." He laughed. "He was adept at finding peers of the realm. Nothing like having Lord so-and-so on your letterhead."

Roland stood up and went out to use the facilities. Isobel checked her mobile phone: 'Gramp's hip hurting. Love u. E x.'

He returned and sat down having looked at his watch.

"Can I just explain one thing, Isobel. Forgive me if you know this, but banking is basically an unstable business. What a bank does is take in a pound and lend it out ten times."

"How does it do that?" she asked.

"A customer deposits one thousand pounds in a bank. That bank then allows ten customers to overdraw up to one thousand pounds and so it has turned one pound into ten pounds."

"Send for Midas," she suggested.

"More like send for Graham de Lille Rutherford because whatever he seemed to touch turned into gold. But let's finish off the banking lecture."

This time Isobel allowed him to refill her glass.

"It works because experience shows that the first customer will not ask to withdraw the thousand pounds deposited." He paused. "As banks grow, their financing becomes rather sophisticated but the general principle I have explained stays in place. In practical terms, banks finance their requirements by borrowing from the wholesale money markets." He sipped his wine.

"I'm trying really hard not to patronise you." he said.

"You are winning the battle," smiled Isobel.

"Let me explain the term 'wholesale markets'," he continued.

"I would appreciate that," she said.

"Think about your personal finances. Money in – monthly allowance, other income, dividends and so on, and money out – household expenses, food shopping, your car, visits to the hairdresser."

Isobel liked that because she had paid extra to the salon stylist the day before to ensure she was looking her best.

"What if expenditure exceeds income?" he asked.

"Off to see Daddy," she replied.

"Exactly," said Roland, "and banking is just the same. If a bank's liquid liabilities exceed its liquid assets, it makes up the difference from the wholesale markets. In other words, your Daddy is a bank's wholesale markets."

Isobel drank some wine.

"Liquid?" she asked. "What does that mean?"

"Cash or convertible to cash," he said.

She nodded her head.

"I know where I can find Daddy but where are the wholesale markets?"

"There's very little cash in the world," he continued. "It's nearly all digital records which means globally there are rows and rows of kids at computer screens. Those with money, rich Arab oil states, Russian oligarchs, corrupt African leaders and Warren Buffet put their funds with investment houses who lend it out to those who need it such as banks. The wholesale markets are, so to speak, in the clouds."

Isobel pushed her glass towards her host.

"No more than half a glass or I'll be joining them," she laughed.

"Back to Rutherford Finance House," he said.

He allowed himself another chocolate biscuit.

"A bank wants to finance an oil tanker for one hundred million pounds. That takes rather a lot of one thousand-pound deposits. They simply borrow what is called overnight money from the wholesale markets. At the end of each day the bank works out its deficit and borrows it for twenty-four hours."

He wiped up the crumbs from in front of him.

"The fundamental requirement for this system to work is confidence. That is why the Bank of England is so important because the markets know that they monitor all that is happening. There are more regulators these days but the Bank is the key player."

"In case you are interested," she said, "I'm following what you are saying."

"The problem occurs when confidence evaporates.

Put another way, it's when Daddy says "no". It's usually when there is too much money in the system but that's more to do with economic theory. In practical terms what happens is that confidence, for whatever reason, disappears, and this can happen very quickly, and the wholesale markets refuse to fund the banks' deficits. Suddenly the banks are in trouble or, even worse, they are bust. The Bank of England will not allow this to happen. This is why it is called the lender of last resort. In 2008, starting in America, banks started to go bankrupt. Over here, two of our main banks hit problems and had to be rescued by the Government. This is where your husband was rather smart."

Isobel sat back, studied his face and decided that Roland really cared about what he was telling her. Over the many sleepless nights when she tossed and turned in her solitary bed, trying to understand what was happening to her and the children, she came to one essential conclusion: she needed to understand things much better; she was hungry for knowledge.

Roland continued by explaining how Rutherford Finance House went to one of the banks and offered to take the toxic (he explained that the word simply meant 'unlikely to be repaid') loans to smaller businesses off their books. This was attractive to the bank as it improved the strength of their balance sheet and helped meet the demands of the Bank of England and of the financial regulators. In doing so, many smaller companies were granted new loans through Rutherford Finance House but the terms were so onerous that many collapsed into receivership. Before that happened, Rutherford had siphoned off huge amounts in fees. When the businesses failed, they often used a subsidiary company to buy the assets from the receiver.

"The case came to court," he continued, "and three of the directors of Rutherford Finance House received prison sentences," he explained. "Graham was never involved because, although he was the managing director and major shareholder, his name never appeared on any documents involving the banking scheme."

"What were they charged with?" asked Isobel.

"It was complicated but essentially the charges were fraud, bribery and money-laundering." He paused. "In my opinion, a decent defence barrister could have defeated the charges but there was an additional problem."

Isobel stood up and went over to the refreshments table where she poured herself a glass of water.

"What was that?" she asked.

"The three men who were charged had become wealthy and they had embarked on a massive spending spree. This involved luxury homes, villas in sunny climates, women, prostitutes, drugs, sex parties and the rest. The prosecution was smart. They showed photographs of them sitting around poolside tables and they each had a self-satisfied look on their faces which was used to influence the jury."

"They were the guilty parties," she said.

"Definitely, they deserved the sentences handed out by the judge," he concluded.

"Were they the only guilty ones?" asked Isobel.

"It depends what you mean. They were the only ones charged."

"What about the independent directors of the bank who allowed this to happen?" She sipped her glass of water. "You will understand that there is a lot of information on the web about the case."

"You have been doing your homework, Isobel." He held up his hand. "No, I promise, that is not me being judgemental. Can I explain the hypocrisy that exists in the business world? The theory is that non-executive directors maintain a control over the executives. In fact, it is more often a case of 'jobs for the boys'." He laughed. "For boys, read girls," he added. "They are paid generous fees for turning up to board meetings. I can't recall any non-executive director being prosecuted for events at the company of which they were directors." He paused. "Graham chose his non-execs carefully. He maintained total control. They simply pocketed their fees."

He paused as he pondered his own words. He often wondered how corrupt the system really was.

"Isobel," said Roland, "I am trying to answer your questions but let's understand one thing. The really guilty party in all this was Graham, your husband."

"And all those who had made huge sums of money out of him, simply ditched him," she said.

Roland stood up and opened a second bottle of wine. He poured some for himself and then held it over Isobel's glass but found she was saying "No more, thanks".

"Isobel," he continued, "there's a danger that this conversation is becoming unbalanced," he said.

"What does that mean?" she asked.

"I'm attempting to answer your questions and you're trying to defend your husband."

Isobel stood up and walked round the room, at one point peering out of the window and across the lawns of New Square, and then she looked at her phone. She read the message: 'Base to Mumsy. Help! Granny has migraine. E x.'

"Please organise a taxi for me," she said. Roland made a call.

"Four minutes," he said. He looked at his guest. "I've upset you," he suggested.

She walked over to him and put her hand on his sleeve,

"You've been helpful, Roland," she said. "My husband is proving to be an unscrupulous, perhaps rather unpleasant person and I must protect my children."

"I know about Hope House," he said.

"You do, I would expect that," she said. "I accept what he is and what he deserves."

A call was made and Roland held his phone to his ear. "Your cab is here, courtesy of the firm," he said.

"But, Roland," she added. "I do not accept that he was alone in his guilt, not by a million miles." She smiled. "Today is the start of my journey," she said.

He looked at her and opened the door. "I urge you to be careful," he said.

"I understand that," she said. She looked intently at him. "Do you think I can be hurt any more than I have been, by what has already happened to me and my family?" she asked.

The solicitor followed her down the steps and opened the door of the cab.

"We can meet again if that helps you," he suggested.

"Perhaps," said Isobel. She sat down on the rear seat and started to pull the door closed. She looked at Roland. "I need to think about all you have told me," she said.

+ + +

CHAPTER FIVE

Turkish side of the border
Friday/Saturday
After being abandoned by the lorry driver, Sarah and Najwa walked for about two kilometres when they came across what appeared to be a small group of derelict farm buildings. They were bitterly cold, the rain was incessant, the road was undulating and the tarmacadam surface was crumbling and offered hidden hazards for the unwary. There were isolated white-washed buildings set back from the road, many of which seem to be guarded by dogs. In the early daylight, Sarah could make out the red-tiled roofs.

The orphan child was struggling and so Sarah decided to gamble and enter into one of what seemed to be several disused barns. The door creaked open on its rusty hinges and she forced her way into the semi-darkness. As the entrance broadened, the daylight revealed small piles of hay, two Angora goats and a number of sacks filled with their fleece which provided Sarah with bedding for Najwa. She had spotted an outside well and, much to her relief, was able to pull up a bucket containing what appeared to be fresh water. She found a plastic container and carried the refreshment back into the barn.

She dressed Najwa's sores, encouraged her to swallow a tablet, made her drink copiously the water from the well and held her tightly until the child went to sleep. As she lay down on the sacking, she tried to prioritise the tasks facing her. She wanted to talk to Max but her phone had been stolen at the airport. They were perhaps seventy kilometres away from

Gaziantep airport on the Turkish side of the border and she knew that Aleppo on the Syrian side was ninety-seven kilometres from the airport. She remembered they were in the Anatolia region of south-eastern Turkey and then her eyes closed and she entered into a deep sleep.

As she opened them, Sarah knew immediately that the sun was blazing down, the rain had stopped and that the man staring down at her was beaming a broad smile. Sarah sat up and checked on Najwa.

"Me, Altan. My wife cares for child," he said.

Sarah put her arms around her charge but Altan threw up his arms in a welcoming sign.

"No, we good people. You English?" he added.

Sarah let go of Najwa and stood up quickly, pulling her clothes around her; through the open doors she could see a bright, warmer day. She refocused on the man who was not tall but rather rotund. He continued to smile.

"Please," he said holding out his arms. "My wife, you can trust her."

As these words were spoken a woman of a similar age and dimensions appeared, looked at Sarah and knelt down by Najwa.

"Bath," she said. "She needs washing."

Sarah let her go and watched as Najwa was carried away.

"Me, Altan," he repeated, puffing out his chest.

She had no idea why she trusted him but he seemed friendly and offered them a short-term period of security.

"Me, Sarah," she said.

They started to walk together and it quickly became apparent that the derelict buildings, which they had first located, were a small part of Altan's farm. The house, which had an ornately-carved front door, was extensive and there were two cars parked at the end of a long driveway. In the distance she could see pine-clad mountains and, when they reached the front, on the far side, there were rows of trestle tables with people having an early lunch. The food was being served from a series of spits over coal fires which were roasting chickens and on each table were bowls of salad, soft flat bread and pots of water.

"You hungry?" suggested Altan.

"Najwa," replied Sarah and he nodded. They walked back to the rear of the buildings and into a kitchen where she was sitting at a table, freshly clothed in items of spotlessly clean warm material. She had fresh shoes on her feet.

"You eat," said Altan.

Sarah held up her hand to her ear and Altan nodded as he registered her request for a phone. They returned to the eating area and sat down at a table where the other diners generally ignored them although several of the women smiled at Najwa. They were served chicken kebabs and, at that point, Sarah realised how hungry she was. She cut up some chicken breast for Najwa who ate carefully and sipped the water from a tumbler. She showed more appetite when the baklava was served: she sucked at the extra honey poured over the sweet pastry.

As the afternoon developed the tables began to empty, Altan returned and sat down with them. He brought with him two children who began to play with Najwa and who, before long, had disappeared. His English was limited but he and Sarah managed to agree that he would arrange for them to be taken to

Gaziantep airport whereupon she took out a fifty dollar note and handed it to him. He nodded, put it in his pocket, pulled out a phone and rubbed his fingers together, resulting in more dollars changing hands. Altan said that they would leave the following day. Sarah argued for a more immediate departure but the Turkish farmer simply blanked her.

Sarah reached Max with her first call and reassured him that she expected to land at Heathrow airport within three days once she had sorted out the paperwork for Najwa. She listened carefully as he explained what had developed with Graham de Lille Rutherford and she frowned when he admitted that he had no idea to where the fugitive had fled. She told him to be careful and then contacted Norman Delamount. He wanted to know about Najwa but he did not ask about her. She spoke briefly to her soon-to-be ex-husband and, for a much longer period of time, to her daughter, Susie. She was told that Marcus was too busy to speak to her; she understood his position and promised herself that one day she would be re-united with her son. Najwa found a friend and the afternoon was spent relaxing in the sunshine.

The following morning Sarah prepared Najwa for the journey to the airport, pleased that her sores were healing, the two stitches in her back were clear of any infection and there was a little more flesh on her stomach. The two travellers ate their breakfast in relative silence. There was no sign of Altan until he appeared just before noon and seemed in good spirits as he led them to the truck. Sarah became confused when he pointed at a woman who he said was the driver but he waved aside her protests. There seemed to be no attempt to load the vehicle and Sarah became increasingly agitated by the continuing delay to their departure.

Altan had spent the last day making himself some money. He had known immediately that Sarah was the English woman for whom the grapevine was searching and he had acquired a picture of her. His link was the local tribal chief who had spoken to the contact in Ankara. A line to Dublin was established and a sum of money was paid; Altan had no idea that his percentage was less than three percent but, for him, it meant a replacement tractor.

The Continuity Irish Republican Army, referred to as the Continuity IRA, traced its roots to the proclamation in 1916 of the Irish Republic. It split from the Provisional IRA in 1986 but did not resume hostilities until 1994 following their cease fire. It remains a designated terrorist organisation in the United Kingdom and maintains links with the political party, Sinn Fein. It has one objective, a united Ireland, and watched the Brexit negotiations with an opportunistic eye. In the last few years, it had strengthened its financial position by accepting contract killing assignments.

Their best operative had known violence all his life. Michael Duggan (his real name was known only to a few top operatives) had been born south of the border with Northern Ireland, he was sent to Chicago where he spent his teenage years and returned in 2016 with a fearsome reputation. He was involved in several killings in London which were hushed up by the security services. Ex-DCI Max Hemmings had come across his face when reading internal briefing circulars. Duggan had flown out of France and was now believed to be in the East Mediterranean area.

Finally, the woman driver indicated they were ready to leave but Altan was nowhere to be seen. The journey to the airport was a little under sixty-eight kilometres and was expected to take around two and a half hours. Sarah and Najwa were in the back, hidden from view by several layers of sacking. The driver had no knowledge of what was about to happen. They had been travelling for perhaps one and half hours when she descended into a valley with a lake on one side and hills on the other and saw ahead of them a broken-down vehicle and an old man waving for help. She slowed to a halt as the bodywork of her vehicle was shredded by machine gun fire. The driver was hit by several bullets which caused her to collapse, so pulling the steering wheel to the right and resulting in the truck overturning. The firing went on until the whole of the metal framework was destroyed.

Michael Duggan waited and then moved in to check upon his success. He pulled the body of the driver out of the cab and shot her in the head to end any lingering signs of life. He moved to the back and carefully started to heave the covering out onto the bank of grass searching piece by piece for the bodies of the two passengers until, slowly, it dawned on him that they were not there.

Sarah held Najwa under the surface of the lake for as long as she dared. She had been on edge ever since they had left the farm and wondered if she had misjudged Altan but thought she had negotiated the right deal for their escape. The other warning sign she had received was Norman's behaviour on the telephone when he failed to talk about her as it was unusual for him not to ask questions and Sarah had noted the signal.

When the truck had slowed down, she thrust Najwa out on the lake side and followed her quickly, taking them both into the tepid lake. She saw the assassin come over to the water's edge and stare out. The light was fading and Sarah noticed, about a hundred yards away, a jetty to which a small boat was secured. She slowly inched their way towards it and boarded the craft and then she laid Najwa in the bottom and untied the retaining rope. She paddled her way out into the lake, helped by a sudden gust of wind, and crossed to the other side where they reached a forest which came down to the water's edge. She carried Najwa into the trees, bundled up some branches and covered her as best she could. She lay down knowing that they had lost everything except for her bag which she had tied around her stomach.

Michael Duggan caught Altan unawares as he was bent over a table slurping some chicken soup. He dazed him by lashing his pistol across the bald palate and then dragging his victim out of the kitchen and into a barn where he used a knife to slice off the clothing of the dazed farmer until he was naked. After securing his feet he threw the rope over an oak beam and pulled violently until Altan was hanging up-side-down with his head resting in a pile of manure. Duggan picked up a shovel which he held at waist level and then he lashed the tortured man across the stomach. As he screamed out his wife came running into the building, only to be quickly tied up and dumped in a corner where a goat came over and licked her face. Duggan returned to the object of his anger.

"You warned her," he yelled out.

Altan shook his head. He already had several broken ribs and suspected that worse was to follow.

The Irish killer reached for his knife and drew the blade across his chest causing Altan to scream out in agony. But there was no time to waste because Duggan calculated that he did not want Sarah to gain any great distance on him. He picked up his weapon, shot Altan dead, left the building, ignored the petrified wife and rapidly spoke into his phone. He decided that Sarah would instinctively continue to try to reach the airport and he knew exactly where he would intercept her.

London
Saturday: late afternoon

It was a clever and uncomplicated plan and the timing was smart. The Continuity IRA exploded a petrol lorry at the southern end of the M1 motorway at its congested junction with the North Circular Road around London and, fifteen minutes later, they triggered a small incendiary device in a parked car in Piccadilly. Then they phoned in a bomb warning naming Waterloo Station and set fire to a block of flats adjacent to the charred remains of Grenfell Tower in North Kensington. When the police, fire and ambulance services were stretched in all directions, two terrorists entered the concourse of Euston Station and shot dead the only police officer in view. They opened up with their automatic weapons, indiscriminatingly firing into the fleeing crowds and throwing two hand grenades. The three security officers who had now appeared were overwhelmed: one died instantly as shrapnel removed the side of his face. A woman police officer lost her lower left leg, a child of four years old was so devastated by the explosions that her body was shredded into fragments and a 'Big Issue' vendor came through the attack without a scratch and carried on selling his publication. An announcement over the loud-speaker system said that trains were subject to delays. As more armed police arrived, one of the terrorists was shot dead and the other, a woman of around twenty-two years of age, was taken down by a member of the public and held until she was arrested by the security forces.

In total, although it took time to ascertain the up-to-date figures, there were eleven fatalities and over thirty people were injured and needing hospital treatment; the transportation infrastructure of the capital city was paralysed. All London railway stations were closed, as was the underground network, and most UK airports were shut down for several hours. The media were fast into action, co-ordinating on-the spot reports from the various locations as the sky above the capital was populated by police and medical rescue helicopters. The London Mayor concentrated on the care of the killed and maimed, their relatives and London people in general, and the Labour leader spoke with some impact and captured the public mood. The Prime Minister said that his thoughts were with the relatives of the bereaved and praised the work of the emergency services. The Home Secretary said that police funding was at an all-time high. On Sunday morning an emergency meeting of selected ministers and advisers was held in the COBRA underground room in Westminster.

Cabinet Office Briefing Rooms ("COBR") are

located in Cabinet buildings in Whitehall, central London. Each is a secure unit seating up to twenty people and fitted with video and audio links to display intelligence information. The first COBR meeting took place in the 1970s to oversee the 1972 miner's strike. The term COBRA gained media usage as various crises were discussed by the Prime Minister, ministers and advisers using Cabinet Office Briefing Room A, which is Conference Room A in the Cabinet Office main building located at 70 Whitehall.

Following the devastation of the Euston Station attack, the Prime Minister tried to calm public nerves by displaying authoritative leadership from his COBRA bunker. He sat nervously fiddling with his pen while the crisis group assembled with the Chief Constable seeming thoughtful and the intelligence chiefs a little subdued.

Terence Barrington wondered who he could trust. The Home Secretary was loyal and under huge pressure because the terrorist tactics had been so devastating. Their diversionary activities meant that the security services were unable to reach Euston Station for nearly nineteen minutes. The media pounced and wanted fast answers.

The Chancellor of the Exchequer was also facing tensions as the aftermath of the post-Brexit settlement began to affect the economy and the Monetary Policy Committee of the Bank of England was split on the direction of money costs, with some of the members wanting a rate increase whilst the rest were 'doves' who argued for low interest costs; there was to be no change as indecision won the day! The Chancellor, William Davidson, was outwardly calm and was enjoying watching the Prime Minister squirm;

he thought that the end of austerity was misguided. The Defence Secretary had managed to reach his hairdresser and still not be late for the meeting.

Prime Minister Terence Barrington was now urging the assembled COBRA group about the need to calm public fears.

"We must demonstrate," he preached, "that nothing will undermine our resolve to defeat terrorists."

In a forest near to Gaziantep Airport, Turkey
Sunday: early morning

Whether the god who was hovering over Sarah and Najwa as they awoke cold and shivering under their bundle of twigs and branches in a forest near a lake perhaps twenty kilometres from Gaziantep Airport, was Muslim, Christian, Catholic, Jewish or some other religious denomination, will never be known. They were fortunate to be alive, following Michael Duggan's unbelievable mistake. He was realising that he had underestimated the resilience of the woman he had been sent to kill. He was not to know that both Sarah and Najwa were struggling with their physical deterioration following an extensive period in the water, on the lake and in the forest.

As Sarah threw the covering off them and stood up, she realised immediately that they were less than twenty feet away from a pathway cut through the wooded area. She could also hear softly uttered sounds and she detected that they were women's voices... were they chanting? There was no choice because it was essential to find help for Najwa and so she stepped out into the middle of the track, stared ahead and was surprised to find that she was facing six nuns.

Events moved quickly as the members of the religious order soon had Najwa wrapped up in a cloak which one of them had taken off. No words were spoken as they hurried along the uneven path for less than half a mile. Sarah saw that they had reached what was clearly a church and watched one of the nuns ring the bell by pulling on a rope which resulted in a copper ball hitting the iron. Almost immediately the door was opened, two women appeared and one took Najwa in her arms and disappeared inside.

They gestured that Sarah should follow them and before long she found herself in a kitchen, the centre piece of which was a huge table covered with vegetables. There was a warming log fire and, as she moved towards it, she began to shake before collapsing to the floor from where she was carried into a side room. When her clothes were cut off her body, a red stain revealed that a bullet had passed through her side. A doctor arrived an hour later, examined and dressed the wound and administered an injection. He left the nuns with an antiseptic cream and a container full of antibiotics and said that he would return on Tuesday.

Providenciales International Airport, Turks and Caicos Islands
Monday: 6.00am

Max sat patiently in the departure lounge waiting for his flight to be called and feeling pleased that his detective skills had not deserted him. It had been obvious that his best route to finding out to where Graham de Lille Rutherford had fled was to locate Zeander. He reasoned that she was still on the islands because this is where she lived and she and de Lille might have agreed to meet up somewhere.

He had spent the previous morning visiting the resort where they had stayed, and then he had travelled in to Providenciales and toured the dress shops. He showed her photograph, taken from Norman Delamount's file, to everyone he met but to no avail – Zeander was not to be found. At around midday he went into a hotel and sat at the bar drinking a beer, trying to decide: what would de Lille do? He had to flee from the islands because he was being chased by people unknown. He could not use the usual channels and so he'd call upon the one advantage he did have: money. Somebody, somewhere, would take him away to a safe haven. There were two alternatives: by air or by water and, as international air routes were too well monitored for the first to be realistic, he had to be in a boat.

After consuming a second bottle of beer he had a thought and within an hour he had located the doctor who looked after Zeander. It proved to be the easiest part of his investigation. He walked into a local surgery, paid some money and was given a name. They even called a car for him and before long he was walking into a small harbour in a village along the coast. As soon as he held up the picture the atmosphere became tense and he found himself being ushered into the back room of a local bar where a man in his fifties was holding a cigarette in tobacco-stained fingers.

Max had the ability to be seriously threatening and it took less than twenty minutes for the other man to write down the name of a boat. Max returned to his hotel and contacted Norman Delamount and, within two hours, he was told that they had the vessel under surveillance. It was three hundred miles into the Atlantic and it seemed to be heading for the Mediterranean although that was not certain. Max decided to fly to Spain, disappointed that there were no further messages from Sarah.

*

'Meryem Ana Evi', South West Turkey
Tuesday: 11.00am

Sarah was awake when the doctor arrived to re-examine her. Only one nun remained as he carefully lifted off her night clothes and exposed the wound. He asked the young woman to take off the dressing which involved unwinding the lengthy bandage around her stomach. The medic examined the one area of damage and seemed to concentrate on the edges of the bruised flesh. He nodded and together they turned her on to her side so that the area where the bullet had exited was exposed. He rubbed some cream onto the damaged skin and helped return his patient onto her back and he then proceeded to give her a full examination including checking heart and blood pressure readings and taking a blood sample. The whole process lasted twenty minutes when he packed his bag and left the room without saying a word. The nun resumed sitting by her side and gave her a pot of water and a bowl containing green grapes and figs.

The door opened and in came a person Sarah immediately assumed was the Mother Superior. She nodded at the nun who went and sat at the end of the bed.

"You have some questions to ask," she said.

"Najwa," replied Sarah.

"She is well. She's being taught by the teachers about our beliefs." She put her hand on Sarah's forehead.

"The doctor says you are healing quickly and suggests that you can start to walk in two days. We'll keep watch but we think your injuries are ones we can tend ourselves. You must understand that it will be at least a week or even more before you can leave here."

"You're English," said Sarah.

"I'm from Dover," she said. "In due course I'll tell you all about Mother Mary's House. What you need to know now is that I came to Turkey ten years ago and I've never left."

Sarah slumped back into the bed.

"What do I call you?" she asked.

"Eslem is my Turkish name." She paused. "Who shot you?" she asked.

"Where am I?" asked Sarah.

"You are at Meryem Ana Evi which translates into Mother Mary's House," she answered.

Sarah's eyes were closing and, before long, she was asleep.

Eslem spoke quietly to the nun at the foot of the bed and left the room. The curtains were pulled across the small window to shut out the day's sunlight as the door re-opened and a second nun came in with Najwa. The young child went up to the bed and kissed Sarah on her head before being led away and out of the room. She had smiles of joy on her face.

*

Michael Duggan was becoming increasingly desperate. His intended victim had completely disappeared and every one of his usual methods was failing to produce anything positive. The phones were dead, no credit cards had been used, the local taxi drivers knew nothing despite money being exchanged and, although her picture had been widely distributed, no-one had seen her. He reasoned that she was in hiding and so, at some point, she would try to escape from Turkey so he decided to stay in the area and await the lead that would surely come his way.

*

Claridge's, Brook Street, Mayfair, Central London
Wednesday: afternoon

The choice was such that, for a few minutes, Isobel de Lille Rutherford managed to forget the mounting pressures which she faced as she read the menu:

Freshly baked raisin and apple scones with Marco Polo jelly and Cornish clotted cream served with a glass of Laurent Premier Brut

The decision was taken away from her as Lady Christel Hemmingway-Brunton called the waiter over and ordered two teas. The lounge at Claridge's was packed with afternoon customers but they were served immediately and a pot of Earl Grey tea was added to their refreshments.

"I'm so grateful you have time for me, Chrissy," said Isobel.

"Nonsense," she replied. "We've been friends for many years, Issy." She paused. "Tell me the bad bits."

The waiter returned and poured their glasses of

champagne before Christel waved him away.

"The bad bits," mused Isobel. "The children are being harassed at school and there have been several incidents of racial chanting. It's because the papers are pinning Hope House on me."

"Hmm," interrupted Christel. "You've seen the teachers?"

"They're doing all they can. Their advice, and I accept it, is that it will blow over."

"Finances?" asked her friend.

"I'm selling the house which is in my name. It's about the only thing that Graham has done for me. A bank has tried to claim it, but they've gone away. We'll move out into the Chilterns and we can live comfortably, I have my own money and my father is being supportive."

"Where is your husband?" she asked.

"Nobody knows," said Isobel. "He's disappeared."

"Surely Lord Mallington knows his whereabouts?" she suggested.

"If he does, he's not telling me." She drank her champagne. "Chrissy, who are 'the Elite'?"

Lady Christel summoned the waiter and instructed him to serve two more glasses of champagne. She waited while he did so and then she dismissed him.

"There are some questions a lady does not ask," she said.

"Every day I find out more about what Graham was doing. Hope House was by far the worst of his excesses but his Finance House was built on his connections and he had debts. A woman from there has come forward claiming sexual harassment."

"As Mandy Rice-Davies once said, 'She would say that'," misquoted Lady Christel.

The two friends laughed together: they had both read up on the Christine Keeler political spy scandal in the early nineteen-sixties.

"What about the banking matter?" asked Christel.

"In a way that makes Hope House seem like a children's bedtime story," she said, "the men in prison have all made statements. They had kept their silence because they believed that when they had completed their sentences their futures would be financed by Graham." She paused. "Hard bloody luck," she said. "Why I'm so grateful that you are here today, Chrissy, is because I can trust you."

She drank some tea. "Hear me out, please." She lifted her napkin and wiped her mouth. "What Graham has done and, in truth, got away with for so long, is because he has been protected by a group of powerful people." She stopped again and drank more tea. "I'm going to find out who they are."

Lady Christel Hemmingway-Brunton stared at her friend.

"That, Issy, might not be such a good idea," she said. "Think of your family."

Isobel looked askance.

"My family! I think about nothing else. Who are these people?"

"The Elite, as you call them, are to be found in every society. They are a group of individuals who are bound together by two things: power and money."

"Who are they?" she pleaded.

"It's a loose association," she continued. "My husband, when he was alive, used to tell me stories. It's about politicians, the armed forces, police, judges and the wealthy." She paused. "There is an association, the Conservative Friends of Washington.

Lord Mallington is the real power there. That's elitist."

"Graham told me he had been asked to be a member," said Isobel.

"Exactly; he was making people serious money which is what the membership is about." She coughed. "He threw it all away."

"Are these people of integrity?" asked Isobel.

"Integrity," laughed Christel. "They are about money and power. Life to them is a game of chess and most of us are pawns."

"Pawns!" exclaimed Isobel. Her immediate memory went back to her meeting with Roland Shaw and the many questions that remained unanswered.

"Pawns," she repeated. "We'll see about that," she whispered to herself.

+ + +

CHAPTER SIX

The Cabinet Room, 10 Downing Street, London
Thursday: 11.00am

Sir Robert Walpole looked down on the assembled group of ministers, a little complacent that his was the only portrait hung on the off-white walls of the Cabinet Room. It was unlikely that the Secretary of State for Northern Ireland, The Right Honourable Elizabeth Shaw MP, was thinking of his reflective words. She had flown back in from Belfast at three in the morning and had foregone sleep for that day and possibly the next. The Whig Prime Minister had said:

I have never been afraid of making patriots, but I disdain and despise all their efforts.

The ministers were sitting in their mahogany chairs according to seniority: only the Prime Minister had a chair with arms, which amused the Minister for International Trade with her permanent suntan. She was listening to the leader's request for an up-to-date report on the terrorist attacks. A number of arms were resting on the oak table as the ministers absorbed the Home Secretary's latest summary of the Euston Station and associated bombings. Heather Cousins could be pompous at times and insisted on using her full title, Secretary of State for the Home Department, but today was different and she gave her carefully prepared report with professional candour. The death toll was now fourteen, and twenty-seven people remained in hospital. The security services had quickly analysed the woman terrorist's background and a raid in Ruislip, west London, led to three further arrests. The individual herself had chosen to

107

remain completely silent and although the dead gunman was known to the police, he had not appeared on their radar for over three years, suggesting he was a 'sleeper'.

"So, Prime Minister, we know for certain that this was the work of the Continuity Irish Republican Army because the coded warning received about Waterloo Station was only known to them. What is really concerning is that we believe they are being trained by a group of foreign terrorists but, as yet, we don't know who they are."

"I'm not sure I understand the point you are making, Home Secretary."

"The point being made, Prime Minister," interrupted another minister of some seniority, "is that the attack on Euston Station was, by IRA standards, incredibly well planned."

"You seem to be glorifying the numbers of dead and injured," snapped Terence Barrington.

"Throughout the troubles in Northern Ireland, Prime Minister," said the Minister, "it was clear to some of us how incompetent the IRA really were." He coughed before continuing. "Much of that was due to the success of our special forces but, if you examine the planning last Saturday, they used diversionary tactics rather cleverly. We've not seen that before."

The Prime Minister sniffed and moved on.

"Secretary of State, you've just returned from Belfast."

"Indeed, I have, Prime Minister." Elizabeth Shaw looked down at her notes. "There are three main issues." She looked around her as though she needed reassurance. "First, the Continuity IRA is re-armed and very aggressive. The Euston Station atrocity was the first time in nineteen years that a Republican bomb has been exploded on the mainland." She paused. "In their world, it has been called a 'spectacular'."

There was complete silence around the Cabinet table and so the Secretary of State continued her report.

"Second, the Confidence and Supply Agreement made with the DUP during the Brexit negotiations polarised opinion and has made discussions with Sinn Fein politicians more difficult. The tension between the two sides is still acute." She paused again.

"I can take no credit, Prime Minister, and your intervention has been crucial, but it is a great step forward that power sharing has begun again after three years. The Stormont Assembly has been restored and the Executive is now working together." She paused. "We hope."

"Quickly, Secretary of State, we have much to cover, but briefly, what are the issues?"

"Prime Minister, there are ninety MLAs, Members of the Legislative Assembly, so take your pick. There's little difference from here: their National Health Service is in crisis and there are too few police."

The Home Secretary, Heather Cousins, snorted and started to interrupt until she registered the stare from the Prime Minister.

"What about the Irish language and the Ulster Scots?" asked a junior minister in a blatant attempt to show off.

Elizabeth Shaw turned on him.

"How many Ulster Scots are there in the

Province?" she challenged. Her questioner was struck dumb. "Perhaps around three hundred and forty thousand but there are twenty-seven million in the United States. The Irish language is important to Sinn Fein and Ulster Scots is recognised as a minority language." She turned back to her colleagues.

"But, Prime Minister, the bigger issue is this: the Dublin Government and Sinn Fein have seen the problem with the border after Brexit as their golden opportunity to force a vote of re-unification."

"That is wholly unacceptable," said Terence Barrington. "I have pledged to Her Majesty and to the British people to hold the United Kingdom together."

"I don't think the Scots are thinking that way," interrupted the Secretary of State for Defence.

William Davidson, the Chancellor, thought that the Defence Secretary always managed to speak the bleeding obvious.

"Perhaps it's a matter of how many bombs and attacks the British people will tolerate, Prime Minister," said the Chancellor of the Exchequer.

The Foreign Secretary, Maurice Henson, looked at the Minister for International Trade and wondered if he could rely on her support in the event of a leadership contest. However unlikely it seemed at that moment in time, following the Brexit settlement, the Irish situation had the capacity to alienate public opinion. The travel chaos which had followed the Continuity IRA attacks suggested that the country's appetite for more disruption was limited. He sensed that there was a lull in the cross-table conversation and realised that this was his opportunity.

"It was interesting, was it not," he said, "what the President of Sinn Fein said when he announced he was stepping down."

"Remind us," suggested a senior minister.

"He said," and he laughed, "leadership means knowing when it is time for change."

As was his usual strategy, the Prime Minister changed the subject and started to talk about building more homes for the British people.

'Meryem Ana Evi', South West Turkey
Saturday: morning

"We are, what is called in England, an off-shoot," said Eslem, holding the soup spoon to Sarah's lips. She spoke a little more sharply. "You need to eat, Sarah, as much as you can. You have a long journey ahead of you."

"You told me what this place is called," she said.

"Meryem Ana Evi," explained Eslem. "It means Mother Mary's House."

"You are Christian," said Sarah.

"We are," she said. "Our name is the same as a much bigger chapel on Mount Koressos at Ephesus. That is an ancient Greek city on the coast of Ionia and is a very religious place. Pope Benedict XVI visited it in 2006 and gave it a papal apostolic blessing." She paused and thought. "I was happy there but they asked that I come here to create a centre in South West Turkey. We grow year by year." She took the soup bowl away. "But we must talk," she said.

"Najwa," said Sarah. "How is she?"

Eslem smiled. "She is a beautiful child; we believe she was born eight years ago. She can remember her mother and her father but cannot recall when she last saw them. She has some recollection of being with a group of migrants who made it into Syria but she may be confused. She must have been in Lebanon for some time because her French is fluent. How she got to the border, we do not know."

"Should I leave her here?" asked Sarah.

"That would be difficult because we would have to disclose her to the authorities," said Eslem. "But there is a bigger matter for you to consider." She paused. "Najwa has attached herself to you."

Sarah thought carefully.

"That is hard to believe," she said.

"She yearns for security and you are giving her that."

"But we've only been together for a few days," said Sarah. "We've fled from a rapist, we've been betrayed by a farmer, we've been attacked by an assassin, we've nearly drowned in a lake, we've no papers and little money." And no phone, which had been lost in the lake.

"Young children are amazingly intuitive, Sarah," said Eslem.

"What does that mean?" said Sarah.

"As far as Najwa is concerned she had poured all her hopes into you."

"Shit," said Sarah. "Oh! I'm so sorry, Eslem, I should not have said that."

"The Lord is understanding," said the nun. "I think we'll pray," she said.

Sarah put her hands together and shut her eyes. She did not understand what was being chanted but she could determine 'Sarah' and 'Najwa'. She opened her eyes.

"What happens now?" she asked.

"The doctor says you will be fit to travel next

Tuesday," said Eslem. "We will get you safely to Ephesus. We'll arrange for you to cross over into Greece where you can claim asylum."

"Does Najwa know all this?" asked Sarah.

"She has had it all explained to her," said Eslem. "I think you should get dressed and go and see her," she said. "I have some good news for you." She put her hand in a pocket of her apron and pulled out a mobile phone. She watched as she registered the look of relief on Sarah's face.

One of the novices had, on a number of occasions, managed to slip out of the church and visit the nearby village. She was permanently hungry and she disguised herself so that she could go into the café where she would order a bowl of lamb stew knowing that she could not pay for it. After the first time, when it came to settling the bill, she proposed a novel solution which the café owner was happy to accept. They slipped out and went behind the building where she lifted her skirt. In their own way they became friends and the proprietor started allowing her a glass of wine with her meal. They then found that they were beginning to enjoy talking to each other She ate onions on the way back to cover the smell of the alcohol on her breath.

During her latest visit to the café she started talking about a little fair-haired girl and so the owner took a photograph out of his pocket which he showed her. The trainee nun showed surprise and nodded her head before leaving to return to the church. The café owner got into his truck and drove to the next village where he met with a provincial organiser.

113

Hotel Don Luis, Madrid-Barajas Airport, Spain
Sunday: mid-morning

Mad Max was not overly impressed that it was raining and he was forced to watch the windswept outdoor swimming pool from the sanctuary of his bedroom in the Hotel Don Luis, which was a five minutes car ride from the Madrid-Barajas airport.

He had Wi-Fi, a fridge full of Spanish beers, and he was worried about Sarah. He had spoken at length to Norman Delamount who advised him that Graham de Lille Rutherford was believed to be on a Russian-owned ocean cruiser and was heading for the Mediterranean. He had not received any further communication from Sarah. He did add to Max's concerns by saying that there was reliable information that Michael Duggan was in Turkey.

He was wondering whether to have an early lunch when the vital communication came through starting with a text message:

'Can I call? D'

A few minutes later, Max and Daisy Maitland were chatting.

"I was with Thelma last night," she said. "She says it's as though de Lille Rutherford never existed. There's new management and all members of staff have been re-employed."

"What about de Lille?" asked Max.

"We don't know where he is," she said.

"For fuck's sake, Daisy, that's what I need to know."

"But we know where he's heading," she said.

The phone went dead and it was twenty minutes before an increasingly Mad Max managed to speak to his informant again.

"Sorry," she said. "I had to move. You cool Max?"

"Where is de Lille heading to?" he asked.

"Cyprus."

"Why Cyprus?" he asked.

"Do you mind doing some of the work?" she said. "If it will help you, I'm going to text you the name and address of his bank and the account details."

"Hell, Daisy, that's brilliant."

"I was in a rather loving mood last night," she said.

"I need to ask: are you fighting it?" he asked.

"Max, keep encouraging me. I'll get there."

He knew the seductive power of soft drugs but she seemed to be speaking in a way that suggested she was making some progress.

"We can help you," he said.

"Not as much as I can help myself," she replied. "Text coming. Good luck, Max."

He went to his main telephone and contacted Norman Delamount by managing to interrupt his boss at the club.

"Max," he said. "That's makes sense. Cyprus is exactly where de Lille might have put his reserves."

"Reserves?" asked Max.

"Most people with serious wealth live their lives worrying that they'll lose it because their prosperity is what makes them a member of the Elite. Many distribute their assets around the world for that very reason. De Lille rather proves the point and he had anticipated that the time might come when he was not welcome in his usual haunts and so he – prudently, I might add – stashed away a fortune in a safe haven."

"Why Cyprus?" asked Max.

115

"It's controlled by the Russians. There are huge advantages there: it's in the EU and the Eurozone which helps money-laundering, there are low rates of interest including corporation tax at 12.5% and it has an attractive Tax Treaty Network."

"What's that?" he asked.

"Put simply, it's a legitimate means to avoid double taxation." Norman paused as, unseen by Max, he gulped a glass of champagne. "But, almost certainly, the attraction to de Lille is that there is no tax on the sale of assets, shares and bonds, and no capital gains tax on the sale of properties. What de Lille is almost certainly doing is amassing enough wealth to allow him to begin a new life." He hesitated. "How do you know he's going to Cyprus?" he asked.

"Sources," replied Max.

"Reliable?"

"Yes," he said. "I will be able to find de Lille. I'm flying out in three hours' time."

*

Claridge's, Brook Street, Mayfair, Central London
Monday: afternoon
"Well, Issy, I didn't think I'd be seeing you so soon," said Lady Christel Hemmingway-Brunton.

"I really am grateful that you said 'yes', Chrissy," replied Isobel de Lille Rutherford.

She paused while Christel berated the waiter on the state of the bread used in the finger sandwiches.

"Brown bread means fresh brown bread and you have used an oil-based butter which is totally unacceptable," she said. She watched as the crestfallen waiter hurried away with the rejected plate of sandwiches.

"It's Monday," said Christel. "No alcohol on a Monday."

She poured the Earl Grey tea.

"You have problems, Issy," she said.

"No, not really. Just a conundrum," she said.

"I love that word," she responded. "It can mean so many things."

"Chrissy. I've seen Lord Mallington and he's been helpful. He's introduced me to a slightly scary lawyer called Roland Shaw who seems to be involved." She paused and wiped her mouth. "He has prepared some papers and my own solicitor has agreed that, once her changes are made, I should sign them." She sighed and seemed to relax.

"At face value, everything is beginning to settle down. The house is up for sale and we've had three offers in the first week." She sipped her tea. "There is no news of Graham and Lord Mallington could not provide an update. I shouldn't say this, but I didn't believe him."

"Interesting, Issy, but what's the conundrum?"

"Your comments about the Elite and us being pawns." She took out her handkerchief and rubbed her eyes. "I asked Lord Mallington about the Elite and, frankly, the door was firmly closed shut."

"Of course, my dear, it would be."

"Why, Chrissy?"

"Misogyny," she answered.

Isobel paused and thought carefully about what had been said.

"Issy," said Christel, "the Elite are contemptuous of women. Our role in life is to look glamorous and perform in bed."

"Are all the Elite, men?" she said.

"They are mostly males but a number of powerful women have managed to make it. That woman at the World Bank is one example. But look around you, at the Conservative Party, at industry, at the Civil Service, at the police. Most of the top jobs are held by men. There are a few women there by merit, the Chief Constable is a good example, and some are there as tokens to the female brigade."

"That's disgusting, Chrissy," said Isobel.

"No, we bring it on ourselves," suggested Christel.

"Not me," said Isobel.

"Yes, you Issy," she said.

"Chrissy, are you trying to hurt me?"

"Issy. You're my friend but you started this conversation. You allowed Graham to run rings round you."

"I did?" she snapped.

"Yes, Issy. You always fancied Graham and you signed paperwork without thinking about what you were doing or what you were signing because he had you in the palm of his hand."

The waiter arrived with a fresh plate of sandwiches only to be told that he had taken too long and neither of them was now hungry and he was instructed to bring a fresh pot of afternoon tea. The distraction was helpful to Isobel who was fighting back her emotions.

"Is that the truth, Chrissy?" she protested.

"Yes, we see it all too often. But you are fighting back in a different way. You have the opportunity to rebuild your life and, Issy, you'll come out of this much stronger."

The two friends left the hotel a few minutes later

having embraced warmly.

Later that evening, after the two children had gone to bed, she put on music by Dame Kiri Te Kanawa who was singing 'I Dreamed a Dream' from 'Les Miserables'. Isobel opened up a document on her computer. The title was 'The Elite' and she recorded all her thoughts; the last heading was 'Action Plan'.

She picked up the glass of vodka and tonic, sat down in her chair and stared at the cupboard opposite where there was a photograph of Graham with Isobel and their children. She stood up, looked at it carefully, put it in the bottom drawer of her desk, locked it away and put the key in her purse. But an inner sense told her it was not over; not by a long way.

*

Nissi Bay Beach Bar, Ayia Napa, Cyprus
Monday: 11.30pm

Max Hemmings sipped his lemonade and shivered slightly despite the outdoor heaters designed to warm the beach area of the Nissi Bay Beach Bar. A native waitress came over and shook her head. He had paid her to ask around after showing the photograph of Graham de Lille Rutherford.

Ever since landing at Larnaca International Airport and hiring a cab to take him the fifty kilometres to Nicosia, he had experienced a series of frustrations. After his conversation with Daisy Maitland, he was sure that Graham de Lille Rutherford was heading for Nicosia because it was the financial centre of the island. It was also the only divided capital in the world, but Max did not care whether de Lille was in the Turkish north or the Greek south.

119

His hotel room was average, the food was average and it was not much warmer than London when he had left. He spent the day trying to locate his adversary. The bank details given to him by Daisy proved worthless as the official he finally managed to speak to denied all knowledge of the Englishman. He telephoned his informant who said that Thelma had told her that de Lille moved his assets around all the time. Max researched the top five hotels in Nicosia and visited each of them, showing de Lille's photograph.

He spent the late afternoon speaking to Norman Delamount who was unusually vague. His mood changed when the call came through from Sarah and she explained where she was and that, in the morning, she and Najwa were leaving for Northern Turkey. As he was trying to assess her chances the line went dead.

The break-through came while Max was using the leisure centre at the hotel. These were an improvement on the rest of the facilities and had a feature where a waterfall cascaded out of rock and into a mosaic of spas and water features. As he marvelled at the deep blue of the water, a woman came through the spray and dived into the largest of the pools. She was stunningly graceful and, as Max ogled at her legs, he realised where Graham de Lille Rutherford might be. He went to the bar and invested in a large scotch which he drank slowly while befriending the barman and giving him a fifty euro note. In return, he was told where he could buy a woman.

The journey to Ayia Napa on the south-east coast took just over an hour and he didn't care that the name meant 'holy wooden valley'. What mattered to Max was that it was where the Nissi Bay Beach Bar was situated. From the moment he arrived, Max not only smelt the money but he sensed a lot more and found it was impossible to ignore the sheer panorama of seduction. It was blatant.

He settled in and a particular girl seemed to be attracted to his table; he gave her twenty euros and showed her de Lille's photograph. She nodded her head, moved off and, after about ten minutes, she returned and shook her head. There was no chance she spoke English but that did not really matter because she understood exactly what Max wanted and she liked his money. More partygoers were arriving and a steel band was entertaining the guests. The girl returned with another girl who, sensibly, was wearing a blouse over her top. She also shook her head and so Max gave them each a further twenty euros and indicated he wanted a drink.

"Beer," said the first girl.

Max shook his head and said that he wanted a lemonade. The one girl stayed and smiled at him while the other went away and returned with a pineapple drink. They then disappeared once more, returning twenty minutes later to Max's table. The first girl took out the photograph, nodded her head and rubbed two fingers together. Max sighed and gave her another twenty euros only for the girl to shake her head. He took out a fifty euro note; she grabbed her friend by the hand and indicated that he should follow them.

He was taken along the beach for around a quarter of a kilometre when they stopped. There was a dimly lit group of whitewashed villas and, as he watched, the door of one opened and a woman came out and shut the door behind her. Max sensed that she was a prostitute. The second girl took his hand and led him down a path towards the back of the area where she pointed to one of the most secluded buildings and then she and her friend disappeared.

Max moved quickly and stationed himself behind the villa amongst an outcrop of rock. He watched for over half an hour, could hear no sound and so he crept up to the door in the rear and found it was unlocked. Pushing it open, he entered a kitchen area and then went into the main room where a girl was lying on the floor, semi-naked and covered with bruises and some blood. Her moans through the mouth gag were pitiful.

Max thought quickly and realised that he could not risk being caught up in this incident but the girl needed urgent medical help. He dashed around the building, opened every door and window and switched on all the lights. As he rushed into a wooded area, he saw two people taking an interest.

He circled round the perimeter and returned to the front of the nightclub where there was a row of cabs for hire. He showed de Lille's photograph to each of the drivers but all shook their heads. Then he went to the front of the queue and asked the driver if he knew where the cab that had been the last to leave had been heading. The driver spoke English and held open his hand which resulted in Max giving him twenty euros as he said that he thought they were heading to the south-east port of Limassol.

"The driver is my son," he said. "I can radio him."

"No, don't do that," Max ordered. "Why Limassol?" he said out loud.

The driver suggested that fifty euros was required to extract the answer from him. Max handed the money over and listened to the information he was given. As his cab took him back to Nicosia, he could not work out why Graham de Lille Rutherford was now heading for Greece.

'Meryem Ana Evi', South West Turkey
Tuesday: 7.00am

Michael Duggan was concealed in the trees outside the entrance to Mother Mary's House, having been in that position since three o'clock in the morning. He reasoned that the white van was the means of transportation that Sarah was using to leave the convent and he was positioned to allow him a clear shot at her as soon as the front door was opened. He ignored the rain and ensured that his rifle was under cover, not reacting to the occasionally claps of thunder although he started to monitor their increasing frequency. The rain was turning into an electrical storm lighting up the skies.

The door opened and the light revealed a woman and a child, each carrying several bags. They hesitated as they realised it was raining and wrapped their clothing around themselves. Sarah stepped out a little further.

Duggan raised the rifle sight to eye level and prepared to shoot, anticipating a clear view of his intended victim. There was a huge thunderclap and a branch above him broke off and fell towards the ground. As he fired, the barrel was knocked off-centre by the debris and the bullet deflected downwards, hitting the pebbles between Sarah's feet. She neither heard nor felt the ricochet. Michael

Duggan swore quietly under his breath as he decided to withdraw.

The journey from the convent to the coast had been prepared meticulously by Eslem. The challenge facing both Sarah and the nun was the lack of paperwork for Najwa and, after several phone calls and much thought, it was decided to drive the two of them to the Mother Mary's House on Mount Koressus at Ephesus. After resting for two days, they would be taken to the port of Kusadasi, on the Ionia coast, thirty kilometres south of Ephesus, where they would be smuggled around two hundred and twenty miles across the Aegean Sea to the Greek island of Rhodes. Sarah would then claim asylum as a British citizen and register Najwa. She was comfortable with the first stage of the plan and expected to reach the sanctuary of the convent at Ephesus without too much difficulty. She reasoned that once they left the security of the religious order and began the crossing to Greece, their passage was likely to become progressively more dangerous.

They said their farewells inside the convent and Sarah ushered Najwa into the front of the van, ready for departure. The driver made no attempt to speak, relying on hand signals to indicate that they should put on the safety belts across the front seat of the van. Sarah noticed that on both sides were painted, in vivid red letters, 'The House of the Virgin Mary' in both English and what she assumed to be Turkish. She was not to know that it was a ten-year-old Mercedes-Benz Sprinter van which Eslem reasoned was as anonymous as possible. What Sarah did understand was the journey was likely to take approximately sixteen hours, assuming there were no delays on the way.

The rainfall continued and was unrelenting. It was not until they were on the Otoyol, the Turkish motorway, having passed through the toll booth, and leaving Gaziantep airport behind them, that the weather began to brighten up. Najwa was seated between Sarah and the driver and kept glancing to her right and staring at him. After two hours, they left the motorway and took what Sarah assumed to be a suburban road heading for Adana if she were to believe the signpost. Once they had crossed the Seyhan river they would make slower progress, not least because of the frequent potholes, but would be relatively more secure on the less exposed route. The driver was careful to stay within the fifty kilometres per hour speed limit. Sarah gazed out of the window at the flat fertile lands and slowly relaxed. She looked at Najwa who was holding her hand.

At around ten-thirty, just over three hours into their journey, the driver pulled into the car park of a roadside café, parked the van and disappeared. Sarah and Najwa followed what appeared to be an entry path and were soon seated in the relatively deserted eating house. Sarah had enough money to see them through to Greece and ordered orange juice, flat bread and fruits. She was encouraged to see that Najwa was both hungry and eating well. Before they had finished their meal, the driver reappeared, pointed at the van outside and so Sarah rushed up to the counter and paid over some euros. She took Najwa's hand and led her into the toilets which were spotlessly clean. When they returned to the van the driver was clearly annoyed at what he perceived to be a delay in starting off again but Sarah smiled and opened her arms in a sign of apology, which he ignored.

The two passengers settled down to the next stage of their journey; the break at the roadside café had been welcome. It was at this point that Sarah made a discovery. Najwa was able to talk in pidgin English. Nobody at the convent, and certainly not Eslem, had mentioned this but events there had moved so quickly the finer details were overlooked.

Najwa pointed out of the window.

"La maison," pronounced Sarah carefully when the van passed through a small village.

"House," said Najwa, and laughed.

For Sarah, it was the sound of an angel and it was a noise she had not heard too often from her orphaned companion. Najwa wrinkled her nose to show that she was happy. They hugged each other despite the restrictions of the seat belts and Sarah registered how thin she was. The words began to flow as they realised that they had found a way to talk more freely together.

"Je m'appelle Sarah," said Sarah, pointing to herself.

"Sarja," laughed Najwa.

"No; non," she said. "Sarah."

"Saha," tried Najwa.

"Sarrrahhh," was the next explanation from her teacher.

Najwa spluttered out another attempted pronunciation.

"Mais oui," sang Sarah. "I am Sarah."

"Sarah," said Najwa. "I am Najwa," she added, wrinkling her nose.

They spent the next hour discovering which words they shared in the two languages and Sarah noticed that Najwa was picking up English quite quickly. She began to drop her rather pathetic attempts at speaking in French and before too long nearly all their communication was in the one language. Sarah looked across at the driver but there was not a flicker from him.

At two in the afternoon, the driver pulled into a petrol station which had only two pumps. He stopped the van and pointed at an outdoor bar-b-cue to the side of the building where there were a series of wooden tables seating four to six people. Sarah and Najwa joined the queue and before long were seated alone, each with a bowl of chicken and vegetable stew. As they were finishing their lunch in the afternoon sun, the driver found them and pointed to the van. Sarah had already paid their bill so she took Najwa's hand and strode towards the facilities, which was a small shed with a hole in the ground. They were soon back in the van and starting the next leg of their journey.

+

The clothes of the novice nun were torn and she was very scared. The owner of the café had dragged her out of her seat and taken her to the rear of the building before

grasping her in a bear hug, with one hand covering her mouth. Michael Duggan was holding a knife to her body.

"Where?" he said. "Ask her."

The local man told her that she was going to

experience great pain unless she told them where the van that had left the convent earlier in the day was travelling towards. She shook her head and then screamed as Duggan used the knife to cut her breast. It took only a few more minutes of pain before she muttered "Ephesus".

He nodded at the café owner who threw her to the ground, allowing Duggan to take out his gun, screw on the silencer and shoot her dead.

*

The next part of their journey proved to be enjoyable for Sarah and Najwa. Despite the bumpy roads and occasional lumps of tarmac, the driver maintained a steady speed and carefully steered his way through the vans and lorries which seemed to collect together in convoys.

"Camion," said Sarah, reverting to her schoolgirl French and pointing to the vehicle in front of them.

Najwa wrinkled her nose and shook her head.

"Camion," repeated Sarah and added, "lorry."

"Holly," tried Najwa.

Sarah laughed and rubbed her hand through the fair hair on her head.

"Llll...lorry," she repeated.

"Lohhy," said Najwa and they laughed together.

"Lorry," she tried again.

A frown crossed Najwa's forehead.

"Lorry," she said and they hugged.

Sarah pointed to their driver who was staring straight ahead.

"Lorry driver," she said.

"Lorry driver," repeated the orphan in almost

perfect English.

Sarah gasped.

At around six in the evening, as the light was fading, the driver pulled into a petrol station and pointed to a building lit up in the front. Before long, Sarah and Najwa were eating mushroom omelettes, drinking warm milk, and finishing with ice cream. The driver reappeared and Sarah could smell tobacco on his breath. They were soon underway and at eleven in the evening, an hour earlier than scheduled, they arrived at the Mother Mary's House on Mount Koressus in Ephesus. The driver fetched their canvas bags from the back of the vehicle, got back in the van and drove off.

Sarah and Najwa found themselves being ushered into a room where there were two beds and, before long, they had washed, undressed and Najwa knelt by the bedside, put her hands together and said a prayer. They lay down on the mattresses and were almost immediately sound asleep.

The following morning, a nun came in and showed them the way to the showers where, to their delight, the water was warm and refreshing and the two travellers found themselves in good spirits. They dressed and were shown into a private room where they were given breakfast. The nun told Sarah that they would be leaving in two hours and explained that they were in the House of the Virgin Mary which was a haven for Catholic pilgrims who wanted to visit the site where Mary, the mother of Jesus Christ, lived some of her life. Many prayed silently at the wishing well which acted as a shrine for the believers. Sarah asked about the alternative name 'Mother Mary's House' and the nun explained that both the terms were used.

Two hours later a car arrived, the driver leaped out and, somewhat to Sarah's surprise, the nun herself said she would be driving them to the port of Kusadasi. Sarah was immediately on her guard. She had understood that they were scheduled to stay at the convent for two days and tried to ask why there was a change in the plan but she was ignored. Events moved quickly and before long they were installed in the back of the vehicle and were driving quite quickly along a rough surfaced road towards the coast. Following the news received from their sister convent, and the death of the young novice, there was a certain relief that the two refugees were being transported away to another territory.

As they turned a sharp corner the coastline lay in front of them and Sarah was dazzled by the blue sea. A shot rang out and the nun grabbed at the wheel of the car which swerved into the side of the road. They were saved by their seat belts. Sarah undid the buckles, grabbed Najwa and leaped into the gully over which the two front wheels were protruding. She suspected the shot had almost certainly come from the front on the driver's side. She therefore made a decision and propelled them backwards along the gully and behind some rocks. As she looked at the site of the shooting, and to her complete amazement, a police car had pulled up and two officers were investigating the incident. Sarah knew they had a moment of opportunity and so they ran as fast as they could. Their luggage remained in the car apart from her bag which Sarah had tied around her middle. Najwa stumbled and grazed her knee but she did not make a sound. They ran on and came across a pebbled shelter where Sarah pushed open the door and they collapsed inside. As the sun beat down on them it became hotter and hotter and they had no water to drink.

At the Mother Mary's House, the community had gathered to pray over the body of their departed sister, which lay covered in a white cloth in front of the altar of the Virgin Mary. One by one the nuns offered incantations. It is not known whether they asked for forgiveness for the person who had shot their colleague dead. In the local mortuary lay the body of the café owner.

Sarah lay alongside her charge, who was sleeping peacefully, and was recalling that the Irish assassin had now made two attempts to kill her – assuming that the last rifle shot came from his weapon. She was reasoning that her luck would not hold for much longer. She thought of Max and wanted him by her side very badly indeed.

+ + +

CHAPTER SEVEN

The Cabinet Room, 10 Downing Street, London. Wednesday: 3.00pm

Prime Minister's Questions had come and gone with the usual torrent of invective from the Labour Party leader about the ever-increasing wealth divide, nurses relying on food banks to survive and the level of personal debt.

Terence Barrington had called a special meeting of eight selected individuals to discuss the Irish situation before the Prime Minister departed for a series of meetings in Brussels, including one with the Taoiseach, the Irish Prime Minister. The Home Secretary started by presenting an updated report on the Euston Station terrorist attack.

Heather Cousins had managed little sleep during the past few days. The conclusion they had reached was that the Continuity IRA attack was a one-off. The terrorists had used up much of their resources in the incident and, despite its effect on public opinion, the security services privately advised that they did not expect a further attack in the immediate future.

"However, Prime Minister," added the Home Secretary, "the threat level is being held at 'critical' for the time being."

The ministers pondered this information: 'critical – an attack is highly likely in the near future'. It was the highest of the five levels set independently by the Joint Terrorist Analysis Centre and MI5.

There was an air of relief in the Cabinet Room because another assault, and further casualties, would blow a huge hole in the credibility of the

Government. The Prime Minister decided to move on and asked the Secretary of State for Northern Ireland to present her latest report.

"Prime Minister," began Elizabeth Shaw. Her colleagues around the table knew that she would be well prepared. "You will be meeting the Irish Prime Minister tomorrow and this is where it is getting complicated."

"We're relying on you to simplify it," said Maurice Henson. The Foreign Secretary was smarting with frustration because his advisers were telling him that it was conceivable that Terence Barrington would survive the post-Brexit negotiations with the European Union and lead the country for the next few years. Once again, he had made a misjudgement with his interjection.

"No, Foreign Secretary, it is not my job to simplify it," she snapped. "That is what you did in Iran, thereby damaging our reputation in the Middle East."

Henson prepared to retaliate when he realised that the Prime Minister was glaring at him and so he left off initiating another attack until the next opportunity arose. Once he gained power, Elizabeth Shaw was history.

Melvyn Donaldson, the Secretary of State for Defence, remained silent. He thought that Henson was obsessional and was certain he would never be prime minister.

"Prime Minister, colleagues," Elizabeth Shaw continued, "the Irish Prime Minster is making an impact within the European Community and, by focusing on the difficulties with the hard border, he is playing his trump card because its rejection was made clear in the EU's negotiating guidelines." She paused.

"We know that until the trading settlement is agreed there is no chance the EU will conclude the Irish situation."

"Secretary of State," said William Davidson. The Chancellor was struggling, following the disclosure in the House of Commons of the deteriorating state of the country's finances and continuing low productivity. He also knew that the NHS had overspent into the billions to counter the winter flu epidemic. "You told us last time that you thought reunification was the real issue." He smiled at his colleague.

"That will always be the ultimate objective," she continued, "but we must remember that it's one hundred years since the Republic fought a bitter civil war following the partition of the island and no Irish prime minister will want to go down in history for signing a treaty leading to the reimposition of a hard border." She paused for effect. "We have a challenge," she continued, as the Prime Minister pondered her use of the word 'we'. "Our Prime Minister – correctly, in my opinion – has committed this Government to keeping the United Kingdom together. Under Section 1 of the Northern Ireland Act 1998, I can call a poll on Irish reunification if, and when, I believe there is a realistic chance of a 'yes' vote." She paused because this time her nose was itching. "That is not the case at the present time but I must warn you that the Catholics are breeding at a faster rate than the Protestants."

"It would also mean, Prime Minister, that Northern Ireland, on reunification, could become part of the European Union again," added Heather Cousins.

There was silence around the table until a voice said, "They voted 56% to remain."

The Prime Minister ignored this interjection and attempted to sum up the situation.

"Thank you, Secretary of State," he said. "I think I'll be talking mostly about trade, not rates of pregnancies!"

"May I make a further point about the Continuity IRA?" said Elizabeth Shaw. "We have picked up some intelligence that they are putting themselves out for contract work," she said.

"Contract work?" asked Maurice Henson.

"Yes," she replied. "Contract killings. It can be lucrative. If we could prove this, it will help our negotiations at Stormont."

One of the people present knew exactly what she was talking about.

Limassol Beach Front, South East Cyprus
Wednesday

Max's journey from the Nissi Bay Beach Bar to Limassol occupied much of Tuesday morning because the taxi he hired broke down on two occasions. It was a distance of one hundred and ten kilometres although, for Max, it seemed much further. The price was extortionate but he had little choice. When the driver suggested that the tip was not enough, Max introduced him to some English words he had probably not heard before.

He found a hotel on the sea front, unpacked his case and established an operational base in his search for Graham de Lille Rutherford. There were two questions which needed answering: first, where was the disgraced banker? Second, why was he fleeing to

Greece? He spoke at length to Norman Delamount who was unable to answer either question and worried Max further by telling him that contact with Sarah had, once more, been lost.

The break-through came late in the evening when he received a text from Daisy.

'Saw Thelma last night. Try Rhodes'

On Wednesday morning, Max found himself outside the Prokymea Sculpture Park overlooking the blue water of Akrotiri Bay. A travel guide in his hotel room had informed him that Limassol is the third most up-and-coming holiday destination in the world but as his only objective was to depart the resort, this rather amused him. He decided to travel by motor boat to the Greek island. It was a distance of around five hundred kilometres through well-known and relatively safe waters but it was not until the late afternoon that he found a skipper prepared to take him. The agreed fee was another lesson in Turkish entrepreneurism and required Max to visit a local bank.

They left early in the evening and almost immediately the skies clouded over and it became chillier. The two men on the boat stayed in the cabin and did not try to talk to Max. He observed how busy the sea channels seemed to be as the lights showed up the fishing vessels and several larger ships in their vicinity. They arrived on Thursday morning as the sun was rising in the skies; Max found him pushed out through the gentle waves and onto a beach and so he walked up through the sand and found several mounds of grass. He lay down and went to sleep, having checked that there no messages on his phone. As he closed his eyes, he wondered how Sarah was getting on.

The Beach at Kusadasi, Western Turkey
Wednesday: 9.00pm

Sarah held Najwa close to her as she was becoming increasingly desperate. She knew that Michael Duggan had made two attempts to kill her but she was not aware of the missed shot at the Mother Mary's House. Her phone was dead and her bag contained a few dollars, some euros and a mixture of personal items including the near-empty tube of antiseptic cream. She felt Najwa shaking in her arms and held her as tightly as possible.

She first saw the single light ahead of her and reasoned it was at the water's edge as she strained to see what it could be. Holding Najwa close to her, Sarah edged closer to the boat and managed to make out what she counted to be perhaps nine people milling around, with two of the women holding young children. She stood up, walked closer towards them and saw that the craft was capable of carrying six passengers seated on the benches.

The tall man was clearly the person in charge of the migrants and so she walked straight up to him and held up her remaining dollars. He shook his head and she noticed that several of the men were moving aggressively towards her. She wrapped Najwa as closely as she could to her body and used one arm to plead with the boss who shook his head again.

She took off her watch and handed it to him as, at the same time, it began to rain. Again, the reaction was negative and so she removed a ring from her right hand and held it up. He tried to take it off her but she shook her head.

"We get in," she shouted.

His attention was diverted by a fight breaking out further up the beach and he began to urge people into the boat and two of the men began pushing it out into the sea. Sarah found herself towards the front, across which there was a plank where there was enough space underneath for Najwa to fit in. As Sarah completed this task, she felt an arm around her neck and a violent pulling action taking place. She managed to feel the skin of the wrist of her attacker and she bit down as deeply as she could. There was a loud scream but the grip eased and Sarah pulled herself away.

The boat was now ploughing through the waves with two men pulling at the oars. There was a single sail which was flapping around as the downpour was turning into thunder-claps. They went through the crashing waves and were propelled into the open seas. The electrical storm was lighting up the area around the vessel and, to her amazement, Sarah realised that there were swimmers in the water trying to reach them. It was not long before three had come close enough to cling to the side and threatened the fragile stability. There were violent shouts as one of the oarsmen pulled his blade out of the stirrup and started hitting the attempted boarders on their heads and shoulders.

One youth managed to gain a hold and was pulling himself into the boat. Two of the women were screaming and trying to resist the invader but the boat lurched and threw all the occupants to the starboard side. Sarah was clinging to the wooden bench and checking that Najwa was safely underneath. She was curled up and her eyes lit up when she saw her protector: they were filled with trust.

The boat was taking in water and several of the migrants were bailing it out as fast they could. The skipper was shouting at everybody and it became clear that he wanted the oarsman to get his paddle back into the sea. As he did so, he hit one of the more elderly men and sliced his head open resulting in his blood pouring out. The victim sank to the bottom of the boat and maintained a loud moaning wail until someone kicked him.

The rain was increasing in its intensity and the conditions aboard the boat, such as they were, deteriorated further. The pole holding the sail broke off and fell into the sea but the restraining rope resulted in it acting as a pull on the side of the boat. There were cries amongst the men until someone produced a knife. His slicing actions resulted in the freeing of the material which disappeared away and allowed the vessel to become vaguely more stable. That was until a wave hit the craft and tipped all the occupants into the sea.

Sarah found herself under the surface about ten feet down. She struck out for the surface and saw the boat upside down in the water with about four people struggling to cling to the wreckage. She dived down as far as she could manage, looking desperately for Najwa, and found herself being hurtled forwards by the swell. To her surprise, her head hit the bottom and she realised that she could now stand up in about five feet of water; she struggled on to the beach.

She managed to reach the sand and cried out as a small child was thrown by a wave onto the pebbles about twenty yards away. She rushed across, picked Najwa up, hugged her as closely as possible, yelled out with joy on finding she was alive and realised she was spluttering out seawater. Sarah turned her over, massaged her back and watched as her lungs cleared.

The two refugees stumbled up the beach and collapsed onto a grassy area whereupon Sarah was violently sick.

During the last three hours they had travelled from Kuradasi on the Turkish coast, across the Mycale Strait, to the Greek island of Samos, a distance of around one kilometre. Three hundred and thirty kilometres to the south, through the Aegean waters, Mad Max Hemmings was also on a Greek island.

*

The Carlton Club, Mayfair, London
Thursday: lunchtime
They had lunch together in the Wellington Room. Coffee was served in the members' lounge and both Conservative grandees chose a glass of brandy.

The Minister of Defence was relaxing in the company of Lord Mallington. They shared much in common, including owning estates in Scotland and making regular visits to New York and Washington, ostensibly as officials of the Conservative Friends of Washington, but mainly to conduct their business activities and to see the bankers in Wall Street. Melvyn Donaldson could have a peerage whenever he elected but he was too focused on the awarding of contracts under the defence budget to choose to leave government. What he did want was an answer to an urgent question and he knew that his guest could provide it.

Initially they talked around the central issue. They

both assumed that the Prime Minister would continue in office and the post-Brexit situation would meander on without further controversy. Interest rates would start to rise, putting pressure on the Government's ability to fund the national debt. They reached the subject for discussion which occupied their real interest.

"I was surprised during the PM's urgent Cabinet meeting," he said, "to hear that our secret services had picked up about the Continuity IRA. The Minister seemed to know that they are accepting contracts."

"These things get out," replied Simon Mallington. "It's important that de Lille Rutherford is neutralised, and quickly. I suppose that in the hurry some information leaked out."

The Minister considered these comments before replying.

"Has the matter been completed?" he asked.

The peer indicated that he would like a refill. The waiter responded and both the club members were provided with further glasses of brandy.

"Melvyn," he said. "We have a complication. De Lille himself has put a contract out on a woman called Sarah Rudd."

"Who is she?" asked the Minister of Defence.

"Do you know Norman Delamount?"

"Yes, but not that well. He gives to the Party."

"He runs a security firm and Sarah Rudd works for him. She's an ex-DCI with an impressive track record. It's taken us some time to piece the whole story together but de Lille's banking cronies bankrupted a business run by Norman's illegitimate daughter. It was Sarah Rudd who exposed him and his paedophile activities at Hope House. Before we could protect him, de Lille put a contract out on her. The Continuity IRA won't move until the contract is fulfilled."

"So, where is Sarah Rudd?" asked Melvyn.

"In the Middle East, we think."

"And where is de Lille Rutherford?"

"We don't know."

Melvyn Donaldson looked at his host.

"This must be sorted out," he said.

The peer put down his half empty glass.

"You know of The Westingham Society, I imagine," he said.

"De Lille has had me there as a speaker on two occasions. The second time was when it was me or Hadley for Defence Secretary. Graham managed to persuade the PM to attend and I said everything he wanted to hear. It's a real shame that de Lille so messed up."

"Yes, he really has gone astray. He does, of course, owe us all rather a lot of money." He paused. "Are you aware who is secretly funding The Westingham Society?" he asked.

"I assume de Lille and the members."

"You've heard of Spartak Grankin," he said.

"We need to be careful here," said the Minister. "He's involved in several defence contracts," and then he paused. "He's a handful," he added.

Lord Mallington looked round the room.

"He's much more than that," said the peer. "He now funds The Westingham Society and is using it as his UK power base."

"With de Lille's agreement?" asked the Minister.

Lord Mallington laughed.

"He owns de Lille." He paused and signalled to the waiter who hurried over with two further glasses of brandy. He sipped his drink. "Grankin has a series of loan notes against him." He paused. "We can be certain that he'll not take current developments lightly."

"Who's our link to Spartak Grankin?" asked Melvyn.

Simon Mallington put down his glass and took off his spectacles.

"I am," he said.

The Caves at Archangelos, Rhodes Island
Friday: afternoon

Events had moved rather rapidly for ex-DCI Max Hemmings. He had now reached the town of Rhodes on the north coast of the island and booked into a hotel. He spent the latter part of Thursday morning on the telephone with Norman Delamount. The judicial process had been moving quickly and a European Arrest Warrant had been issued by London magistrates for the apprehension of Graham de Lille Rutherford on seven charges including the inciting of child pornography. This had been sent to the Chief of Police in Rhodes who had delegated Sergeant Ajax Kanakaris to find the fugitive. 'Ajax' means 'powerful eagle' and that is exactly the approach the Greek police officer took. They knew they might be receiving a visit from a British agent and so when Max arrived at the police headquarters, he was soon talking to Sergeant Kanakaris. It was a meeting of blood brothers.

The situation was helped by a text message that Max had received from Daisy. She had found out that de Lille had a property at Malonas about thirty kilometres south of the capital. By late on Thursday afternoon the Greek police had located the villa and ascertained that there were thought to be four people in residence. Early on Friday morning, when Max returned to police headquarters, Sergeant Kanakaris informed him that they were certain it was Graham de Lille Rutherford, a woman and two bodyguards. Ajax nodded towards Max.

"Russians," he said.

The only area of disagreement was that Max was refused permission to carry a weapon. He took his seat in the back of the police vehicle and absorbed the bumps and bruises as the wheels bounced over the poorly surfaced road. When they reached the villa, Max was perspiring. Two local police officers were observing the property and told Ajax that the four occupants were all on site and believed to be at the rear of the building around the swimming pool.

Max was told to stay in the vehicle. Six police officers, led by Sergeant Kanakaris, moved in to execute the arrest warrant. It was unfortunate that, before they were all in position, one of the bodyguards went to the side of the building and started to urinate. The police officer in the lead to the left of the property froze but was a nanosecond too late as the Russian fumbled his fly, pulled out his gun and started shooting indiscriminately. He was quickly joined by the second bodyguard who also fired rather wildly. The Greek police force was, in effect, in a semi-circle around the front of the property and to the one side. Sergeant Kanakaris broke away, ran to the other wall, added to the burst of gunfire and Max could see that one of the police officers was wounded and the second of the guards had stopped firing his weapon.

There was a further outburst of firing and then suddenly it all went quiet except for the sound of a single shot. Max ran forward and round to the right-hand side before he reached the poolside where he saw, in the middle of the pool, a woman floating face down, a bullet wound in the centre of her back. Max dived in and pulled her out on to the side but she was already dead.

He realised that Ajax was looking down at him.

"We've got both the bodyguards," he said.

"Where's de Lille?" asked Max.

From around the corner of the next house came a young lad perhaps no more than eleven years old. He was pointing and so Ajax went over and spoke to him. He came back and told Max that de Lille had fled down a single track that led to the Caves at Archangelos.

"Why would he do that?" asked Max.

"He'll have a boat there," replied Ajax.

"And he's ahead of us," said Max.

At that moment a helicopter came over them and slowly landed a hundred yards away in a parched field. Ajax and one of the officers ran towards it. Max followed and they all boarded the craft; there was already a police officer sitting in the rear. It rose quickly into the air and Ajax explained to him that they were liaising with a patrol boat about a mile offshore. Fifteen minutes later, two officers, Max and a woman were lowered onto the deck of the vessel. Ajax gave out instructions and explained to Max that there has been a sighting of a boat just off the shoreline. He could see that they were heading towards a vivid rock formation which was the Caves at Archangelos.

At one time, the area was inhabited by farmers who grew wine grapes and olives amongst the cypress forests. Then the pirates came, raped and pillaged and forced the peasants inland into collective hamlets which offered greater security. The coastal caves had been deserted ever since with just the heron, cormorants and butterflies for company.

The captain of the patrol boat was in heated conversation with Sergeant Kanakaris who came over and told Max that they were near to the limit of their engagement area. Almost as the words were spoken, the afternoon thermals started to create waves and Max sensed they were moving offshore. The female officer began gesticulating and the boat thought to be carrying de Lille came into view. Max asked if he could use her binoculars and focused on the shore line.

"Is that crabs I see running all around the rocks?" he asked.

"They're blue crabs," said Ajax. "Keep away from them. They're omnivores."

He could see that the vessel was being buffeted onto the rocks and it was clear it was breaking up. Max urged Ajax to persuade the captain to take the boat in but he shook his head. He pointed at a dinghy stowed in the bow and said he would go in alone. Ajax shrugged his shoulders and within minutes, Max was on the rubber craft paddling vigorously as the tide swept him in. As he neared the shore he leaped into the sea and began swimming for a gap which seemed to offer a haven beyond.

Max was not used to this type of physical activity

and was soon floundering; he went under the surface and swallowed some seawater. Then the waves came to his rescue and he was thrown up onto the pebbled entry to the caves. He looked up and saw that Graham de Lille Rutherford was staring down at him.

"We're both survivors," he smirked.

Max was both recovering and thinking hard.

"You're alone," he said.

"Just you and I," said de Lille. "I think you're a detective from England. Your name is Max."

"Ex-detective," said Max. "I work for SC Group."

"Ah, yes, Norman. I seem to have upset him," said the fugitive.

Max was regaining his strength and stood up. De Lille looked at him.

"I've two options, haven't I?" he said.

"You tell me," said Max.

"I can kill you or give myself up. I'm beginning to tire of the running away caper."

"Difficult decisions require courage," said Max.

"I've always made decisions," said de Lille. "The problem I face is that I'm no longer in charge of the outcomes." He laughed. "But enough, I've made mine. You should have stayed in London."

He pulled out a revolver and pointed it at Max. He was a fraction of a second too slow as his right foot slipped away from under his weight. Max lunged and knocked him over. The gun was lost in a pool of seawater. Max straddled the banker and hit him very hard indeed on the side of his face causing De Lille to gulp and look up at his attacker.

"I've had enough," he said. "You can take me in."

Max hauled him up and hit him in the stomach resulting in de Lille keeling over. Max brought his knee up into his face and de Lille collapsed onto the rocks with Max looking down at him.

"Do you seriously think I came here to take you back to England for trial?" he said.

He went over, stripped de Lille's clothes off him and threw him roughly against the rock face. He then piled fresh stones around his feet, took his right hand and broke several fingers by slamming a piece of rock on the limb. De Lille screamed out in pain.

He looked around, spotted what he wanted and went to one of the pools where he located a blue crab. The red ends on its claws showed it was a female – not that Max cared; all he wanted was for it to be hungry. He picked it up and watched it wave its claws in the air. He hid it behind his back and, with his other hand, he felt in his pocket and took out a photograph which he extracted from a plastic cover. He held it up in front of de Lille's eyes.

"Her name was Gabrielle," he said.

De Lille stared and began to shake with fear.

"She pleaded with me to help her," he cried out.

Max was struggling to control his anger.

"You stole the business she and her husband had worked for years to build up."

"It was the bank's idea, what we did," said the shaking prisoner.

"You made an error," said Max.

Even in his vulnerable state, the accusation angered de Lille.

"She was nothing," he said.

"She was Norman Delamount's daughter," informed Max.

De Lille's eyes opened in panic as he realised his mistake.

"You used vulnerable children to satisfy your obscene desires," Max said. "Although I believe in the British justice system, I think that solitary confinement for the rest of your life is just too good for a pervert like you."

"How much do you want?" pleaded de Lille. "I'll pay you a million dollars to let me go."

"How do you put a value on my promise to Norman to exact revenge?" said Max. "It was his daughter you drove to commit suicide!"

"I've said I'll give myself up," pleaded de Lille.

"You're about to experience pain beyond human imagination," said Max. "As you scream the time away, I want you to think about the little girl at Hope House who ended up in hospital because of what you did to her."

De Lille went mute as he realised what was going to happen. Max had pulled his hand from behind his back and held the crab in front of de Lille's eyes.

"As you know, they will go for your orifices and in time will reach your eyes," said Max. "First, I think our friend would like a juicy steak."

He took the crab and placed it on de Lille's genitals. For a few moments the only sound was the crashing of the waves. Then de Lille gave out a piercing scream as the crab began to eat his scrotum and reached a testicle. Max went over to the pools of seawater and captured two more crabs which he brought over, placing one on de Lille's shin and the other on his right nipple. His body began to shake and his veins were almost bursting through the skin of his arms.

Max gave him one more look, then turned around, ran to the water's edge, dived in and began to swim out to sea. He located the vessel from its lights and struggled to reach its sanctuary. He tried to climb on board but needed the help of two of the officers who pulled him in and laid him down on the deck whereupon Max felt very tired. The sea was now calmer and the captain edged the patrol boat inwards before launching a second, smaller rubber craft. Sergeant Kanakaris guided himself and his colleague through the opening where they moored their vessel. As they reached Graham de Lille Rutherford, they were horrified by the physical injuries inflicted on the victim. They picked the crabs off his body and laid him down: he was still breathing. They carried him through the waves to the dinghy, paddled back to the patrol boat and prepared to return to their base. De Lille was laid down on the deck where first aid was initially applied. The trained medical officer went to the captain and she asked that the air ambulance was called. Once an oxygen mask was attached to his face, de Lille started to recover and began uttering what sounded like gibberish.

The helicopter arrived in a little over eight minutes and de Lille was winched up into the fuselage. The doctor on board blinked when he began to examine his injuries, quickly injected antibiotics and then sedated the patient. When de Lille was landed and taken to the main hospital, he was immediately transferred into the intensive care unit.

As the police patrol vessel made its way back to its base, Ajax smiled at Max.

"He must have knocked himself out when he was dashed against the rocks," he said.

"It was a lucky day for some hungry crabs," said Max, looking out to sea.

A House in Thames Ditton, Surrey
Sunday: lunchtime

"It really is good of you, Chrissy, to invite me round," said Isobel.

"I'm having a sherry and you're driving," replied Christel Hemmingway-Brunton as she poured her friend a cup of tea. "What's this news you have for me?" She hesitated as there was a crash upstairs and then the sound of laughter. "They're getting on well," said the mother of two teenagers.

Isobel gave a slightly weary smile.

"Emily has been relatively unaffected but Nick's been quiet." There was another bang and some shouting.

"Issy, come on, what's your news?" asked her host.

"I've had a call from Norman Delamount," grimaced Isobel. "He said that Graham is in a hospital in Greece and is seriously ill."

"Meaning what?" asked Christel.

"I'm not sure; he was vague. I suppose I should be grateful that he phoned me but it was a bit frustrating. Graham is in intensive care in a Rhodes hospital, and is unlikely to recover in a normal way."

"This is like a Hercule Poirot mystery," chuckled Christel. "We must use our little grey cells."

"Norman said he had been shipwrecked."

"More clues for Hercule," laughed Christel.

"And that he had been attacked by some crabs."

"This is becoming more Stephen King than Agatha Christie," she said.

"Norman said he'll phone me again later in the week."

"Are you thinking of flying out to Greece?" asked

Lady Christel.

"Why would I do that?" replied Isobel.

"He's your husband," she said. "Whether you like it or not he's the father of Emily and Nick upstairs," she added.

An hour later Isobel drove her children back home in London and they spent the rest of the day quietly in their bedrooms. Later that evening, she opened up her computer and accessed her document titled 'The Elite'. She recorded the details of her telephone call with Norman Delamount and her conversation with Lady Christel. She decided that she would wait for the next conversation with Norman before making any further decisions.

She checked up on Emily and Nicholas both of whom were asleep in their rooms. She went back downstairs, poured herself a vodka and tonic and picked up the unopened Sunday newspaper which had been delivered earlier in the day. She immediately became absorbed by the headline:

'Opposition demands emergency debate on defence contracts'

She turned to pages three and four because one name caught her attention. She drank quickly and read the whole feature. The newspaper had succeeded in having a Government attempt to prevent them publishing the story overturned in the High Court. They were now free to reveal evidence which had come into their possession suggesting an alleged link between the Ministry of Defence and the awarding of three multi-million-pound contracts to a Turkish company thought to be controlled by a mysterious Russian oligarch.

Isobel stared at the name given by the journalists.

She stood up, poured herself a second drink, sat

down and thought carefully: Spartak Grankin. She placed her glass on the table, stood up once more and went upstairs to her husband's study. After the police had completed their searches, she had tidied the room and then locked it. She entered the room and smelt the dust that had accumulated. She sat down, looked at the photographs on his desk and after opening one drawer after another she found what she was looking for. She had only seen the letter once when she was tidying up but it was the embossed note paper which had stayed in her memory because the Hyde Park address was impressive.

The handwritten note was a letter of thanks to her husband for an introduction he had made. The name of the writer was typed in bold with a signature above it.

'Your friend, Spartak.'

She took the letter, closed the drawer and went into her own room where she opened up her computer. She recorded the contents of the newspaper article and listed the feature and the letter under 'documents'.

She typed in: 'Action: who is Spartak Grankin?'

As her head rested on the pillow, she organised her plans for the coming week. She needed to understand the exact nature of her husband's injuries, she wanted to talk to Lord Mallington and this should free her up to pursue her understanding of 'The Elite'. Sleep started to arrive until she opened her eyes: she realised that the newspaper had not shown a picture of the Russian oligarch.

+ + +

CHAPTER EIGHT

The Greek Island of Samos
Thursday - Sunday

When Sarah and Najwa woke up early on Thursday morning, the sun was beginning to appear over the horizon; they both stared around the beach of Samos island. There were a few people scattered along the front and several fishing boats were about two kilometres offshore. Her first instinct was to assess the risks they faced, with one looming up more than any other because Sarah did not know where Michael Duggan was. For that reason alone, she grabbed Najwa's hand, found her bag – the only luggage they had between them – and moved into a small copse on the other side of the coastal road. She spotted a refreshment area and took out of her bag the remaining, rather soggy, twenty-dollar note. Sarah decided that they must lie low for a day and so she and Najwa found a stream running through the trees which gave them fresh water and they settled down beside it. It broke Sarah's heart that she knew Najwa was hungry but she could not compromise their safety.

They spent a restless night together and early the following morning they moved in towards the catering facilities. She and Najwa sat down at a wooden table and, much to Sarah's relief, the man who approached them nodded his head to indicate that he would accept the currency and they were soon eating omelettes and fresh fruit and drinking tea. At every possible moment Sarah was looking around to see if she could see any danger. Najwa was relishing her breakfast and decided to practice her English.

"Me, Najwa," she said, wrinkling her nose.

"Me, Sarah," said her guardian.

"Eggy," she said, pointing at the breakfast plate.

"Eggs," corrected Sarah.

"Eggs," repeated Najwa. "Date," she added pointing at the fruit in the bowl on the table.

A couple of people approached them and Sarah was furious with herself that she had not seen them coming. To add to her apprehension, they sat down at their table and the man called the waiter over and ordered a pot of tea.

The two people immediately focused on Najwa.

"Your daughter?" asked the lady.

Sarah explained that she was an orphan from Syria and she was in charge of her.

"But you're English," said the man. Before long they were telling her their story of retirement following his forty years in local government rising to chief executive of a Midlands city and now it was holidays around the world and then back to the grandchildren.

Sarah looked at the man.

"Do you have a phone?" she asked. He nodded, took a mobile out of his pocket and handed it to her. His look told Sarah she could use it.

She phoned Norman in London, woke him up, and brought him up to date with the situation. He said he would arrange for her to collect money from a bank in Vathi. The call was abruptly terminated and, as she was re-dialling, she spotted a man walking along the path leading up from the beach. She instantly sensed he was trouble and so she grabbed Najwa by the hand and threw the phone on the table.

The English couple were mystified as they watched them run towards a group of trees fifty kilometres away with the man yelling out that he could help them.

Norman Delamount made three phone calls and instigated an urgent search for Sarah Rudd because his sixth sense told him she was entering into a period of great danger.

Sarah and Najwa laid low for an hour and then carefully moved inland. They walked for a little over two hours when, somewhat to her amazement, Sarah realised they were moving downhill to a beach. They were on the island of Kasonisi which was separated from the Samos mainland by a strip of water two kilometres wide. Sarah searched in her bag and unexpectedly found two more ten-dollar bills. She and Najwa reached the beach and, after several futile attempts, found a fisherman who spoke English and not only was he willing to carry them across the strait but he told Sarah that Vathi was around eleven kilometres to the north west.

They landed on Samos and the fisherman found them a peasant farmer whose shorts were torn and who was willing to take them on his horse and cart to the capital. They left as the sun was setting and after a short period of time the cart came to a halt and the driver gesticulated towards a barn on the side of a farm building. He tethered the horse and ushered them into the hay-filled building. Sarah sensed that he intended bedding down with them and so she wrapped the straw around her and Najwa and before long they were sound asleep.

The following morning when Sarah awoke, she

immediately realised that the peasant was missing so she left Najwa to sleep on and went outside. The horse was still roped to the barn but there was no sign of the farmer. She decided to answer the call of nature and rounded the side of the building only to find, lying face down on the pathway, there was a body. She checked the man, felt the warmth of his skin and saw that he had been strangled – and it had happened recently.

Sarah flew back to the barn entrance, picked up Najwa, fled out into the fields, ploughed through a stream and started to climb the hill in front of them. They reached the tree line and secured some cover. Sarah peered back to see if she could see the man who she knew was coming to kill her. She felt Najwa clinging to her and she began to wonder if she could fight this killer any longer because her strength was draining from her and she looked at her charge with a feeling of utter desolation. Ex-DCI Sarah Rudd rarely shed tears but she found herself wilting and unable to offer any further resistance.

They remained concealed for the whole day and huddled together through the night. The following morning Sarah reached a decision that they could run no more. They would walk back to the road and stop the first car that approached them hoping, at best, that the authorities would take Najwa off her and knowing, at worst, the gunman would find them. Najwa sensed the change in attitude and wrapped herself around Sarah. They walked slowly down the gradient and she realised that they were returning to the building where they had been the day before. The sun was high in the sky but not yet generating real warmth.

As they neared the entrance a dark, tall figure came out and indicated they were to stop. Sarah knew immediately who it was.

"You can let the girl go," she said. "This has nothing to do with her."

Michael Duggan raised his weapon and pointed it at Sarah. For one of the few times in her career as a police officer, and now as a security consultant, she had no answer to the danger she was facing. She thought of Nick, her soon-to-be former husband, and of her lovely daughter Susie and her son Marcus. Her eyes filled with tears; the tears that had rarely come. She wanted Max more than ever before and she was riddled with guilt. She had so wanted to take Najwa home and give her a new life but she had been crazy and selfish. Sarah realised it was all over because she could not protect Najwa and save herself. She stared at the killer sent to complete a contract paid for by a paedophile.

She sensed that the weapon had been fired and felt a bullet pass her head and then she watched, her mouth wide open, as Michael Duggan slumped noiselessly to the ground. This was because a man had wrapped his left hand over his mouth and, with his right, drawn a knife across his throat. He allowed the dying body to slump down onto the earth and, for some unknown reason, he kicked it.

He then rushed forward and grabbed Sarah who collapsed into his arms.

"Max," she cried as she clung to him.

Almost immediately she freed herself and felt for Najwa who was laughing as she sensed the joy of the reunion. Sarah held her and pointed towards their rescuer.

"Najwa," she said. "This is Max."

"Hax," she said as she wrinkled her nose.

It was only at a later stage when Sarah realised that Najwa had seen the death of another person within a few feet of her and seemed to accept it as a normal event.

"What have you really been through?" Sarah asked herself.

Paradise Hotel, Vathi, the municipality of Samos
Monday: evening

Sarah looked down at the flatbread and olive oil which the waiter had placed in front of her, she drank some more retsina and put her glass back on the table.

"My favourite Greek wine," she said and then she giggled.

The waiter reappeared and put a pot of a pink fish paste on the table.

"Taramasal…" she spluttered. "I think I'll try that again; taramasalata." She wiped her forehead.

Max looked across and was consumed with desire. Sarah probably had one button too many open but it didn't matter because nobody was going to bother them. He poured her the remainder of the bottle of the wine and indicated to the waiter that they were ready for the bottle of Ellinas red. The menu told them that it was from the island of Thessaloniki but Max was not that interested because he was enjoying the Kantada music which was from Kefalonia. The romantic serenades were being performed by three male singers accompanied by guitars and mandolins. Max and Sarah were both relaxed and listened for some minutes until their dishes were cleared by the waiter. Max stood up, went behind Sarah, put his arms underneath her shoulders and lifted her up.

"No," she said. "Najwa."

Max nodded his head, allowed Sarah to slump back in the chair and hurried over to the lobby of the hotel where he climbed the stairs to the first floor. He opened the door to their room, crept over to her bed where Najwa was sound asleep and kissed her on the forehead, exited the room and returned to the restaurant.

As he wandered towards their table, he reflected on the events of the last two days. Norman Delamount had come into his own with his organisation of the clear-up processes. He was elated when Max had telephoned him and explained how Graham de Lille Rutherford effectively ended his normal life due to the appetite of the blue crabs in the caves at Archangelos. His security consultant was made to repeat the whole episode and to confirm the screams that came from the mouth of the deranged banker.

He arranged a private plane from Rhodes to Samos International airport and gave Max the directions to where it was thought Sarah was hiding with Najwa. He warned him that Michael Duggan was close and very dangerous. When, the next day, he heard that the assassin had been eliminated he was ecstatic. He repeatedly asked questions about Sarah and began to show an interest in Najwa.

Norman then managed to sort out the protocols with the local police and arranged for Sarah, Max and Najwa to stay at the Paradise Hotel in Vathi, the capital city of Samos. It was going to take about three more days to obtain registration papers for Najwa and a replacement passport for Sarah and he sent through a considerable sum of money to a local bank for his two employees.

Max arrived back at their table.

"Is she safe?" asked Sarah.

"She's sound asleep," said Max. "Shall we dance?"

Sarah stood up and took Max by the arm.

"I never thought that you would ask," she said.

They hurried towards the wooden floor on which a number of couples were following the music of Samos with variations of a canoodling waltz. At one point she was ahead of her partner and the fluorescent lighting made her white dress virtually transparent. Max could see that she had lost some weight which, for him, added to her seductiveness. They danced for a few minutes and then returned to their table where they relaxed.

Sarah suddenly stood up.

"Where are you going?" asked Max.

"To check on Najwa," she replied.

"I've just done that," said Max. "She's completely secure."

"Back soon," sang Sarah. She was as good as her word and returned within five minutes.

"She looks so happy," she said.

They sat and listened to the idiosyncratic 'birp' of the night bird.

"Max," said Sarah. "When we were in the woods and I knew Duggan was near, it made me think about things," she said.

"I'm not surprised," said Max. "He was one dangerous individual."

"He did not scare you, Max," she said.

"Sarah, I was wetting myself."

She paused and wiped her eyes.

"Did de Lille deserve what you did to him?" she asked. Before he could answer she continued her commentary, "Bloody stupid question," she said.

"No," said Max. "I think you're right to question all we do." He drank some wine. "When we were in the force it was different. Everything was process and as police officers we had to ensure that everything we did was by the book or else the CPS threw the case out. But Norman has given us a new opportunity: we have so much freedom." He put his glass down and took Sarah's hand. "I've never enjoyed a job so much."

"You're good at what you do, Max, and I think Norman knows that."

Sarah paused and sipped her wine.

"You're gasping to raise the issue, aren't you Max?" she said.

He looked at her and said nothing.

"You want to know if I'm going to sleep with you," she said. "Is that right?"

"It crossed my mind," he said.

"I've been thinking about an alternative," she said.

Max looked puzzled and stretched his legs.

"What I said at Holborn," she said. "I think it was along the lines of..."

"You said, "Never leave me, please, Max"; those were your words."

"Yes," said Sarah.

She stood up, went around to his chair, encouraged him to stand up and then she wrapped her arms around his shoulders and kissed him with a passion that came from deep within her heart as the recent dangers and escapades exploded into a ferocious physical desire.

"I'm ready Max," she said. "I want you to never leave me."

They strolled quietly back into the hotel lobby and up the stairs to their room. Sarah took Max into her arms.

"You're about to discover what I'm truly about," she said.

Max opened the door and tiptoed towards their bed, relying on the light from the corridor shining through the partially opened door. He stopped, rushed to the switches and put on the main lights. The bed in which Najwa had been sleeping was empty. He felt the sheet, which was still warm, and then saw there was blood on the cover.

Sarah dashed to the side of the bed and looked askance.

"Max," she cried out. "Where is Najwa?"

Twenty-four hours later the chief of police in Vathi told them that they could find no trace of Najwa. They had questioned all the hotel staff and unfortunately, there were only two CCTV cameras and neither showed anything of interest. She had disappeared and no-one had seen anything. He faced a torrent of questions from both Sarah and Max but his explanation that he had limited resources simply did not wash with them.

Later in the evening Sarah found herself walking alone at the water's edge. She was listening to Najwa trying to say 'Max' and she smiled as she recalled her attempted "Nax". Her body shook with inner anger; she was becoming more emotional as the traumas of her perhaps ludicrous odyssey to rescue an unknown child lost in the Middle East were manifesting themselves. She felt a long way away from home.

She stubbed her toe on a pebble lying in the sand. The pain shot up her leg and perhaps reached her brain: it was time to pull herself together. She looked out to sea and at the lights of the fishing vessels.

"Najwa," she said to herself. "Wherever you are, I will find you."

She turned and started to walk back to the hotel.

*

Paradise Hotel, Vathi, the municipality of Samos
Wednesday: morning

They had finished breakfast, for which neither Sarah nor Max had showed much appetite, each picking at a bowl of fresh melon. She poured him a coffee and replenished her own cup. They had an hour to prepare for the visit of the chief of police. Tuesday had been a frustrating day as they were restricted to the use of a smaller bedroom while the forensic team searched the room from which Najwa had been taken. Max spent several hours on the telephone to Norman Delamount, who arranged for further sums of money to be transferred to a local bank. He confirmed that Sarah's replacement papers were being couriered out to them and he arranged for a meeting in the afternoon with a local solicitor. That was helpful in that they were able to understand better the local policing procedures and by the end of the day they were overtaken by a sense of utter inadequacy.

Sarah seemed to be in better shape on the Wednesday morning as they sat together at a table in the grounds of the hotel and allowed the sunshine to brighten their moods.

"Right," she announced. "Detective Chief Inspector Max Hemmings," she said, "you are in charge of the search for a missing child and I'd like your report, please Inspector."

Max stared at her and understood immediately the role playing she was suggesting.

"Ma'am," he responded, "we know that the child was abducted at around eleven o'clock on Monday evening."

"Abducted, Inspector?" she interrupted. "Where's your evidence that the child was taken?"

"The guardians had been checking the room regularly throughout the evening. They are saying the last visit was by the woman at 10.30pm."

"What did she find?"

"She reported that Najwa, the missing child, was sleeping soundly."

"Inspector, what happened between ten-thirty and eleven o'clock? Are you telling me they left the child alone late at night for thirty minutes?"

"They left her alone for thirty minutes late at night, ma'am," he said.

"Why?" she said. "They are telling us that they had fought through great odds to rescue this child. Now you are telling me they left her alone for thirty minutes."

"If I understand events correctly, the couple had been drinking and their conversation had turned to, shall we say, more personal matters."

"Are you telling me, Inspector, that they compounded their irresponsibility in leaving the child alone by becoming romantic?"

"That is certainly a possibility, ma'am," he said.

"The visit made by the woman at ten-thirty. Had she been drinking?"

"We've spoken to the waiter, Ma'am. They were merry, shall we say, after drinking two bottles of local wine. One was white and the other red." He hesitated. "The bar manager has told us that they were seen on the dance floor together and were, in his words, all over each other."

"They abandoned their little girl," she accused.

"They left her alone for thirty minutes when they had been checking her every fifteen minutes," he said.

"The visit made by the woman at ten-thirty, Inspector," she continued. "We know that there had been heavy drinking going on."

"Heavy, ma'am?" queried the police officer. "They admit that they were merry."

"My point to you, Inspector, is this. Is it possible that the child was, in fact, not there at ten-thirty? She had been drinking, there was romance in the air and of her own admission she had been through difficult times," She banged her fist on the table. "Is there any chance the child had been taken before ten-thirty?"

"It can't be ruled out but she says she is certain that Najwa was sleeping soundly."

"Did she kiss her?"

"Well ma'am, it's interesting you ask that question. I don't think she did."

"And usually she would have kissed her?"

"Yes, ma'am."

"She didn't kiss her because she was rushing to get back to her lover."

Max stared at Sarah.

"Inspector. The couple were having dinner in the pool area and using the dance floor. Where was the child?"

"In their bedroom on the first floor of the hotel."

"Could they see the room from where they were in the grounds?"

"No, ma'am, they could not. Their room did not have a sea view. It overlooked the car park and part of the reception area."

"Are you telling me, Inspector, that from ten-thirty to eleven o'clock, they could neither see their room nor have any idea about the safety of the child – assuming she had been there at ten-thirty?"

"That is correct, ma'am."

"When they returned to the bedroom at eleven o'clock who opened the door?"

"The man. He led the way."

"He used his key?"

"Yes, ma'am. They both had keys to the room. We've checked. They have now given up those keys."

"And the door was locked?" she asked.

"Yes."

"What happened then?"

"The man opened the door and made his way to the bedside table. There was a double bed and the child had been sleeping in a single bed between their bed and the window."

"He did not turn on the lights?"

"Not at that point. He realised the child was missing and then he turned on the lights."

"Had either of them turned on the lights on their previous visits?"

"No. They relied on the lights from the corridor. They did not want to wake up Najwa."

"The bed was still warm."

"Yes. The man felt the sheets and there was

warmth in them."

"Had Najwa wet the bed?"

"I've no idea, ma'am."

"And there was blood on the sheets."

"There was blood on the top sheet. Just a smear but clearly fresh blood."

"Were the windows checked?"

"Not to my knowledge."

"What happened then?" she asked.

"They searched the whole room but there was only the bathroom and shower and they were clear. Then they went down to reception, the police were called and they were told to remain in reception. They were placed in another room and went back to collect their personal luggage about two in the morning."

"Was there a wardrobe in the room?"

"Yes."

"Did they look in it?"

"I don't know the answer to that question," he said.

"What happened when the couple were in reception?"

"They tried to talk to the staff but a policeman was stationed with them and stopped them from doing that."

"What are your conclusions, Inspector?" asked the woman.

Before their conversation could continue, they were interrupted by the appearance of the Chief of Police who was accompanied by a female officer. They both sat down and stared at the distressed couple.

"I'll get straight to the point," said the Police Chief. "Najwa was abducted at, we believe, around ten minutes to eleven on Monday evening. The criminals had keys to the window locks and they scaled the fire escape on the wall outside the floor on which you had your bedroom. They were able to stretch across and gain access. We think it was Najwa's blood on the sheet." He paused. "We have one sighting from a couple of German tourists who had arrived back late in the evening. They reported seeing a man and a woman carrying a fair-haired child". He took a deep breath. "There are no fingerprints. The two CCTV cameras show nothing."

"Who has taken her?" asked Max.

"Almost certainly a tip-off from inside the hotel: a fair-haired young girl has a price. There are gypsies and migrants all over the island. We are asking the fishermen; that's our best hope."

"That's not good enough," snapped Max.

"Mr Hemmings," said the police chief. "There are security notices all over the airport and in the hotels. You left Najwa alone in the room." He paused. "You'll excuse me saying so, but that's not good enough."

He stood up and walked off. The policewoman put her hand on Sarah's shoulder.

Max was angry. He watched Sarah walk off towards the hotel, went down to the water's edge and kicked around in the gentle waves. The sun beat down and he watched the holidaymakers having fun. He went back to the table where he found Sarah on her phone. She finished the call, put the mobile in her bag, felt in her pocket and took out a key which she threw at Max.

"You've moved to another room," she said.

Max stared at her.

169

"What does that mean?" he asked.

Sarah turned and he saw the look he had registered on previous tense occasions.

"We have to find her and pretty bloody quickly," she said. "Or she'll be gone."

The Island of Samos, Kokkari
Wednesday

Former Detective Chief Inspector Max Hemmings was certain of three things. First, they might have moved her to Turkey the night before, in which case the chances of recovering Najwa were remote. His experience told him that it was possible, because it was a late evening kidnapping, that they'd lie low for the first night and move her on the second. Second, the police in Samos would not find her because their system was riddled with corruption and they did not have enough officers. Third, his one hope, and perhaps his only hope, was to find the fishermen who would be crossing the waters to Turkey. He finished his beer at the bar and summarised his analysis which was that he had one chance to find Najwa and that was tonight.

He went to his new room where he found his luggage thrown onto the bed. He changes into his fatigues and checked his two knives and his revolver. He used a taxi to reach Samos where he went to the local bank where he withdrew a substantial sum of euros. He did not have a photograph of Najwa but a fair-haired, eight-year-old girl would remain in people's memories. He walked down to the coast and located a number of fishing boats. He needed an English speaker and found an older man who spoke fluently so he gave him one hundred pounds in euros.

His eyes bulged as he listened to Max, nodded his head and they began talking to the locals. After he had spent a further two hundred pounds they were getting nowhere. Max stopped at a coffee shop as the sun was setting, asked the old man where he would cross. He replied that the seas might be rough and so he'd go from Kokkari to Kusadisi on the Turkish coast. He suggested it might take two to three hours, depending on the boat. He then pointed up the coast when he realised that Max was asking the way to Kokkari.

"Ten kilometres," said the man.

Max shook him by the hand and began walking, twice hiding in the rocks as he came close to several groups of men, and managed to reach his destination within three hours. He decided to cut inland and approach the village across the fields. He reached a group of gypsies and took the risk of speaking to them but, without a translator, it proved impossible and frustrating. They took Max's money and went back to their fireside smoking.

He entered the small town down a dark roadway and realised that the beach and sea lay in front of him. As he turned a corner, he noticed that further along there were bright lights and music. As he was deciding what to do, he spotted a group of three men and a woman, who Max could see was carrying a child. He edged nearer and watched as they prepared to board a small boat. He checked that his revolver was readily to hand and held one of his knives in his left hand.

There were two other vessels on the beach, and he was able to inch his way towards the cover they provided. As he watched through a gap, he became increasingly certain that the woman was carrying Najwa.

With her was a huge, dark-skinned man who was carrying an oar. Next to him was a smaller white man hugging a bag to his chest. The woman with Najwa had a satchel on her back. The fourth person was also dark and thin. They were about twenty yards away from the boat and Max knew he had to act.

He had one chance to overcome them. He could not use his gun because, although he could take out one or even two of the gypsies, he could not guarantee that in the subsequent shooting that Najwa would be safe; he also had no idea what the woman would do. His best guess was that she would run up the beach carrying the abducted child. He knew that he must take out the leader and hope the others would panic. He gave himself five seconds to decide who was the general. The fifth second arrived, he stood up and ran at the group.

The clue was the bag. He reached the target in four seconds which gave the giant time to raise the oar. Max hit the white man in the middle of his chest and felt the leather container bite into him. As they went backwards, he felt for the man's face and put his thumb into the corner socket of his right eye. There was a loud yell as the victim of Max's assault clutched at his face. He had called it correctly and the two other kidnappers hesitated momentarily. Max had dropped his knife but grabbed the thinner man and twisted his arm behind his back until he felt the bone fracture. He turned as the giant came charging at him, took out his gun and shot him in the knee. He stepped over the groaning body and looked at the woman who was holding the child out for him.

Max sighed with utter relief. He had lost Najwa and he had recovered her. His thoughts went back to The Paradise Hotel and he imagined arriving back and handing Najwa to Sarah. He took the child in his arms just as the woman buried a knife deep into his thigh. Max just managed to allow Najwa to land safely on the sand before he half turned to see the gypsy nomad preparing to dive on him. The knife was pointing towards his stomach and was dripping blood.

As she closed in, he managed with his left leg to push her foot away and caused her to stumble. He leapt on top of her and hit her jawbone with his left fist. She released the knife and clutched at her face. Max picked up Najwa and stumbled up the beach towards the road where he collapsed and lost consciousness.

*

Sarah was fighting her demons as she replayed again and again her failure to protect Najwa. The sweat was pouring down her when she realised that there was a knocking at her door. She struggled out of bed and put on her tracksuit top. As she opened the door she saw being held out to her the one person who, at that moment in time, she wanted to have in her arms. The police woman entered the room and, in halting English, told Sarah that she had been examined by a doctor and she was in good health.

"Fancy," said Najwa, pointing at the officer.

"To onoma mou einai Nancy," she said and ruffled her hair. She put her on the bed and struggled to tell Sarah that she would be staying to look after her.

The Chief of Police appeared in the doorway.

"We need to take you to the hospital," he said.

*

Mad Max was in intensive care as Sarah looked at him, adjusting her face mask. She now knew the whole story. The worst piece of news was given to her by the duty doctor. To her relief his English was near perfect as a result of a four-year secondment to St Bartholomew's Hospital in Central London.

"The gypsies have a nasty little trick," explained Dr Villios. "They rub their knives in cow dung thereby causing infection as well as trauma." He looked at the monitor. "We've given him massive blood transfusions and filled him with antibiotics. He will need rabies injections in due course." He paused. "I know that you have questions," he said. "We can't guarantee anything but he is strong and he's fighting."

"How do you know that?" asked Sarah.

"We can tell," said the doctor. "It helps if he has something to focus on."

The nurse came, altered the speed of the drip into his arm, tidied the sheets and stepped back.

"I ask that you stay for just a few more minutes," said the doctor. "He needs a lot of rest."

They left and Sarah took up her position besides Max. She whispered quietly to him, leaned over and kissed his forehead. As she reached the corridor she ran into the medical practitioner.

"Doctor," she said. "You said he needed something to fight for."

"Yes, it will help," he responded.

Sarah smiled.

"I've told him what he's fighting for and, I promise you, he'll recover."

Dr Villios nodded and moved on to his next patient.

+ + +

CHAPTER NINE

The offices of Hannings & Richards, Lincoln's Inn Fields, London
Saturday: 11.00am

Isobel was fighting hard to say 'no'.

Her strength of character won through and she settled for a cup of coffee rather than the glass of white wine that Roland Shaw offered to pour for her.

"I was pleasantly surprised to receive your email, Isobel," said her host.

"It was your suggestion," she said.

"Indeed, it was." He smiled. "After the forms were signed, we heard no more from you. We were impressed by your solicitor and found that her amendments to the documents were all valid. We are still waiting to hear back from her on the status of the divorce process."

"You offered to meet again; "if it helps you" is what you said."

The lawyer drank some wine.

"Why don't you update me," he suggested. "Once the forms were signed, I reported back to Lord Mallington and my role was complete."

"I'm going the check my mobile phone," she said. There was one message.

'Gramps wants to play cards Granny cleaning kitchen. Love E x'

"The house will sell and we'll move out, probably to Chesham"," she said. "I am receiving medical reports from Rhodes. Graham is a vegetable and it is thought there will be difficulties over the divorce papers."

176

Isobel watched as Roland's legal brain pondered the issue.

"There are various ways of approaching that situation," he said.

"I'm well advised, thank you," she said. "The children are more settled and my parents are supportive."

"I'm so pleased to hear all that," said Roland. "If I may please ask one question?"

"Yes, as you wish," she said.

"Isobel, why are you here?"

"You are going to explain to me all about the Elite."

He reached for the bottle of wine and poured himself a second glass. He then hesitated, filled another glass and pushed it towards Isobel.

"Still no peanuts," he laughed.

She lifted the glass and drank the wine with a certain sense of relief.

"Why do I want to tell you about what you are referring to as 'the Elite'?" he asked.

"Because I intrigue you," said Isobel. "My lawyer has checked you out. You've been divorced twice and, according to her, you're playing the field at the moment."

"And paying out huge sums to two greedy women," he said.

"You'll manage," she said. "Your firm is late filing its accounts but you earned over eight hundred thousand pounds in the year to April two years ago."

"Do you know why I earn so much money?" he asked.

"I suspect you're going to tell me."

"First, I work very hard; second, I keep myself

very fit; and, third, I understand people."

"Apart from your two ex-wives," suggested Isobel.

"Let me make an observation," he said. "I think I'm correct in saying that your presence here today has nothing to do with the possibility that there is a vacancy for a third Mrs Shaw."

"Poor soul, when you find her," said Isobel. "But, Roland, what I am basing my strategy on is that you enjoy my company and, if I tickle your ego, you'll explain to me the mysteries of the Elite."

Her mobile phone indicated a second message.

'Granny and me cooking. We're cool. Love E x'

Roland pondered her words: circumstances were forcing him to change his male superiority attitude and he had voted for the first ever female partner in his firm. He scanned Isobel through semi-closed eyes. She excited him and, just for once, this was a professional judgement.

"I think it's time to start work," he said.

He cleared away the glasses and the half empty bottle of wine and put between them a flask of water and two clean glasses.

"Tell me what you understand by the term 'the Elite'," he said.

Isobel reached down, picked up her case and took out a plastic binder.

"I've prepared an initial report," she said, handing the document over to Roland.

He looked it over and flicked through the eight pages. He nodded in approval.

"Can you summarise them for me?" he asked.

"The Elite is a loose, global group of powerful and wealthy people. They are bonded together by privilege, elitism, connections and greed and have the ability to use legal, royal, political, judicial, masonic and any other form of the system to achieve their aims. They are to be found at the top of countries, government, banking, investment and other political bodies. Their god is the worship of wealth, the seduction of making money and the privileged lifestyle it brings. They are generally without scruples, are outside the law and because they believe they are the Elite. Their membership brings with it an unspoken responsibility to protect each other. There is an occasional relationship between elitism and sexual perversion."

Isobel had spent two days rehearsing in front of the mirror and was now hugging herself as she judged that she had delivered a word-perfect presentation. She watched Roland's reaction and realised that she was feeling fulfilled.

He seemed transfixed by the woman sitting opposite him.

"In my research," she continued, "I came across a reference to an elite group known as the Order of the Companions of Honour."

"Have you researched it?" he asked.

"Briefly," she said. "I have so much to do at the moment."

"It's part of the Honours process," he said. "It's a Commonwealth award headed by our Queen and goes to notable figures from the arts, science and politics."

"Recipients can use the title CH after their name," said Isobel. "JK Rowland is one."

"It's not what you mean by 'elite'," he said.

"I know that, Roland," she answered. She hesitated because a text message had arrived.

'Emergency call. Brother is having nose bleeds'.

"Damn," exclaimed Isobel. "I have to go," she said.

Roland made a call and told her a cab would be outside in a few moments. Isobel stood up and was clearly flustered.

"Will you have dinner with me?" he asked.

"Yes, I will," she replied.

"Next Wednesday. The Holborn Dining Room." He paused. "A driver will collect you from your home at six forty-five and will take you back afterwards."

"Do you need to check your diary?" she asked.

"I'm already looking forward to it," he said.

The General Hospital, Kallistratou, Samos
Saturday: 2.00pm

The entrance to the intensive care unit on the ground floor at the General Hospital in Samos was guarded by a rather serious looking local attendant. Whether he spoke any English was not obvious as he was saying very little to anyone. What he did make clear was that Sarah and Najwa must keep their paper filter masks firmly in place.

The previous twenty-four hours had been one of the most worrying times Sarah could recall. Even when being chased by Michael Duggan she had options and choices to make. At this point in time she was in the hands of the doctors and other medical staff at the hospital. The couriered letter that the general manager had received from Norman Delamount created an additional degree of tension. He reiterated that it was essential that his associate Max Hemmings receive the best medical care possible, that he would be making a donation to the hospital and he provided the names of two London based specialists who were willing to fly out to Samos to advise on the treatment required.

Dr Vallios read the communication and told his manager that one of the named specialists had taught him how to treat infectious diseases when he was at St Bartholomew's Hospital in London. What he did do, which proved helpful, was to take Sarah and Najwa into a private room and allow them to ask their questions. The position was that Mad Max Hemmings was poorly and the next twenty-four hours would be significant.

"There are usually two possible outcomes, Mrs Rudd," explained the doctor. "He will respond quickly to the drugs and transfusions and we'll simply nurse him back to full health over the next two weeks."

"And the second?" asked Sarah.

"He's vulnerable to several illnesses. The cow dung, and its intrusion deep into his flesh, is a real threat."

"What's the main threat, please," asked Sarah, as she held Najwa close to her.

"There are two," replied Dr Villios. "There's diphtheria although that is less likely. The real problems are tetanus and hepatitis A."

"I had a friend who contracted hepatitis while on holiday and she recovered," said Sarah.

"She almost certainly had hepatitis B. It's hepatitis A that we must guard against," he said. He answered his phone and replied in Greek.

"Mr Hemmings is vulnerable for two reasons. One, the spores that are to be found in animal faeces and two, the depth of the wound. They will attack the liver. The medical term is tetanospasmin but you will understand it better as motor neurons."

"That's a nervous disease," said Sarah as her worry lines increased across her forehead.

"We must ensure we consider every possibility," said the doctor, reading a text message on his phone.

"And what about rabies?" asked Sarah. "My understanding is that it has all but been eradicated."

"That is what the tourist industry would like you to believe," he said. "It's still here and in Greece it is mainly carried by bats."

He again looked at his phone.

"Hax," said Najwa as she pointed her finger at the doctor. "He better."

Dr Villios looked at the two of them.

"We'll know a lot more in twenty-four hours." He put his phone in his pocket. "I'm sorry but I must go."

They idled away the afternoon at the gardens of the Paradise Hotel. The water was warm and, for Najwa, more enjoyable as she made several new friends in the swimming pool. Sarah was left with her thoughts apart from a telephone call with Norman Delamount.

*

**The Cabinet Room, 10 Downing Street, London
Sunday: 11.00am**
"I'm sorry Prime Minister but this Sunday morning meeting is inconvenient."

"But you're here," said the Secretary of State for Northern Ireland.

The Foreign Secretary had enjoyed a rather

gastronomic dinner the evening before, at The Ivy, and missed his early morning run. He was planning his leadership challenge and was trying to find the right diplomatic response to the latest bombshell from the President of the United States of America.

"I've family responsibilities," he said.

"But you're a minister of state," said the Chancellor. "Surely your relations understand that there are priorities?"

"Which is why I am here," said Maurice Henson. "My duties come first."

The Prime Minister tapped his hand on the table.

"I do appreciate your willingness to come in today; it is the only way we can deal with several rather urgent matters." Terence Barrington paused and looked around him. "Let's try to make some progress. Home Secretary: the terrorist threat."

"Thank you, PM," said Heather Cousins. "The security services are saying the Continuity IRA is biding its time. The Irish border issue is dominating the political agenda and we think they are waiting."

"For what?" asked the Foreign Secretary.

"We don't know."

The Prime Minister looked at Elizabeth Shaw.

"Northern Ireland Secretary," he said. "Can you add to that?"

"Prime Minister," she began, "the agreed strategy is to present a united front while the post-Brexit settlement negotiations continue." She hesitated. "That is somewhat easier now we have devolved government in Stormont and the rift between DUP and Sinn Fein is less fractious. There is still no real clarity on the border issue and the Taoiseach, the Prime Minister of Ireland, is proving illusive. At one point in time he wants to align with the twenty-six other EU leaders and, at a different moment, he seems to realise that twelve per cent of Ireland's trade is with the UK."

"But you are sticking with your belief," said Heather Cousins, "that the underlying objective remains re-unification?"

"Without a doubt," she said. "They will do anything to achieve it."

The next twenty minutes were taken up with a general discussion on the state of play in the post-Brexit negotiations. The Prime Minister's position was easier because the Commons majority was such that he had total authority. The opposition parties coughed and spluttered and the Scottish Nationals went on about their own referendum.

Terence Barrington decided it was now time to deal with the most pressing issue facing the Cabinet. He had been told that the opposition party was asking the Speaker for an emergency debate the following day.

"Melvyn," he said. "Thank you for joining us. As the newspaper story is about you, can you please take this opportunity to brief us about the position of these contracts."

"Prime Minister," replied the Secretary of State for Defence, "I appreciate the opportunity to do just that." He opened up a newspaper in front of him. "Lots of pretty pictures," he said "and not a grain of truth." He wiped his mouth with his handkerchief.

"The article tries to suggest that a contract recently awarded by the MOD to a Turkish company involved the payment of bribes. You can all understand the dynamics: we spend perhaps twenty billion pounds a year on equipment. This particular transaction totals around two hundred million pounds and is for the building of a helicopter simulation centre which will train aircrews for both the army and the navy. It will be built at RAF Benson in South Oxfordshire." He looked angry. "The article makes no reference to the fact that it will create fifty or so new jobs."

"Thank you, Minister of Defence," said Terence Barrington. "I think the suggestion made in the paper is that the supplier company is owned by a Russian called Spartak Grankin who resides in London. They have used a Freedom of Information request and are saying that there is no evidence of a tendering process having taken place."

"An investigation is taking place, Prime Minister, but the idea is preposterous. We place thousands of contracts every year and there is a proven process."

"Do you know this Russian?" asked William Davidson.

"I think I've met him once," said the harassed minister.

"At this moment in time, the last thing we want is an opposition assault on the integrity of one of our ministers," said Heather Cousins.

"Thank you all for coming," said Terence Barrington.

As the room cleared, the PM invited Melvyn Donaldson to join him in his private office. The minister looked at his watch and knew he must accept. A few minutes later the two men were seated in the privacy of the PM's sanctuary.

"I think," said Terence Barrington, "you might want to look at these. They were sent over by a newspaper editor who is supportive of our party."

Melvyn scanned quickly through nine photographs showing himself with Spartak Grankin. Three were in restaurants, two in parks, two at navy dockyards and two in which the backgrounds were rather dark.

"When a minister is lying," said the Prime Minister, "the end is nigh."

"I think, Prime Minister," responded Melvyn Donaldson, "that now is the right time to announce my retirement and take my peerage." He was beginning to relax. "My wife is not well and I need to spend more time with her."

"I will immediately accept your resignation," he said. "Here's my response to the letter you'll write to me."

Melvyn read it quickly and nodded.

"There's no mention of my peerage," he said.

"That's because you'll not be recommended for one," said the Prime Minister.

Melvyn Donaldson smiled.

"The Conservative Friends of Washington might find that unfortunate," he said.

"Are you threatening me?" asked Terence.

"Of course not," replied the soon-to-be former minister. "But several of my committee colleagues may choose to discuss the matter in Washington and you are relying on a trade deal, aren't you?"

"Would you like to name any of the committee members involved?" asked the PM.

"May I suggest, Prime Minister, that you should focus on the reaction from the White House," he said.

Terence Barrington realised that he had been outmanoeuvred.

"I'm so sorry to hear about your wife," he said.

"Please pass on to her our best wishes." He paused. "I'm sure the news of your peerage will help her recovery."

No further words were spoken. The soon-to-be former minister left Downing Street and rushed to the airport to catch the flight to Zurich.

Terence Barrington poured himself a large scotch and soda and sat back in his chair. It was, at times like this, that he so missed her. His two daughters were caring and phoned him regularly but each had their own lives to live. It had been a routine operation and it went horribly wrong. Even now, when he was defending the Government's record on health spending, there would be a dryness in his throat.

He wanted to tell someone that he had just been out-manoeuvred. He went over to a table and picked up a photograph of the four of them in Florence. It was when boarding the aircraft for the return flight to London that his wife had fallen on the steps and slipped a disc in her back. He never really understood why the surgery led to an infection and a lingering death. He looked at her and just wanted to take her in his arms: there was something so pure about her.

At that moment in time it was one of the few decent thoughts he could manage amongst the avalanche of corruption, greed and ambition which seemed to be dominating the political world.

The General Hospital, Kallistratou, Samos
Sunday: afternoon

The clock outside the intensive care unit was showing five minutes past four o'clock. Sarah was more than agitated following a frustrating morning call with the hospital when she was told not to attend until late

187

afternoon. The attendant twice reminded them to keep their masks over their mouth and nose. The members of the medical staff were in and out; Sarah stared at them in the hope that it was their turn to enter. Four o'clock came and went and Najwa indicated that she needed the facilities. When they returned, they were again reprimanded by the attendant who supplied them with fresh masks.

When the clock showed four-fifteen Sarah decided to act. A nurse went to enter the unit and so Sarah stood in front of her and demanded to see the person in charge. It was clear that the recipient of her request did not speak English. She smiled and rather firmly indicated that Sarah should sit down. She did, however, reappear a few minutes later with a middle-aged woman.

"I'm so sorry," she said. "Mr Hemmings has been moved."

"Moved where?" pleaded Sarah.

"I'll go and find out," she said.

Ten further minutes passed and Sarah knew that she was soaked through with perspiration. She held Najwa close to her and kissed her cheek. She looked up and saw Dr Villios.

"What are you doing here?" he asked.

"I'm looking for Max," said Sarah.

"He's on the second floor in a private room. I checked him a few minutes ago."

"The drugs have worked?" asked Sarah.

"I think the focus you gave him, helped, Mrs Rudd," he said. "He's a man fighting for something."

He took a step towards her and smiled.

"It's early days," he said, "but he's a determined patient." He paused. "Off you go," he suggested. He looked at Najwa and ran his hand through her hair. "Hax better," he said.

They rushed up the corridor, climbed two flights of stairs and located the private room where Max Hemmings was to be found. A nurse opened the door for them.

He was lying in the bed with a tube attached to his arm and appeared to be asleep. Sarah sat Najwa in a chair, went to the side of the bed, put her hand on the top of his and gently squeezed. He opened his eyes.

"You're late," he said.

Davos, Switzerland, the World Economic Forum
Sunday: evening

A famous, if slightly hypocritical, British politician, who was later to decide that 'One Nation' politics might propel him into 10 Downing Street, said in 2013 that the World Economic Forum was "a great big constellation of egos involved in massive mutual orgies of adulation". He justified his use of tax-payers money to pay for the cost of attending by saying, "You do meet people here who you can encourage to invest in London. For most politicians, who want to 'big up' their cities, it's an important place to come". He was seen to be 'whacking back the vodka'.

This politician was also misguided because Davos was about wealth. It was where the Elite met with the objective of making more and more money. In many cases, they were above the law and protected by the tentacles of power. It was where diners met and discussed increasing their personal fortunes in the knowledge it was, perhaps, crude but it was fool-proof.

The Restaurant Extrablatt in the Promenade had a

rather modest exterior. Inside, its exclusively placed tables were the location for a number of secretive, and occasionally furtive, dinners involving visitors to the World Economic Forum. The highlight for some, over and above the fine wines, was the nine vegetarian dishes on the menu. Lord Mallington did not even bother to read it. He and the head waiter had, over a period of time, reached an understanding: he and his guests were there to talk.

He had been coming to Davos for a number of years. He had fallen in love with the Parsenn skiing facilities, which neighboured Klosters, and which were part of the Grisons canton in the easterly border area of Switzerland. He, his wife and three sons all used the chalet in Davos throughout the year but, for the forty-eighth event, he had travelled alone. He admired the founder's vision and shared his commitment to social mobility. Professor Klaus Schwab was an extraordinary entrepreneur, as evidenced by the hundreds of global leaders and businesspeople gathering for the various events. They were bonded together by the theme of the Forum: 'Creating a Shared Future in a Fractured World.'

Lord Mallington worked industriously throughout the whole occasion and was looking forward to his breakfast the next morning with Martine Newcross, his American political ally. The other key engagements for him were the various meetings and dinners which allowed the sharing of strategies with others aimed at the dual objectives of cementing further political influence and creating personal wealth.

"You've had an eventful time, Melvyn," he said.

"Spartak is rather a handful," he said. "The PM is

focused on the EU settlement so this was a good time to move on." He drank some champagne. "There will be no further deals for him from the MOD."

"Win some, lose some," said his host. "Your payment is in your account."

He waited while the fish course was served and then turned to another of his guests.

"Roland is here to update us on the de Lille situation."

"I'll try my best," said the London-based lawyer. "I must tell you it's complicated."

He gathered his thoughts and then pushed the plate away.

"De Lille himself is in a hospital in Rhodes. I think you know that Norman Delamount's hatchet man brutally attacked him in some Greek caves by putting flesh-eating crabs on him. He's physically recovering but the local specialist is saying that his brain, to use his words, is pickled. We can only wait."

"For what?" asked Melvyn Donaldson.

Lord Mallington sighed and agreed with the lawyer that the situation was decidedly complex.

"A group of us," he explained, "financed de Lille's little banking venture and we've made serious money from it. We also shorted the bank's shares and currently that has netted us around five hundred million pounds."

"What are we waiting for?" repeated the former Minister of Defence.

"De Lille has much of the money in about seven different banking jurisdictions around the world. I had been pushing him to distribute it when the Hope House matter blew up." He hesitated as he gathered his thoughts. "He confided in me that the details of the seven bank accounts and the access codes were written down on a piece of paper in his study."

"That's crazy," said Melvyn.

"Indeed, it is," agreed Lord Mallington. "In this modern world it is exactly what people do." There was a pause. "I recall de Lille telling me that he does not trust computers."

"We wait for de Lille to recover, return to London and find a piece of paper?" The former minister grimaced. "Then we can get our money."

"That's one option, although the specialist is not optimistic. Spartak has a guard at the hospital."

"There is another possibility," said Roland Shaw.

He waited until he was sure he had their full attention.

"Simon asked me to work with Graham's wife which involved obtaining her signature on certain forms. This has been mostly done and makes things much easier."

"Well done again, Roland," said the peer.

"Yesterday Isobel asked to meet again with me. In short, she's obsessed by what she is calling 'the Elite' as being responsible for her husband's misfortunes."

"He's a fucking sexual pervert," said Melvyn.

"She knows that. One of the papers she has yet to sign starts the divorce process." He drank some water. "But she appears to want to fight on and expose the group that she believes was responsible for the banking scandal."

"She's misguided if she thinks she can do that," said Lord Mallington.

"I agree, she's not a hope although she is seriously bright and determined." He smiled. "I'm having dinner with her on Wednesday."

"Ever the charmer," said his host.

"She does have access to his study," he smiled.

"Where there is a piece of paper detailing the bank accounts wherein lies our money," said Simon.

"Exactly," smiled Roland Shaw.

Scott's, Mount Street, Mayfair
Monday: 12.45pm

"That's the gossip completed," said Christel Hemmingway-Brunton. "Issy, you have not, rather generously, invited me to Scott's to muse over teenage mood-swings."

"Chrissy, you know me too well," said Isobel. "Well, first the news." She was showing little interest in her choice of lunch. "I've had a call from Norman Delamount," she said. "Graham is recovering physically but is mentally a wreck."

"What, darling, does that mean?" asked Christel.

"I'm not sure. Norman said that there are serious doubts as to whether he will regain a normal state of mind."

"Put it another way, he's a vegetable."

"The only way I'll really know is to go out to Rhodes but I have my doubts, Chrissy." She paused. "I've yet to start the divorce proceedings partly because I'm not sure what now happens as it seems he'll not be able to understand the process. There is, apparently, a legal way but it has its complications."

"Surely it only matters if you fancy another man," she laughed and stopped eating to sip her wine.

"His name is Roland."

Isobel was later to reflect that, during their years of friendship, starting at Oxford University long ago, she had never seen a speechless Christel. She handed her a paper tissue.

"You've spilt your wine," she chided.

"Who is Roland?" she asked.

"Chrissy. It's crazy, I'm crazy, I'll sober up," laughed Isobel.

"Who, Issy, is Roland?"

"He's a solicitor," she replied.

"How many times has he been married?" asked Christel.

"How on earth did you know?"

"You silly girl, Issy. They'll target you. Phone him now and end it."

"This is different, Chrissy, I promise you."

"Do you remember Sylvia, my Pilates teacher? Husband dropped dead on a business trip to Japan. They were queuing at her door. Chose the wrong one and lost a fortune investing in his travel business. He actually hit her."

"Roland is different," said Isobel.

Christel stared at her and sipped some wine. She waved at the waiter and told him what they wanted. She knew she had to allow her friend to tell her more.

"We're having dinner together on Wednesday evening," she said. "Chrissy, before you deliver the next sermon, I'm serious about exposing the Elite and their involvement in Graham's affairs. But," and she paused, "I'll be honest. I've found it rather stimulating to find myself in a conversation with an interesting man on my own terms." She hesitated. "I now realise that I was a little dominated by Graham."

"Darling, we all are to a certain extent. You were totally supportive and it never occurred to me that you were in any way downtrodden. Graham was like a hurricane and you did well to keep up with him."

"Roland has a style about him," she said.

"And two broken marriages," added Lady Christel.

"We're only having dinner together and he seems keen to help me with my investigation into the Elite."

"Let's have a wager," said her companion.

"What's the stake?" asked Isobel.

"Afternoon tea together at Claridge's," she proposed.

"What's the wager?"

"You'll start relations with him within a month."

"Really, Chrissy. That is just utter piffle."

The General Hospital, Kallistratou, Samos
Tuesday: afternoon

Max Hemmings lay back on his bed and sighed. The drip had been removed and, apart from the nurses dressing his wound twice daily and an injection and prescription drugs morning and evening, he was beginning to return to a more normal existence. Dr Villios visited him every day and, a few hours earlier, had suggested that he would able to leave the hospital in around ten days.

"Where is Najwa?" he asked.

"Playing in the hotel pool," said Sarah. She put her hand on his arm.

"Relax, Max," she said. "There's a Scottish couple staying in the hotel and they've agreed to take care of her."

"We can't lose her again," he said.

Sarah took out her phone and showed him a picture that had just arrived. It featured Najwa and another girl waving to the camera from the top of the water slide.

"The girl's father is reliable," she said. "He sends

me a picture every hour."

"There is a risk," said Max.

"I've paid the hotel security officer one hundred euros to keep an eye on her."

Max, at last, began to unwind.

"The food is awful," he said.

"Norman has been helping me with the immigration process," explained Sarah. "An iPad is arriving for you tomorrow. I want you to have a look at a website 'Home for Good': there are thought to be perhaps ten thousand British people wanting to adopt a migrant orphan. They are referred to as 'refugee foster-carers'."

"There are still some good folk left in this world," suggested Max. "How do we get her in?" he asked.

Sarah started to explain the process when she noticed that Max was closing his eyes. He had been badly wounded by the gypsy woman and, in Dr Villios's estimation, he would need a minimum of a further ten days in hospital to reach even a basic recovery. The medical staff were well aware that Max wanted to go home to England.

"Max," she said, putting her hand on his arm. "We'll fly her into Heathrow airport in about three weeks' time."

"It must be the drugs," said Max. "I seem to be hearing fairy stories."

She chuckled. "We both know that Norman is the master of pulling strings. He has discovered that her name is Najwa Malak and next week we will be receiving the official papers naming us as her foster-carers."

"As simple as that?" he said.

"I wish it was," continued Sarah. "Najwa and I are

visiting a private hospital tomorrow where she'll have a full medical examination." She stood up and tidied his sheets. "Norman needs the report in London."

"That sounds reasonable," said Max.

"There's another form that you and I must complete," she said.

"I never doubted that," said Max. "What form?"

"We will be named as her official foster-carers."

"Susie will love her," he said. "You'll make great carers."

"Yes, Susie's always wanted a sister but you're not paying attention. You and I have to complete a form which is six pages long."

"Just write 'no' to every question and I'll sign it," he suggested.

"There is one question where the answer must be 'yes'" she said.

He knew the warning signs. On so many occasions there had been moments in the questioning of a suspect where Max knew a key point had been reached. The bells were ringing. He decided to exact an immediate answer.

"Tell me," he said.

"The foster-carers must live together. There is no way that Norman can circumvent that requirement."

"Your place or mine," laughed Max.

"We have another option," she said.

"I can't keep up with this," said Max. "Nurse, the flannel," he jested.

"Norman has offered to buy us a terraced home in Fulham. It's ideal." She wiped her forehead. "He's even checked out the local schools." Sarah reached into her bag and took out the printed agent sales particulars which he had emailed to her. She handed them to the patient who was showing signs of taking a greater interest. He read the five sheets of information and then went back to the outside photograph of the property. He re-read the explanation provided on the parking of vehicles.

"What are his conditions?" he asked.

"Just one," she said.

"No wife beating," he said. "It'll annoy the neighbours."

"I'm not your wife," she said. "We both have to sign five-year employment contracts with SC Group," she said. "Max, I'm going to fetch us some drinks."

Sarah returned a few minutes later with a tray of fresh fruit juice and cakes. She put her arm around his shoulders, kissed him, helped him sit up and served him the afternoon refreshments.

"Have you discussed this with Najwa?" he asked.

"The couple who are looking after her both speak French. They have a holiday home near Toulon. I've explaining some of the information to them, they've spoken to her and they are smart people. When I was at Mother Mary's House in Turkey the sister told me that Najwa had attached herself to me. The mother had worked this out herself." She paused. "Max, you and I are all that Najwa has."

"You've been saying "no" to me for quite a time, Sarah. You must understand that I'm wondering what your motivation is really all about."

"I've been saying "no" to permanency, Max. I have found the work at Delamount Security, whoops, I mean SC Group, rather demanding and I need to prove to myself that I can make it."

"You've just defeated an IRA hitman," he said.

"I think you helped," she smiled.

Max pulled himself up in the bed even further and took Sarah's hand.

"We have much to talk about but you know that all I've wanted is us."

"Yes, I know that," said Sarah.

"Has Norman discussed the issue of personal safety?" he asked.

"The news is good, Max." she said. "Obviously Michael Duggan is dead and Norman has ascertained that the Continuity IRA will not pursue the contact. They were paid in full by Graham de Lille Rutherford. He's in a hospital in Rhodes because someone put flesh-eating crabs over his body."

"He was alive when they rescued him from the caves," said Max.

"He's alive now," she said. "Norman says he has lost his marbles. De Lille is in the past." She sat close on the edge of the bed. "It's just the three of us now, Max. If you say "yes", we'll catch a plane in three weeks back to London and we'll start a new life together."

Sarah stood up, went over to the windows which she closed together with the curtains, went back and told him it was time to get some rest. As she reached the door, she heard Max speak so she looked round.

"Please bring Najwa tomorrow," he said.

CHAPTER TEN

10 Downing Street, London
Wednesday: 9.20am

The Prime Minister poured the Secretary of State for Northern Ireland a cup of coffee and offered her a croissant which she refused.

"Thank you for coming in," he said.

"Happy to oblige, Prime Minister," said Elizabeth Shaw.

"You are flying to Belfast later, I understand."

"More talks," she said. "That, Prime Minister, is what I seem to do most of the time."

The Prime Minister studied his minister. With over twenty Members of Parliament in the cabinet, he found it difficult to maintain the level of contact he would wish especially as full cabinet meetings were being stage-managed to cater for the differing opinions over the inevitable difficulties with the European Union on reaching a trading agreement. Elizabeth had come into parliament in the two thousand and ten general election and had slowly created an impression. Her appeal lay in her ability to withstand the inevitable bruises and find the right phrase at the important moment. The reports received in Downing Street suggested she worked hard in her West London constituency and in her first two years as Secretary of State for Northern Ireland she crushed her doubters by managing to fall out with no one.

"I'm sorry if you must maintain that role," said Terence Barrington.

"I don't see it that way, PM," she said. "We have

had twenty years of peace in the Province and if talking maintains law and order, then I will keep on talking."

"Do you find the position lonely?" asked Terence.

"I like that question, PM; thanks. The answer is "yes". I'm living alone with my two cats and I'm forever in a plane."

"Where are we going?" the PM asked.

"I'll give you a positive and a negative," she said. "This is just my opinion but I think the Irish people are enjoying living peacefully and, yes, there are the occasional outbursts and the recent attack on Euston Station left me dumbfounded. Where I worry is that the Continuity IRA seems to be well-financed. I mentioned in Cabinet about their willingness to undertake killing contracts but, to be honest, that's not really where their spending power is coming from." She paused and straightened her skirt. "There are rumours about Russian money but I've spoken to the security services and they are not sure."

"Was that the plus or the minus?" laughed Terence Barrington.

"They like their peace," she said. "The minus, PM, is that the Irish Government and Sinn Fein will never rest until there is reunification." She wiped her eyes. "I sometimes wonder why the popular press seem confused at times. The DUP will fight to their dying day to remain within the UK."

"What are your options?" asked the PM.

"It's a matter of timing and politics. If I ever judge that there is a realistic possibility of the Northern Ireland people voting to agree to reunification in a poll, I can call it." She laughed in her lovely soft manner. "It would certainly solve the post-Brexit issue."

"What about the threat of violence?"

"The Continuity IRA might become more militant but, and I'm not supposed to know, we have somebody on the inside."

"You have a plane to catch," said the PM.

"Yes, more talking."

"Thank you for coming in, Elizabeth." He paused. "You may think that I say things out of duty but I want you to know that, in my opinion, and that of others, you are quietly imposing yourself on the situation in Northern Ireland."

"Thank you, Prime Minister."

As Elizabeth Shaw left the building, Terence Barrington sat back and reflected on times past. She reminded him of his wife and they shared the same gentle laugh.

The General Hospital, Kallistratou, Samos
Wednesday: late morning

"This is bloody silly."

"Bloody hillie," laughed Najwa.

Max was confirming what was rather apparent to the medical staff at the General Hospital: that he was not the most tolerant of patients. His daily flirting with two of the nursing staff was accepted with amusement and yesterday's late afternoon bed bath ended in some hilarity. The truth was that the wound in his leg was taking a long time to heal, although there were no signs of infection and Dr Villios was pleased with the results of the latest blood test. The simple prognosis was that Max needed time and rest to ensure his complete recovery.

"I push," announced Najwa.

It took nearly four minutes to transfer Max from his bed into the wheel chair. There was a further delay as a nurse insisted on applying sun block to his face.

Between them, Sarah and Najwa pushed Max out of the room, along the corridor, into the lift, Najwa pressed the ground floor button, the doors opened and, almost in an instant, they were in the grounds of the hospital. They parked the wheelchair and its occupant at a table and Sarah went to buy them each an ice-cream. Najwa, who was wearing a pink top and shorts, smiled as Max ran his hand over her head.

"You better, Hax," she said.

"Najwa," said Max. "It's Max. I am called Max."

"Yes, you Hax," she said. "You better, Sarah tells me."

"I think you can speak more English that you are letting on," said Max.

"Hmm?"

"What is the capital city of the Lebanon?" he asked.

"Beirut," she replied.

Sarah returned with their treats. Her obsession with food not only reflected a daily loving of sweet things but her concerns over their charge.

Najwa's weight was slowly increasing although the doctor who had examined her, and submitted a report to Norman Delamount, advised that he would like to see her gain another two kilograms.

Sarah watched as Najwa attacked a Neapolitan ice cream covered in fresh cream, nuts and chocolate sauce which she managed to spill all down her front. She finished it in a record time.

She stood up, took off her outfit and ran to the swimming pool in the centre of which was a castle.

She swallow-dived in and swam confidently to the island where there were two other children playing. Max laughed at her swimming costume, which was covered with cartoon characters.

"When you think what she's been through…" he said.

"Sister Eslem at Mother Mary's House talked to me about that," said Sarah. "I was going through one of my wobbles and she told me that it never ceased to amaze her how resilient the children can be."

"How much does Najwa understand about what is going to happen?"

"I've talked to her and her English is improving daily. The people at the hotel have also discussed our plans in French with her. I'm fairly certain she knows what is happening." Sarah smiled. "I've noticed that she's trying to read English papers. She found one in the hotel lobby."

Max was enjoying Sarah's mesmerising company.

"Dr Villios told me this morning that it will be at least another eight days before he'll release me."

"Eight days," pondered Sarah. "I've prepared a list for you. Max. It splits into three sections: the first are the arrangements to get us back to London. Norman has said the house in Fulham is ready and he's had some people prepare it for us. Second, the paperwork that's needed, what's already here and the items still outstanding, and third, us."

"Us?" he said.

"Norman is asking for details about our relationship. There's something bothering him but when he wants to be obdurate, you know Norman."

"What have you said to him? I thought this was written on the form?"

"I've confirmed separately to him that we are partners and we'll jointly bring up Najwa."

There was a commotion in the swimming pool and it became apparent that the three swimmers were racing round the island. Sarah beamed with pride as she saw that Najwa was in the lead.

"What's wrong with that?"

"Detective Rudd has been doing a little ferreting of her own. From what I can glean the lovely Daisy has been putting doubts in Norman's mind."

"Daisy!" exclaimed Max. "What's it bloody well to do with her?"

"She influences Norman, we all know that," continued Sarah. "She has suggested to Norman that you are not stable enough to maintain a relationship with me." She paused. "Max, I need to know. Has anything happened between you and Daisy?"

"Fuck," said Max under his breath. He then told her the whole story including their meeting in Norman's office, his discovering of her drug dependency, the link with Thelma and the invaluable information she had provided on Graham de Lille Rutherford. Sarah questioned the link with Thelma and seemed rattled by the answer that they had a lesbian relationship.

"What's wrong with that?" he asked.

"Max, she has the hots for you," she responded. "It's obvious." She smiled. "I had picked something up in the office but your belief that all women fancy you is such that I couldn't bring myself to fuel it further."

"So how do we sort this out with Norman?" he asked.

"It's sorted," she said.

"Where are you with your divorce?" he asked.

"There's been a delay but it will be all over in about a month's time." She finished her tub of strawberry delight. "I've been in touch with Nick. He managed an outburst about me being irresponsible and the usual other accusations. Susie says he has a new girlfriend who is much younger than him."

Max explained that he needed to stretch his legs and so she helped him lift himself out of the wheelchair. She pulled down his pyjamas and examined the wound by lifting off the dressing and then gasping as she viewed the yellow and black bruising and the five stitches still in place. It was perhaps only then that Sarah realised what Max had risked in rescuing Najwa. She eased him back and kissed him.

"We are partners," he said. "In whose name is the house registered?"

"Mine," said Sarah. "Norman has gifted it to me."

"Interesting," he said.

"Don't react, Max," she said. "What else could Norman do? He wants to give us stability and registering the property in both our names is more complicated."

"Yes, I get it." He smiled. "I'm relaxed about that."

Najwa came running up and Sarah quickly dried her down, removed the swimming costume and replaced it with a fresh multi-coloured outfit. She then applied suntan lotion over her exposed skin which contrasted with her fair hair, such were the ravages of the years in the Middle East sun.

Najwa pointed at Max and made a chuckling sound.

"You come swim tomorrow, Hax," she said.

They collected their packs and pushed Max back into the main building, up to the first floor and into his room. The transfer into the bed took a little time but eventually he was settled and so Sarah tidied the sheets around him.

"Come tonight," he said, closing his eyes.

Sarah kissed his forehead and Najwa squeezed his hand.

"Hax better," she said, as they closed the door behind them. Najwa skipped down the corridor and then stopped. She held up her hand, paused and waited for Sarah to take hold of it.

Max smiled as he heard her words. His leg was throbbing and his mind was racing. He needed to talk to Daisy because he wanted answers to several important questions. The detective's warning bells were ringing and, for his liking, rather too loudly.

*

The Rosewood Hotel, Holborn, London
Wednesday: evening
Isobel read the words with a surge of excitement about the evening ahead. Her son, Nick, and daughter, Emily, were entertaining Granny who would be staying the night. She had spent a lot of time trying on dresses. She knew from the beginning what the final selection would be but she had to be certain. The weeks of coping with the fallout from the implosion of her life and the departure of her husband had left her in a rather trim condition. She decided there was a silver lining somewhere: her dress fitted perfectly. She read the words again.

"A kiss makes the heart young again and wipes out the years."

She was having the carefully pre-planned approach to her evening with Roland Shaw swept away by a tidal wave of charm and seduction. The executive car had arrived on time to collect her from her home and, after the chauffeur had opened the door for her, she found a single red rose and the anonymous quote written in ink on a perfumed card.

As the driver pulled away, he opened the divide and apologised for disturbing his passenger. Isobel said that was fine and then found herself intrigued when the chauffeur said that he had been asked to play a special piece of music for her. She mulled over the possibilities. The romantic Roland will have been predictable and so the most likely choice was 'There's a Place for Us' from 'West Side Story', followed by 'Imagine' sung by John Lennon or, perhaps, the song that Emily played over and over again: 'Lovesong' by Adele.

"Is it in order to play the music?" he asked.

"Yes, please" agreed Isobel. "Can you tell me what we're going to hear?" she responded.

"I've been told that it must surprise you, Madame."

Within four minutes Isobel was tempted to ask the driver to stop so that she could get out of the car and find a stranger with whom to dance. The vehicle was filled by the disco beat of Donna Summer rendering the Jimmy Webb classic, 'MacArthur Park." It was a magical, trumpet blowing, captivating track as the singer claimed, "I don't think that I can take it, 'cause it took so long to bake it". The crazy lyrics, vibrating music, and, because it was on repeat play, a sensational way to arrive for dinner at the Rosewood Hotel in Holborn.

As the car pulled through the Edwardian arches, the porter opened the door and said,

"Mrs Isobel de Lille Rutherford, we at the Redwood Hotel welcome you here, Ma'am."

She was directed through to The Holborn Dining Room and she knew that her choice of a black cocktail dress was right. When she was shown to the table her host was awaiting her: Roland was standing still and made no attempt to greet her. The maître d' arrived and handed them each a glass of champagne.

Roland raised his glass to his guest.

"To you, Isobel," he said.

They sat down and she gazed around her.

"Who said it?" he asked.

"Said what?" replied Isobel.

"A kiss makes the heart young again and wipes out the years."

"John Keats," she suggested.

"Good try. You've two attempts left."

"W.B. Yeats."

"Phew, rather close."

Isobel pondered his reaction because she didn't know the answer.

"Rupert Brooke," she suggested.

"You win twelve dozen roses," he announced with a smile.

"He died in Greece at the age of twenty-seven," she said.

"I've an obsession," he admitted.

Isobel decided that its revelation might be interesting.

"I can't relax until we have placed our orders."

He called for the waiter who handed them both menus. Isobel then caused her host to have to conceal his impatience as she took ages to make her selections. The waiter displayed immaculate style and then hurried away with their choices.

They sipped their champagne and smiled at each other.

"I'm nervous," said Roland.

"Is it the first time you've had dinner with a lady?" asked Isobel.

"Usually," he said, "it's business with high-powered barristers, lawyers, corporate financiers and the rest. In that case the rules are known. There's a deal and we all have a part to play. Some of the women are impressive but generally that is incidental."

"You're making money," she suggested.

"I prefer the word 'fees', but yes."

"Surely there are times when you dine with a woman for social reasons?"

"I married two of them," he laughed. "That is the difference. They were chasing me: it was a game."

"Marriage is a game?" said Isobel. "I've never thought of it that way."

"You understand I have a massive ego. That is what drives me. These women know it, play me along and I fall for it."

"An expensive pastime," she said.

"No. At the time I was genuine and thought I had met the right person."

"What went wrong?" she asked.

"Bluntly, evolvement."

Sarah held her empty glass and pondered on his choice of words.

"These women, they disappointed you?" she suggested.

"Quite the opposite," he mused, thinking of the first night in Paris with Naomi. "They were sensational. The problem was that, once the initial thrill had passed, we found we had little in common." He paused and waved at the waiter. "I said "no" to children and Naomi reacted rather petulantly so that was the start of the end of the first marriage and the second Mrs Shaw ran off with her swimming coach."

The first of several courses had come and gone and they decided to wait for a few minutes before enjoying the red mullet. The white wine was poured but both host and guest were limiting their consumption.

"You're going to talk to me about the Elite," said Isobel.

"I'll start with my professional advice," suggested Roland.

Isobel reached across and put her hand on his sleeve.

"We're not here as solicitor and client," she said. She then realised that he was sneaking a look down her dress. "We're here by choice to enjoy each other's company," she said, enjoying the moment.

She sat back and decided that he was a mixture of a younger George Clooney and David Tennant. What she would have given to have been Olivia Colman in *Broadchurch*.

"I've read your report on the Elite," he said.

"You found it disappointing?" she asked.

He groaned as the seductive sound of her voice weakened his resolve. Lord Mallington wanted the bank accounts details and they were secreted in her

211

husband's study.

"As the Irishman said when asked the way to Dublin, "I wouldn't start from here"," he said, and was pleased when Isobel smiled at the oft-repeated humour. "Much of the content in the first part tries to examine the Rutherford Finance House scandal and seeks to apportion blame. We discussed this when we first met. The guilty parties are in jail and the one exception, your husband, is badly injured." He paused and thought about what he was going to say. "You have tried to trace tentacles to various groups to identify accountability. You are making a mistake. The actual concept of lifting the toxic loans off the bank's balance sheet and moving them one removed was legal and considered by the Bank of England to be constructive." He looked around him before continuing. "I accept it is popular to bash bankers but it's the banking sector that creates much of our wealth. The dividends which the banks pay account for part of many people's pensions."

"Are you telling me that the Boards of Directors of the main banks are all upright, hardworking people?"

The main courses arrived and the two diners continued in silence. Roland was confused and elated. Isobel was enjoying the ambiance and being an individual in her own right.

"Isobel, let's go and sit in the gin bar," suggested Roland.

They were shown a secluded table and Isobel rather liked it when he sat down beside her. They were served with gin cocktails which she tried to drink slowly.

"I'm going to take a risk," he said.

"I'm wearing my crash helmet," she replied.

"Isobel, your thinking is all awry. What you are really trying to understand is the wealth divide – a posh term for it is social mobility."

"I've always thought that when politicians run out of ideas they talk about social mobility."

He put his hand up.

"Before I receive a verbal lashing, let me try this on you." He paused and watched his guest remain thoughtful. "Suppose I decide that my life's ambition is to become general manager of the Rail, Maritime and Transport Workers Union, what they call the RMT, what are my chances?"

"Nil." She laughed. "Why would you, anyway?"

"I'm a Labour convert. Up the workers. I'm going to dedicate my life to making life better for the eighty thousand members of the RMT. Down with the bosses."

"I'm ahead of you, Roland," she said. "You don't stand a chance because it's a closed shop. You have neither the connections nor the compatibility with the union members. Equally, you're never going to be a Tory grandee because you don't own vast tracts of farmland in Scotland." She sipped her gin cocktail. "Life's unfair, why haven't I won the lottery?"

A second cocktail was placed in front of her.

"The problem with your line of thinking is that it's not what I'm pursuing," she continued. "Inequality is fine provided there is equality of opportunity. When I look at what happened to Graham, I sense a group of nasty, greedy, avaricious, power-crazed individuals who'll do anything to increase their wealth and influence. They think they are above the law and in most cases they are."

"What's your end game?" he asked.

Isobel put her hand on his outstretched fingers.

"In truth, I don't know, but I cannot let matters rest. I just want to expose someone and perhaps others will follow me."

"Enough shop," he said. "Let's talk about you."

"What do you want to know?" she smiled.

"Favourite book?"

"'Bossypants' by Tina Fey."

"Never heard of it."

"Way-out American comedian. It's her biography in one-liners."

"Film?" asked Roland.

"'Mamma Mia!'" she said, "With 'Paddington' not far behind."

He nodded. His second wife had dragged him to the Meryl Streep classic and it turned out to be one of their best evenings together. It didn't last.

"Song?"

"'MacArthur Park' by Donna Summer," she smiled.

"You liked it?" he said.

"Together with a red rose, what more could a woman want?"

"A man to go with them," he said.

Isobel stood up and found him in front of her.

"I've had a wonderful evening, Roland, thank you."

He kissed her on the cheek.

"I hope you like the music on the way home," he smiled.

He waited while she used the facilities and then walked her slowly to the car where the driver opened the rear door. Neither spoke but expressed themselves with a hug, and then she slid quietly onto the rear seat. She looked back: he was watching her leave.

As the chauffeur opened the glass divide, she said, "No need to ask, just play it please."

The glass divide was closed.

"What," she thought, "will he have selected?"

Somewhat to her surprise, some piano music filled the car. She knew it so well but why choose a concerto? She listened and began to realise that it was a film theme. It was so famous: she was being dim. The melody meandered on and she decided there was an edge of sadness in its progress and then the trumpets came, only to be replaced by the violins. The pianist was playing with hope and expectation and was reaching a crescendo. Her heart was racing as she gripped the seat belt across her.

Then she guessed right. It was Rachmaninov, and the film…? She knew it so well. What was it called? Her mobile phone vibrated. Emily should be asleep and her mother would be slumbering in the chair ready to quiz her about the evening she had enjoyed. She looked at the message.

'I hope ours is not a brief encounter. R x'

Isobel pondered and was uncertain about her reply. Slowly her fingers hovered above the letters.

'I think Celia Johnson made a wrong choice. Isobel x'

The reply was almost immediate.

'We have choices. R x'

She responded without hesitation.

'Yes, we do, x'

She turned off her phone and sat back in the car while the music of Rachmaninov played on.

215

"Chrissy," she said to her friend, "I think I'm going to lose the wager."

The Ballroom, The Park Plaza Hotel, Westminster
Thursday: 9.00pm

"George," cried Lord Mallington, hurrying over and hugging his American friend. "Our evening just would not be the same without you."

"Always charming," he responded. "Simon, I shall be leading the applause at the end of your speech."

"Shouldn't you hear it first?" laughed his host.

"I hear the Secretary of State for Homeland Security is here and speaking. How did you manage that?" he asked.

"She's creating quite a stir in official circles," he said. "She's completed seven meetings around Westminster and the security services."

The American visitor looked around him.

"The Conservative Friends of Washington seems to get stronger as each year goes by," he observed. "I'll head for my seat."

The eight hundred guests were taking their places and the formalities efficiently completed. The meal and wines ensured a lively atmosphere and the contributions to the bank account of the Conservative Friends of Washington came in at a pleasing rate. The Chairman, Mark Rollings, a former junior minister and now chairman of a London Health Trust, rose and said all that was expected of him. He introduced the guest speaker to warm applause. Martine Newcross, the American Secretary of State for Homeland Security, felt the part, looked the part and was the part.

"Mr Ambassador," she began with impressive self-confidence, "Mr Secretary of State for Defence, my lords, ladies and gentlemen," and then she paused, quite deliberately, because she wanted her audience to look at her. Her speech coach had drummed into her that nearly all speakers cannot wait to get to the prepared joke which usually results in a ripple of laughter. A number of men were more than happy to stare at her.

"Mae West said, "It is better to be looked over, than overlooked.""

That worked a treat.

"I was in the Oval Room of the White House when the President of the United States of America handed me a letter. When I read it, he was delegating me to represent him here tonight. Right guys, I've not been overlooked!"

The applause started and she knew that she could milk it.

"My boss, Felix Merryweather – to all of us, Mr President – wanted to be here but we all understand the issues he is facing. I hope you'll consider me an adequate representative."

More applause, more stares, more empathy and the start of a great speech. Martine revisited the Presidential election campaign, the unexpected victory, some of the key appointments and several of the important issues of the moment. She was allowing herself no more than thirty minutes in total, again at the urging of her coach. He repeatedly chided her that the best speeches left the audience wanting more. She looked furtively at her watch and saw that she had seventeen minutes remaining of her self-imposed deadline. She covered several policy matters which she knew would interest a British audience and then moved on to creating a real impact.

"What do I want you to take away tonight from my speech?" She paused and then, with perfect timing, rang the victory bells. "Just three things." A pause. "I hope you find them helpful."

That was going to cause problems because her coach preached a maximum of two. True, Tony Blair won the 1997 General Election with a mantra of five promises but he had six weeks on the electioneering campaign for their continual repetition. She knew that the Conservatives had won with just one, 'Get Brexit Done', but Martine Newcross had three things to say and was building up to their pronouncement.

"First, Felix Merryweather will prove to be perhaps the greatest ever American president." She smiled. "He is willing to challenge the Establishment and it's working."

The applause went on and rose to a climax until she put her hand up.

"Second, he will serve his full eight-year term. Nothing can stop him."

Martine hoped that her statement proved correct and knew that one event could be his undoing, but tonight was an evening for dreams.

"Third, he believes in the special relationship between the United States and the United Kingdom."

There was more applause. She allowed the moment to linger as she moved towards her finale.

"That's a phrase the media loves to question: 'special relationship'," she added.

The CFW members and their guests muttered restively.

"My friends," she said, and she knew she had

timed it to perfection, "I'll tell you what there is and I want you to take this away with you. There is an umbilical cord between us that will never be broken. It is what binds the United States of America and the United Kingdom together with a friendship and mutual respect that no other pair of countries can match."

She waited and waited until the applause slowly died down and even then she needed to raise her hand.

"Ladies and gentlemen, on behalf of the President of the United States of America, I ask you to take this away with you, my dear friends." She paused just a fleeting moment. "We are one."

She sat down and gazed out at the panorama of tables, faces, flashing phones and table lights.

The applause went on and on. It was not until Lord Mallington stood up that it quietened. He remained still until the audience was ready for him to speak. He explained that he had been asked to propose the vote of thanks to their guest. He held up two pieces of paper, explained that they contained his pre-prepared words, and then dramatically ripped them in half.

"No words can possibly do justice to one of the greatest speeches I have ever heard," he cried, and then allowed the applause to resonate around the room.

"Secretary of State for Homeland Security," he said, "please tell the President that we, the Conservative Friends of Washington, send him our best wishes and our total support."

The President of the CFW, Mark Rollings, closed the formal proceedings and personally thanked

Martine for her speech. He told her that it would remain in the thoughts of a vast number of members present and their guests.

Martine explained that she needed to use the restroom facilities and the security guards led her to the privacy of a segregated room. A few minutes later she returned to the after-dinner noise and found herself shaking hands with people whose names she was never going to remember. The announcement was made that their guest was about to leave. She was cheered all the way to the hotel lobby where her car and security staff were ready to take her back to her Mayfair hotel. She found that she was walking with Lord Mallington. As they exited the ballroom he stopped and faced her.

"It's all arranged," he said. "You'll be having breakfast tomorrow morning with Isobel de Lille Rutherford."

"Thank you, Simon," she said. "The President will be pleased to hear that."

The General Hospital, Kallistratou, Samos
Thursday: evening

Sarah sat quietly at the side of the bed and watched Max struggle to cope with the confinement of the hospital bed. Dr Villios had been less than encouraging when he made his morning visit and decided to take a blood test. Frustratingly, he would not tell Max why. Sarah told him it was just a precaution but didn't believe her own suggestion.

"We rarely talk about you," said Sarah.

"What do you want to know?" said Max.

"Your wife: she was a police officer, I understand."

"No, Sally was a primary school teacher. She was good at what she did. We met as teens and never thought about anyone else." He asked for some water which he drank quite quickly.

"Why has Dr Villios taken a blood test?" he asked.

"Relax, Max. He'd have come back if there was a problem."

"Perhaps," said Max. "Sally was quite a gentle person and as my career developed and the rough stuff started, she found it increasingly difficult. I had an elbow broken when arresting a car thief and it caused me problems for some time." He asked Sarah to help him sit up. "It was on a Sunday that it happened. We were sitting at the breakfast table and suddenly she said that the marriage was pointless."

"How long did it take you to find out who the other man was?" said Sarah.

"Yep, that was the route I took. I managed it badly and it got worse when it became apparent that there was no other man. In the end, her father came to see me. I think I scared them all but, in fairness, he handled it rather well. There were no children and Sally made absolutely no demands apart from asking for a certain amount of money which was far less than half the equity in the house. I remortgaged the property and paid her off. Before she left, she cleaned the house from top to bottom. I thought that I would probably never see her again but, about a year ago, she came to the house. Her father had died and he had left me a letter in which he said he wanted to thank me for giving Sally her freedom. He wrote that I could have made things difficult and I should take credit for acting reasonably. I asked her if she had someone and she avoided the question. She was,

221

frankly, more self-confident than I had even known her to be."

They were interrupted by a nurse coming into the room and suggesting that Sarah might think of leaving in the next fifteen minutes. She stood up and said that she would leave as Max needed a good night's sleep. She tidied his sheets and kissed him good night. She left her lips on his forehead for a little longer than usual

As she moved to the door she turned.

"I'm nothing like Sally, am I, Max?"

Max did not reply because he could see Dr Villios coming through the door.

"We should talk," he said.

Sarah stood by the bed as the doctor took a sheet of paper out of an envelope.

"This is your blood test result, Max," he said. "It's good news. This morning I sensed some tenderness around the scar tissue and I suspected an infection. We must be so careful about the amount of antibiotics we prescribe and so I decided to wait for the results, which clear you. A secondary infection can be a problem; I am so pleased for you."

He said he wanted to examine Max's leg, which he did.

"One of those things," he said. "Much less swelling tonight, hardly any in fact, and I suspect that it will be completely healed in the morning. We'll manage it."

As he was leaving, he looked at Sarah.

"You look tired," he said. "A gin cocktail and then bed."

Sarah went back to Max and repeated their ritual before exiting the room. She reached the end of the corridor, went over to a window which overlooked the floodlit grounds and sank to her knees. The inner strain came as she became overwhelmed with the emotion of Max, his ex-wife and his injuries.

CHAPTER ELEVEN

The Dorchester Hotel, Park Lane, London
Friday: 8.00am

"I am so pleased to meet you, Isobel, I've heard wonderful things about you."

The American Secretary of State for Homeland Security, Martine Newcross, smiled across the breakfast table at her guest. She picked at the fruit bowl and contented herself by drinking cups of English breakfast tea. The atmosphere in the restaurant of the Dorchester Hotel was quiet and relaxed as business people prepared for the day ahead.

Isobel laughed and smiled all at once.

"I received a phone call from Lord Mallington and here I am, chauffeur-driven to breakfast with an American politician," said Isobel. "I know what the internet tells me about you but why I am here is, shall we say, a surprise."

"I understand you have two children," said Martine.

"Why are we here, Martine?" said Isobel.

"Because the President of the United States of America has asked me to meet with you," she responded.

Isobel brushed her hair off her forehead and frowned.

"But you know nothing about me?" she said.

"Not true," said Martine. "I met with Roland Shaw yesterday. You've a great supporter there," she said.

This stopped Isobel in her tracks. She was trying to tie the various strands together, starting with her husband, Graham, Lord Mallington, Roland Shaw, the President of the United States of America and now Martine Newcross.

"What's the latest news about your husband?" asked Martine.

"I suspect you know the answer better than I do," replied Isobel. "This meeting is all about the Conservative Friends of Washington. There's a report on one of the websites about your speech last night."

The American politician stared at her guest. She was already liking her.

"It said that you were sensational."

"I said what they wanted to hear," said Martine.

"And what the President told you to say," suggested Isobel.

"You Brits need a trade deal with the United States and the President is ready to deliver. You are having difficulties negotiating with the European Union and, if I might remind you, the President told your Prime Minister that is exactly what would happen."

Isobel decided to butter a croissant and then spread strawberry jam over it. Martine continued to face her.

"The President has asked me to deliver you a letter. He sends his personal best wishes and asks that you take the contents seriously."

Isobel studied the embossed envelope, the handwritten address and the seal on the back. She put it in her handbag.

"I gather you've a plane to catch," she said.

"The President wants me back in Washington as soon as possible." Martine looked at her watch and then across to a dark-suited sentinel standing at the entrance who was also pointing to his wrist.

Isobel gazed at the stranger across the table.

"I'm sure the President wants many things," she said. She pushed the half-eaten croissant to one side, stood up and held out her hand. "Fly back safely and thank you for breakfast."

She walked out of the restaurant, ignored the staff, went into the lobby and sat down. She took out the envelope, looked again at it, put it back, closed her bag, took out her phone and sent a text.

'Roland. We must talk and soon. Isobel'

She looked up and, to her surprise, saw that the Secretary of State for Homeland Security was staring down at her. There were several security guards near and around her.

"You are cross with me," she said.

Isobel stood up, faced her accuser and frowned.

"Not with you, Martine, just with the underlying circumstances."

"Will you come up and have a chat with me in my room?" she asked.

"I'd like that," accepted Isobel.

The US politician spoke to one of the security officers, told him that her flight back to the States should be pushed back an hour and led the way for she and her guest to walk to the lift and travel to an upper floor. They were soon secreted in a palatial suite; a maid appeared to serve the refreshments.

Martine Newcross resumed their conversation with an impassioned plea that she was merely the messenger; the contents of the letter were confidential and known only to the President and that she had no option but to follow his directions.

Isobel responded in kind and apologised for her abrupt behaviour during their breakfast. She developed this by telling Martine the background to her husband's demise and her involvement in trying to piece together the various factions involved in his complex business affairs.

"We seem to be bound together by Lord Mallington," suggested Martine.

"He keeps popping up," said Isobel but what I want to understand is why you met with Roland Shaw yesterday."

"He really is a charming man," said Martine.

"He certainly thinks so," smiled Isobel. "Why did you meet with him?"

"It was at Lord Mallington's suggestion," she replied. "The President has asked me to try to understand your husband's sudden fall from grace."

By the time Isobel had completed the details of Hope House, Martine was better informed and seemed to relax. Isobel told her American companion about the medical reports they had received from a specialist at the hospital in Rhodes. She then directed the conversation back to her main area of interest and delivered an outpouring of her resentment of the Elite. "One of my girl-friends told me we are pawns in their game," she said.

"I don't think she's only referring to gender," said Martine. "The reality is that the Elite, as you refer to them, are mainly men but there are some tough women in the States I promise you," she laughed.

"Where does sex come into this, Martine?" she asked.

Isobel wondered whether her question was misplaced as her companion seemed to drift away into her private thoughts.

"It's an ever-present," she said. "I'll say nothing you don't know. But the combination of wealth and power seems to unleash a tornado of expectations amongst the most powerful of men." She paused. "One of our problems is that there are too many women who want to play the 'poor me' role both for attention and the possibility of a pay-off. The media love it as it generates headlines for them."

"There are some seriously evil predators out there," said Isobel "but I get the impression that the authorities are getting their act together. Women who deserve justice are beginning to see that happen."

"Which is great, Isobel," Martine replied, "but, as you said, there are some women out there who will try to milk the system for what they can get." She looked at her watch. "I have to fly home," she smiled. "Promise me that you will read the President's letter."

Isobel collected her coat and walked to the door, knowing there was a secret service agent on the other side. Martine came up to her and held out her hand, in which there was a card.

"Can we stay in touch?"

"I'd like that," said Isobel.

As she reached the end of the corridor and allowed the agent to call for a lift, she checked her phone:

'Lunch. Car will come at 11.45am R x'

The General Hospital, Kallistratou, Samos
Friday: 11.00am

Sarah was annoyed and she left Max in little doubt about how she was feeling.

"Max, you've upset Najwa. Her friends left early this morning for the airport and then you text me and say she must not come to the hospital." She continued pacing round the room. "You cannot treat her in this way. She had made you a garland of red roses."

"Where is she?" he asked.

"There was a playschool open for the hotel guests and she was accepted without a problem."

"Come and sit down, Sarah, you need to hear this."

Her sixth sense rang some warning bells and she did as she was requested. Max did not waste any time.

"Daisy rang me this morning. She met Thelma last night and they are fairly sure that the information is genuine."

"What information?" asked Sarah.

"Graham de Lille Rutherford has escaped," he said.

"Rubbish," replied Sarah. "I've had it from two separate sources that he's in a vegetative state."

"He was – he was poisoned by the crabs and his brain was affected. But a doctor in Rhodes found an antidote and nobody realised how quickly he was recovering. Thelma has told Daisy that her sources, which we assume are in Rutherford Finance House, say he escaped two nights ago."

"But he was being guarded," said Sarah.

"They were not expecting him to try to get away."

"What is he planning?" asked Sarah.

"He'll have a plan alright but what it is we have no idea."

Sarah went over, kissed Max and apologised for the opening salvo.

"Time for more detective work," she said, "you need some writing paper."

Before long the two of them were trying to work out what options were available to de Lille Rutherford and which was the most likely. After an hour, they paused and decided to make their way into the hospital grounds. Ten minutes later they settled down at a table near to the swimming pool and started to enjoy the sunshine.

"Right," summarised Max. "We have settled for five possibilities. In no particular order: *One*: he's coming for me because he objects to having live crabs placed on his naked body. *Two*: he's coming for you because he's heard you survived Michael Duggan. *Three*: he's returning to the Caribbean because he's missing Zeander. *Four*: he's meeting somebody, somewhere. *Five:* we haven't a clue."

"There is one other possibility," said Sarah.

"Try me," invited Max.

"He's being aided by the Elite," Sarah suggested, "and they only care about money. They protest about Hope House and his activities with the little girls but they couldn't really give a damn." She paused. "I think there is some unfinished business which Graham de Lille Rutherford intends addressing." She paused. "We must speak to Norman as soon as possible."

"And he needs to quiz Daisy," thought Max to himself.

Sarah suggested that the staff would return him to his room as she wanted to get back to their hotel.

"Please bring Najwa this afternoon," requested Max.

"Try and keep her away, Hax," she laughed.

The Bunghole Cellars, Holborn, Central London
Friday: 12.30pm
They were seated at a remote table in the basement of

230

the Bunghole Cellars in Holborn about half a mile away from Roland Shaw's office in Lincoln's Inn Fields. They had placed their orders and agreed to share a bottle of carbonated water.

Isobel was dressed to reflect her anger and frustration but decided to allow Roland to begin their conversation. She studied his face to try to gauge his mood but he was, as ever, implacable.

"You've met our American visitor," he said.

"To be accurate, Roland, Lord Mallington asked me to have breakfast with her. During this morning's conversation, Martine mentioned that she had met with you."

"She's given you a letter from the President," he said.

"Would it not be better if you told me what is going on?" suggested Isobel.

"Yes, that's the reason I cancelled my lunch appointment so that I could be with you," he said.

Isobel held up her hand as though as she was trying to push him away.

"Stop just there, please. Your attempt to seduce me into making an application to become the third Mrs Shaw is over. Today, Roland, is strictly business."

"That is what I feared," he said. "You are not going to believe me when I tell you that since we first met, I have thought about little else apart from being with you."

Isobel hated herself but she was enjoying his protestations.

"I'm flattered, thanks," she snapped. "But forget it. I want to understand exactly what is happening and what's your role in all of this."

Their meal arrived and they waited while the waiter

sorted out the table. Isobel spooned some salad onto her dish, selected the French mustard but showed little appetite as she fiddled around with her fork.

"You leave me only one option," said Roland.

Isobel changed gear, sliced her sirloin steak into small pieces and busied herself with her lunch.

"I'm trying hard not to upset you," he said.

"Telling me the truth might help," she suggested.

"That is what I'm going to do but you must allow me one moment of latitude," he said.

"You're in love with me. Move on, Roland."

"I'm in love with you," he said. He was perspiring and used his napkin to wipe his forehead.

Isobel looked at him. Strangely, she later wondered whether to believe him.

"Now you have cleared the decks, let's get on with the truth."

He drank some water and coughed.

"Your husband, Graham, was an unbelievable businessman. He had three great qualities in that he worked assiduously, was a clever deal maker but the most important attribute was his instinct for building up his network. Rutherford Finance House was amazingly successful and it allowed him to spread his influence in political circles through his patronage of The Westingham Society. He became a member of the CFW, the Conservative Friends of Washington, and built in particular his association with Lord Mallington."

He paused and looked at his guest.

"How am I doing?" he asked.

"Keep going," instructed Isobel.

"You're not going to like the next bit," he warned.

"Try me," she said.

"There were questions being asked about his sexual habits but, to some extent, he used you rather cleverly."

Her mind flashed back to the evening at The Westingham Society. He had taken her into Mayfair to buy her an outfit and, before the evening event, he had worked out where she was to sit and at what point she was to stand up. He even suggested how she should turn her head and look around the room. She was to count to four and then sit down. He added to the subterfuge by using a family photograph extolling the joys of their children.

"I'm not enjoying being lectured to and told that I was a puppet," she said.

"I'm not enjoying telling you," stuttered Roland.

"I asked for the truth, didn't I?" she said.

Roland's heart sank. He was trying to work out if there was any way their relationship could survive the lunch.

"His unusual exploits that you've mentioned," she said. "The suggestion that the pretence of a happy home life was just a façade," she mused. "It never seemed like that to me because all I can recall is a great marriage, our two children who had a loving father and lots of laughter."

Roland could sense her pain.

"Where Graham showed himself to be rather special was his banking deal. We were all hit by the recession and he was seriously in debt. He managed to convince a group of City backers to fund him out of his problems and into the Rutherford Finance Deal. This created vast wealth and it was here that Graham took his eye off the main chance. The executives running the scheme went bananas; I think we covered this. Their new-found wealth went to their heads and, with it, a requirement for more and more money and they ended up with lengthy prison sentences."

He stopped while their table was cleared; they agreed to order coffee and green tea.

"At this juncture there were two main developments; first, there was Hope House. The Elite, as you call them, will tolerate almost anything but as the stories emerged his supporters became nervous. They were also dealing with another issue in that Graham had never distributed the profits owing to his backers. He was a master at travelling at such a speed nobody could keep up with him. The bubble burst, he fled to Greece and Lord Mallington found out that there were millions of pounds which he owed, in seven bank accounts around the world. It was then discovered that Graham was nervous about computers. The details of the bank accounts are written on a piece of paper which is believed to be in his study."

Isobel looked at her watch and sent a text message to her daughter.

"This is where our relationship collapses," he said.

Isobel looked askance and, for a fleeting moment, decided that she was not in control.

"I've not indicated that," she said.

"The forms, and Lord Mallington's introduction, were genuine and I think we managed to help you regain control," he said.

"That's fair comment," she said.

"The next part is less tasteful. I'm so sorry, Isobel, but Lord Mallington has hinted that I might be able to find a way into your affection and gain access to

Graham's study, and, with your help, find the piece of paper."

She pushed her plate away and grabbed at a glass of water.

"You could have saved yourself the dinner, red roses and Donna Summer music. You simply should have asked me," she said, fighting back her frustration.

"The wisdom of hindsight," he said. "I've agonised over how this situation built up."

"Where does Martine Newcross fit in to this?" she asked.

"The President is a committed backer of the CFW. It helps him with his own funding on Capitol Hill. He wants the backers' money found and is owed some himself. Have you opened his letter yet?"

Isobel began to collect her possessions.

"I'll call a cab," she said.

Roland stared at her as they both stood up.

"We're blown, aren't we?" he said.

"You've been honest, I think," she said. "Thank you for that." She made sure her coat was in place. "I'll be straight with you, Roland. I just don't know what to think." She held out her hand. "Please don't contact me again," she said.

"Do you really mean that?" he asked.

She looked at him and decided the emotion might be genuine.

"I didn't say there would be no further contact," she replied, as she moved towards the stairs and into the fresh air of High Holborn. After attracting the attention of a London cab driver, she sat in the rear compartment with just one thought on her mind.

"Where," she wondered, "would Graham have

235

hidden the details of the bank accounts?"

*

10 Downing Street, London
Friday: 3.00pm

"Thank you for seeing me, Prime Minister," said William Jarvis, a member of the Democratic Unionist Party and a Northern Ireland representative in the British House of Commons. He was known as 'Willie' and spoke with a magical Irish cadence.

"We are on the record, Willie," said Terence Barrington.

"But of course, Terence." He paused. There was a history between the two politicians due to their time together, some years earlier, when the Prime Minister was starting off his political career and wanted to understand better the Irish situation. He had managed to persuade the then Secretary of State for Northern Ireland to allow him to accompany him on a trip to Belfast. This proved a success in that Terence Barrington quickly became a name being mentioned in the corridors of power and the protégé befriended a junior member of the main Unionist party. He and Willie shared a passion for rugby union and Guinness and both were dedicated to finding a peace settlement forever in the province.

"Willie, it's Friday and my doctor won't allow me to drink much alcohol so, while I sip this awful fruit juice, you can pour yourself a can of Guinness."

"You're a true gent," said the Irishman, filling his glass and holding it up. "I told everybody after we first met that, one day, you'd be the head man."

"You never wanted leadership, did you Willie?"

asked the PM.

"Terence, I love the life I lead. You pay me a load of money and a pension and yet I'm able to spend time with Maeve and our daughters."

Terence laughed.

"You've something to tell me but first I'd appreciate an update," he said.

"Your Secretary of State's just been over so I guess you know the headlines," he said. "The post-Brexit issue is something to discuss but, in the end, Terence, it will get sorted. Trade overcomes everything and the border, or no border, will be subsumed by the commercial reality."

"What was your thinking on the Euston Station attack?" asked the Prime Minister.

"The humanitarian cost was huge, Terence. We couldn't believe the loss of life and those maimed." He drank some Guinness. "If you look back over the Irish troubles, the IRA only occasionally inflicted such atrocities."

"Do you know why this attack was so successful – although the word itself is repugnant?"

"Yes, I know what you mean." He coughed. "My understanding is that the attack was financed from the outside and also the Continuity IRA received some training."

"Who provided the money, Willie?" asked the PM.

"It was Russian funding, Terence," said Willie Jarvis. He held up his hand. "Can I add one more thing, Prime Minister. I attended a briefing with your Minister and, to be sure, she was impressive. There is one thing on which I completely agree although I'd not say this outside this room." He looked at his host. "There is only one outcome although the timescale is difficult to estimate. My guess is sooner rather than later, but eventually there will be a united Ireland outside the United Kingdom." He hesitated. "I think your Minister was trying to suggest this could be a consequence of the post-Brexit issues but that's unlikely. My guess, Terence, is five to ten years."

"And Scotland will have gone," sighed the Prime Minister.

"Oh, to be sure."

"Why are you here, Willie?" asked the PM.

"There is something we don't like, Terence."

"Try me."

"I think you know that the relationship between Sinn Fein and ourselves is closer than realised or we allow to be known. Sometimes the leaders are at war when we, the rank and file, can't see the argument." He wiped his nose with his handkerchief. "I've been speaking to a pal in Sinn Fein and he's close to Dublin." He stopped and held up his glass. The PM handed over a second can of ale.

"Terence, there's someone talking. That someone is in your Government. They are talking, we are convinced, because they want to stir up tensions."

"Why?" asked the PM.

"Power, pure and simple." He sighed. "While Northern Ireland is in the UK its politicians assume much greater power. Look at the 2017 Confidence and Supply Agreement. It would never have happened unless the DUP had offered so much influence."

"Can you tell me who it is?" asked the PM.

Willie Jarvis handed over a piece of paper which Terence Barrington looked at and read.

"Fuck me, Willie, are you certain?"

Willie Jarvis finished off his Guinness.

"I am arranging to obtain a more complete confirmation for you," he said.

Terence Barrington looked around his office. He was utterly bewildered by the information which he had just been given.

The two men completed their conversation and the Northern Ireland MP left to return to his own country.

Terence Barrington dealt with a number of phone calls and two visitors before closing the door, pouring himself a scotch and sitting in his favourite chair. He read again the name on the scrap of paper.

"Why," he cried. "Why you?"

Graham de Lille Rutherford's home office, Mayfair, London. Saturday: mid-morning

Isobel sat at his desk and looked around her; the windows were open and a fresh winter air was blowing in. Nick was playing junior hockey at his school and Emily was singing in the church choir. She looked around her husband's office which, in fairness, the police had tried to return to its previous condition after removing the computer and support equipment. Certain files were missing but she had received a list of each. It was simply not possible for her to absorb so many memories without experiencing a certain family emotion.

There was a photograph of Graham in Washington with a smartly dressed companion at the hotel where they had shared breakfast together. Isobel looked again: it was Martine Newcross. There were a series of framed press cuttings, mostly capturing the success of Rutherford Finance House and its banking scheme. Isobel looked round and saw Winston Churchill gazing down on her. She picked up a painting of Margaret Thatcher at the dispatch box in the House of Commons. Next to that was a bottle of parliamentary whisky signed by the former Prime Minister. There were six family scenes in the room.

Isobel looked around at the oak-panelled walls and the storage areas. Her eyes came across a floor to ceiling book case catalogued in her husband's meticulous style. The fiction section included every title written by Wilbur Smith and quite a few of the Jack Reacher books by Lee Child. The political section was populated by autobiographies and the lives of politicians over the last hundred years.

Where had Graham hidden the list of seven bank accounts which contained the vast wealth generated by the banking scheme, she wondered? She drank her cooling cup of coffee, absorbed in her trip down memory lane. She did not know where to begin and she wondered how Roland, even if he had gained access, would have known where to look. She stared again at the photograph of Margaret Thatcher and her mind went back to the evening of The Westingham Society when Graham was perhaps at his peak. A thought flashed into her mind. She used her mobile phone to ascertain a number which she rang. It would almost certainly be necessary to ring back on Monday but she wanted to check the answer phone message to ensure she had made the right connection. To her surprise, the call was answered.

"Robin Pargetter, Wilton, Wilton & Ashurst," said a voice.

Isobel stumbled but quickly recovered her poise.

"Robin," she said, "I'm surprised to find you in

your office on a Saturday. It's Isobel de Lille Rutherford."

"The tax man collects money seven days a week," he laughed. "Mrs de Lille Rutherford, I'm feeling a little sheepish because I should have contacted you. I will need to do that because our friends have some questions."

"I'm sure they do, Robin. Please, it's Isobel."

"You must be having a difficult time," he said.

"Robin. This may be a waste of your time but I am wondering if you can help me solve a riddle."

"Try me," he said.

"I'm in Graham's study and somewhere there is a piece of paper on which he has written some important information. I need to find it and I simply do not know where to look."

"What sort of information are we talking about?" he asked.

"That's not material," she said.

"It might help, but on we go," he said. "It's not on the computer?" he asked.

"The police still have that but I am certain he has secreted a piece of paper in here and I need to find it."

"I solved 'The Times' crossword in thirty-five minutes last night," he said.

Isobel raised her eyes to the ceiling.

"I've never been in his study but I can imagine that it's immaculate and well organised."

"Exactly," confirmed Isobel.

"That's a clue you've already given me," he suggested.

"Have I?" she said.

"Graham will have had to put it somewhere he'd

remember himself," he said.

"Isn't that rather obvious, Robin?" asked Isobel.

"Your husband worked at a pretty frenzied pace, Mrs de Lille Rutherford. He'll have realised himself that it must be secreted somewhere he'd always remember."

Isobel gasped at this logic. She was quietly congratulating herself on phoning the tax accountant.

"Do you remember the night of The Westingham Society," he asked. "What did Graham highlight?"

"Yes," she exclaimed, "Margaret Thatcher."

"Almost, Mrs de Lille Rutherford," he responded, "but not Maggie. "Graham thought she was reckless sending the fleet six weeks across the Atlantic and losing the lives of British soldiers for some threadbare islands."

"But, Robin, that evening. He was venerating her."

"That was an act for his audience. The chap at the back who answered, "No, no, no!" was one of my partners."

"Where does that take us? Shall I go through his Thatcher memorabilia?"

"I have a better suggestion," he said.

"Go on, please."

"Graham's real hero was Winston Churchill. He idolised him simply because, against all the odds, he won the second world war by managing to bring in the Americans."

"Did not the Japanese, Pearl Harbour and all that, have something to do with it?"

"It played a part but the attack on Pearl Harbour was a failure because the Japanese failed to knock out the American aircraft carriers. Many Yanks were against fighting Germany. It was Churchill's relationship with Roosevelt that was the key and then, later, with Eisenhower."

"Robin, while you've been talking, I've looked on the shelves. There are perhaps twelve books about Churchill and many of the ones he wrote."

"Behind you, Isobel, I think there is a photograph of Churchill. Graham showed a slide at The Westingham evening of himself at his desk and I think I remember seeing it behind him…"

"Yes!" interrupted Isobel. "It'll be behind Churchill in the frame. Hold on," she said. She put her phone down, turned and lifted the photograph off its bracket. She turned it over, put it on the desk, unhinged the holding clasps and removed the back cover and then the photograph. She checked again and then again. There was no hidden piece of paper.

"Nothing," she said.

"It's like a *Times* clue," he said. "So often you're on the right track but you miss the obvious." He hesitated. "Graham had a favourite saying: 'Difficulties mastered are opportunities won.'" Robin laughed. "However low I managed to reduce his tax bill, he would say, "Difficulties mastered"."

"But what book do I look in?" pleaded Isobel.

"Is there a book of quotations in his collection?" he asked.

Isobel again put down her phone and went over to the shelves. She had to brush off the dust to read some of the titles but one after another failed to provide the answer she sought. She was just about to report in the negative when she decided to run her hand over the top of the shelf of books. She felt it and pulled out a small, hardback and blew off the dust. She was looking at 'Quotable Churchill' by Max

243

Morris. She opened it and groaned with disappointment as she realized that the inside pages were empty. She spoke into her phone.

"Robin," she said, "I've found a book of Churchill quotations but we've drawn a blank again."

He instructed her to return to the desk and sit down. He then asked her to read out the list of chapter headings. She did as he requested: 'Life and Living', 'Power and Authority', 'Toil and Trouble' until she reached 'Education." He told her to stop and turn to the page. She did as he asked and read out the saying she had reached: 'Personally, I'm always ready to learn, although I do not always like being taught'.

Isobel did not think much of that piece of Winston philosophy and told Robin Pargetter that they were getting nowhere. She flicked through to the end of the short tome and, as she opened the penultimate saying (under the title 'Philosophical Thoughts') a piece of paper was attached to the page which read 'Difficulties mastered are opportunities won'. She took the paper off the page and opened it. There, in Graham's handwriting, was a list of seven bank accounts.

"We've got it," she said triumphantly.

"And not on chargeable hour time," said the tax accountant.

"Pardon?" exclaimed Isobel as she wondered if Robin Pargetter was proposing to levy fees for the assistance which he had given her.

"Just my sense of humour," he said. "Glad to have been of help, Mrs de Lille Rutherford. As I said, I need to speak to you over Graham's affairs but that can wait until another day. Cheerio."

She realised he had terminated the call.

She picked up the piece of paper and went over to the photocopier where she made three copies. She knew exactly what she was now going to do. She went back to her phone and sent a text message.

'Roland. I have something you want I.'

She added a kiss but then deleted it.

+ + +

CHAPTER TWELVE

Dereboyu Avenue, Northern Nicosia, Cyprus
Sunday: midday

Spartak Grankin stared at his guest in the small, fan-cooled office on the first floor of an office block in Nicosia. He was shocked by the appearance of his associate, who was holding a piece of cloth in a trembling hand.

"You do not seem yourself, Graham," he said. "I trust that my staff have brought you back in a comfortable plane?" He nodded at the security guard who understood that he was being dismissed.

"We have things to discuss," continued the Russian oligarch. "If you wish, I can have you returned to your hotel and we can continue tomorrow."

Graham de Lille Rutherford lifted his head and faced his mentor.

"I'm recovering, Spartak," he said. "The infection is cured. I just need rest, sun and decent food."

"All of which you will have, Graham, once we have talked about some important matters."

"Yes, I understand that," said de Lille Rutherford.

"The man who attacked you in the caves at Archangelos. His name is Max Hemmings and he works for Delamount Security who are now called SC Group."

"Yes, Spartak," he mumbled as the memory of the first bite from the blue crab into his testicle caused him to dribble. He used the cloth in an attempt to cover up his embarrassment.

"He went on to murder Michael Duggan, yes?" He

laughed. "I am told he is known as 'Mad Max'."

Graham began to explain to Spartak the connection between Max and Norman Delamount and the role of Sarah Rudd in attacking his empire in Britain.

The crime chief seemed to hesitate on hearing the name, 'Sarah Rudd'.

"You seem to have made several mistakes, Graham," said the Russian, who had poured himself a glass of vodka. "I do not want to add to your pain but you allowed the banking deal to implode; your activities at Hope House were, shall we say, careless; and, when we get you to Cyprus, you go to the Nissi Bay Beach Bar, assault a local girl and have to flee to Rhodes."

The visitor simply nodded his head.

"We do not wish to cross Norman Delamount. He is well regarded in London and it will not help us in any way."

"I want Max Hemmings dead," he said.

"You are not in a position to demand anything," snarled Spartak. "Please remember that I hold a series of loan notes from you."

Graham looked at the Russian in bewilderment as he could not reason how he was in a position to honour any of his outstanding commitments at the present time.

"What do you want, Spartak?" he asked.

"The chief executive of The Westingham Society, the man called Martin Balcombe, can I trust him?"

Even in his anguished physical and mental state, de Lille was alive to this confusing question: Spartak Grankin funded The Westingham Society.

"He'll sell to the highest bidder, Spartak. There is a

file on him in my office safe and that might be useful. Why are you asking me about him?"

"I am rearranging my affairs globally and I want to make London my permanent residence. It is a liberal financial centre and is in Europe and it is where I will deposit my money." He swallowed some more vodka.

"Perhaps I should say "bal'shoye spasiba" to their regulators," he laughed. "A big "thank you" to them!" he roared. "It is good that there is a Conservative Government in place." Then he smiled. "I intend using The Westingham Society much more in the future to give me greater influence."

De Lille Rutherford was enthused by this proposed development and was, gradually, beginning to feel re-energised.

"I'm surprised to hear this, Spartak, because I thought you always preferred to stay in the background?"

"My wife likes London and our children are settling in well. But, more importantly, as I have said, the banks are porous and I can move my money around the London financial markets and nobody asks any questions."

"Is there a role for me?" asked Graham.

"There is another issue," he continued. "I was damaged by the leaking of the connection with the Minister of Defence, or rather the former minister. But you British have a wonderful way of dealing with failure and corruption." He laughed and refilled his glass. "Melvyn Donaldson is now in the House of Lords and they've put him on one of the finance committees." He looked down at some written notes on his desk. "Here it is," he said. "The Economic Affairs Finance Bill Sub-Committee." He bellowed with laughter and then turned his attention back to de Lille Rutherford.

"Lord Mallington is watching events. He's a valuable friend. But now, Graham, we need to talk about you,"

The fugitive sensed a change of atmosphere and realised that they were approaching the real reason for the meeting.

"You have been a little naughty, haven't you?" said Spartak.

Graham looked at his mentor and sensed that trouble lay ahead.

"You've not distributed the funds owing to me from the banking deal and my understanding is that you have seven bank accounts around the world where you have deposited the proceeds of your various enterprises. Are we understanding each other?"

Graham nodded his head.

"I would like you to retire back to the Caribbean where you can recover your health and where there are plenty of local girls for your amusement. You will have enough money and a nice home." He paused and drank some more vodka. "As a bonus, Eugene, who is outside, will kill Max Hemmings."

De Lille had worked out that he could not do it himself. There was no hope of putting a contract out with the Continuity IRA. The Russian assassin was a perfect answer.

"And what do I have to do?" asked Graham although he already knew the answer to the question.

"Give me the details of the bank accounts," said Spartak. "I need to replenish my reserves."

Graham, for some inconceivable reason, suddenly

recalled a favourite Winston Churchill quote which had sustained him during the 2008 recession:

'If you're going through hell, keep going'

He needed to play for time and Spartak Grankin had dropped his guard.

"I've never known you short of finance," he said.

"The Irish are asking for more, there are no further defence contracts and there are many mouths to feed," he explained. "Once you pay me what I am owed, I shall be back in a strong position."

It was an example of 'mind over matter'. Graham de Lille Rutherford remained in a badly damaged physical state but his thought processes were gearing up. This was where he had always excelled: the ability to think the unexpected.

"Bring me a photograph of the body of Max Hemmings and we have a deal," he said.

"You don't bargain with me," said the Russian. He banged his fist on the desk. "You have my word that Hemmings will be killed."

"I'm going back to the hotel, Spartak," said Graham. "When I see the photograph of his body, I'll move on the bank accounts."

He'd read the situation well and before too long he was installed back in his room. A package had arrived bringing him an iPad, mobile phone and a wad of euros and dollars. There was a pleasant note from Thelma wishing him a good recovery.

He was planning his various moves. The details of the bank accounts were a key factor and he visualised the shelves in the office in his London home and a book of Winston Churchill quotes in which there was a piece of paper.

He rested his head back on the pillow of the bed

in the belief that his trump card was secure.

The Bunghole Cellars, Holborn, Central London. Monday: 12.30pm

Isobel and Roland sat at the same table in the Bunghole Cellars that they had occupied three days earlier. A waitress took their orders and served a carafe of iced water.

The solicitor had responded to her text message on Sunday evening and confirmed that a car would collect her at 11.45am on Monday. By now, Isobel had considered her personal letter from the President of the United States of America. She valued the warm comments and his concern for her and the family's welfare 'in these difficult times'. The key part of the communication was a request that the termination of Graham's affairs should be completed quickly 'under the radar', that she might consider joining the Conservative Friends of Washington and continue the work undertaken by her husband. In the cold light of a Monday morning, on its third reading, it made no real sense to her.

"I'm sorry there was a delay in responding to your text, Isobel, but I was out of range for a day," said Roland.

"Climbing mountains with the third Mrs Shaw," she laughed.

He looked at her and she realised that her flippancy was not what he wanted to hear.

"You have it," he said.

"Yes, Roland, I have it."

"You're sure it's the list that we want," he said.

"I'm certain it's genuine," she replied. "Roland, it's the real thing."

"Where did you find it?" he asked.

"Winston Churchill was looking after it."

He fixed his guest with a legal stare.

"Winston Churchill? What are you talking about?" he challenged.

"Shall we agree I have it?" she said.

"How did you find it?" he asked.

"I did 'The Times' crossword."

It was helpful that, at this moment, the waitress reappeared with their lunch orders and there was a pause as the table was rearranged to allow them freedom to eat. Roland immediately started fiddling around. Isobel cut up her steak, poured an oil-based dressing over her salad, picked up her fork and began to eat with a certain relish.

"Can I take it with me?" he continued. "I'm assuming you've brought it with you."

"Your rhetoric is misplaced, Roland". There was a hesitation because Isobel was silently applauding the chef on a well-prepared meal. Her appetite was returning.

"I'd like a glass of wine, please," she said.

The waitress was summonsed, the selection was an Italian red wine, and Roland raised his eyebrows on hearing that she wanted a large glass.

"What music can I expect on the way home," she said. "How about the Rolling Stones?"

"What are you going on about?" he asked.

Isobel was now consuming, with a certain relish, a glass of Chianti Classico.

"One of my favourite tracks is, 'You Can't Always Get What You Want'."

Roland slammed down his knife and fork which he hadn't been using for their main purpose but more as pointers.

"Isobel. Stop playing games with me and pay attention," he ordered.

She concentrated on her nearly empty glass.

"Your attitude is probably the reason why you've already been through two wives," she suggested.

"It was they who lost out," he said. "Stupid bitches; always wanted something different."

Isobel laughed and called over the waitress. She asked for a small glass of wine.

"We'll add misogyny to your growing list of faults," she said. "Now Roland Shaw, solicitor, of Lincoln's Inn Fields, there are two lines in that song which apply to you."

He was regretting his 'stupid bitches' comment and remembered that Naomi, his first wife, had said something along similar lines. He looked back at his guest.

"But if you try," she sang, using a raised tone of voice, "sometimes you might find," and then she stopped.

"Are you paying attention, Roland?" she asked, but did not wait for a response. "You get what you need."

He called the waitress and told her to clear the table. He ordered coffee for the two of them.

"Why didn't you ask for the table to be cleared?" said Isobel.

"Pardon?"

"You told our rather polite waitress to clear the table."

"I want the table cleared," he snapped.

"Why didn't you ask her to clear the table and use the word 'please'?"

"What I want, Isobel, is that list of bank

accounts."

"Yes, I know that," she said. "It will help your case if you learn to speak to other human beings in a pleasant manner."

Roland sighed and let his shoulders droop.

"Winston Churchill, 'The Times' crossword, the Rolling Stones," he sighed. "What the fuck do you want, Isobel?" he asked.

"Don't swear in front of me," she chided. "And stop taking me for a complete fool." She paused. "I think you men, when you are not patronising us weak females, have a phrase for it: 'when the gloves come off'." She put her hand over her glass and asked the waitress to serve the coffee. She added "thank you" to her request.

"The events that are taking place are making more sense to me and I think I am more fully understanding the role of 'the Elite' in all of this. I've studied the banking scandal case and while the money stolen and defrauded from all those innocent small business owners is obscene, in terms of the wealth you lot have, it was petty cash. That means, Roland, that the seven bank accounts must have very substantial funds in them. Enough to create this search for the details that now involves the President of the United States of America." She had finally cracked the hidden meaning in his letter. She stopped and left the table, returning after a few minutes and picking up from where she had left off.

"Now here's a thought, Roland. My research into the Elite lead me to understand better what is money laundering."

Isobel stopped and called her friend, the waitress, over and ordered another small glass of red wine.

"I just wonder," she continued, "whether the vast amounts of money resulting from the defence contracts awarded to the Russian, Spartak something, might somehow have been passed through Graham's bank accounts?"

Roland Shaw was sitting still with his mouth open.

"So, in my best Miss Marple manner, I've worked out that the details I now have, and you want, are the key to something much, much more important. Here's the good news, Roland."

His eyes lit up as a hint of a resolution appeared.

"You can have the details I hold in a safe place on one condition."

"What is that?" he asked.

"You clear Graham's name."

"What on earth are you talking about, Isobel?"

"I want him home and I want him to be able to resume a family life."

"Impossible," he snapped. "You're out of your depth."

"I think 'misogyny' was putting it mildly," she smiled. "Thank you, Roland. You've just told me what I suspected."

"Which is what?" he said, looking at his watch.

"When it gets to the really challenging task, you are a limp watermelon."

He pondered the description and hesitated.

"How do you expect us to clear Graham's name?"

Isobel laughed and finished off her final glass of wine.

"Your Elite group can do whatever it wants. You told me that yourself."

"You're involving yourself in a dangerous game," he said.

Isobel smiled and prepared to leave the table.

"Text me when you are ready to meet my condition," she said.

She stood up, put her hand on his shoulder, went over to the waitress, took out a five-pound note, handed it over while thanking her for looking after them, walked out of the wine bar and decided that spring was in the air. As she strolled along the high street of Holborn, she whispered something to herself.

"I'm fighting for you, Graham. I really am."

Her next move, on returning home, would be to contact Martine Newcross.

*

The General Hospital, Kallistratou, Samos
Monday: early evening

Dr Villios seemed a little flustered as he shook Sarah's hand and rubbed Najwa's head. He indicated that they should sit down and he closed the door.

"I'm sorry to have kept you waiting," he said, "but at least I can make amends with some good news."

As the two hospital visitors sat down in the chairs around the bed, the doctor read the chart fixed on the bottom of the iron frame and then moved up to be near to Max. He felt his pulse and looked at the readings on the heart monitor. He read a sheet of paper he was carrying with him.

"Looking good, Max," he said. "The blood test is positive and, all in all, you are mending well. The most important result is that you are free of any infection meaning that we can stop the antibiotics and I'll just leave you with two pills a day to build up your resistance." He smiled at his audience. "You're free to return to the hotel tomorrow and Sarah tells me you are flying home on Thursday."

He looked around.

"Hax is better, Najwa," he smiled.

Sarah came across and shook his hand.

"Max," he said, turning to his patient, "doctors build up alliances with their patients." He paused as he looked down at the incoming message on his pager. "It has seemed that we've been fighting this together. The cow dung trick that the gypsies use is so difficult to combat." He paused. "Especially when it goes deep into the body."

He looked around at all three of the group.

"You're a tough man, Max, but it seems to me you also have some rather determined support."

Najwa came up and hugged his leg and then laughed.

Dr Villios waved and left the room.

"We are going home?" asked Max.

"Norman has organised flights for us on Thursday. We fly out in the afternoon which means we can have two days at the hotel and you can relax."

"The paperwork; is it all through?" he asked.

"When Norman decides, Norman delivers," said Sarah. "There is one more form which will be here tomorrow," she said. "He's been really worried about you."

They looked at each other and silently agreed not to talk about Graham de Lille Rutherford in front of Najwa.

"Najwa is attending a swimming gala tomorrow so I'll come for you around ten in the morning."

As Sarah leaned over him, he whispered in her ear.

257

"We're on the way home," he said, for which he was rewarded by a tantalising embrace.

"Norman has said he's having the house made ready for us," she said.

"Bye, Hax," said Najwa as they left the room.

Wiltons Restaurant, Jermyn Street, Mayfair, London
Monday: 9.00pm

"Thank you for securing a confidential table, Lord Mallington," said the Secretary of State for Northern Ireland. Her security officers were outside with another guard in the location itself. Elizabeth Shaw did not really need to make an effort with her appearance in that she was naturally attractive with a facial innocence which had created a long line of suitors.

Their orders were taken and the wine poured. She was relaxed from the moment they greeted each other. They engaged in some small talk and exchanged some gossip on the latest infidelity in the House of Commons.

"I've always thought," said Simon Mallington, "that with six hundred and fifty of you, a little bit of 'how's your father' is inevitable."

"What surprises me," said Elizabeth, "are the various couples. Several of the women choose the most unlikely lovers."

Their meals arrived and, for a few moments, they concentrated on their choices.

"I'm so pleased we have been able to meet," said the peer. "It gives me the opportunity to tell you how impressed we are at the results you are achieving." He smiled. "Please call me Simon," he suggested.

"Your praise is valued," she said, "but, in truth, all I do is listen to Sinn Fein and the DUP be rude about each other. There is simply no way that that they'll ever really co-exist and so I have no issue with trying to hasten a united country." She put down her knife and fork. "It's the only solution, Simon," she said.

"Will they stop fighting each other?" asked the peer.

"They play rugby together, Simon," she laughed.

"What does the PM say to you?" he asked.

"He just wants me to try to ensure that Ireland is not one of his many problems," she replied. "The attack on Euston Station was a bad move, if I may say so," she added.

"It was a disaster," he acknowledged. "It achieved exactly the opposite to what was intended. The Russians, who trained the two members of Continuity IRA, misunderstood their brief. It was meant to remind the British Government, and the public, that the Irish situation needs a solution. How the two terrorists managed to acquire the weaponry and kill so many people, amazed us." He wiped his mouth. "We've suggested to Dublin that a hold is placed on further activities at this stage."

"I think that is wise, Simon," she said. "The hard border issue is beginning to take up people's attention again and although I don't think our objective can be achieved that quickly, it is going to help – for the simple reason it makes the border the problem."

"We've picked up a rumour that you told a meeting of the Cabinet that there is someone on the inside."

Elizabeth Shaw laughed and Lord Mallington allowed his thoughts to wander for a brief moment.

"I threw that in the mix," she said. "It makes me cringe when I watch that pompous lot hug themselves when they think they have some information that others do not."

"Just as I thought," he said. "Did you catch up with Martine Newcross when she was over here?" he asked.

"No, I was in Belfast. I've heard she delivered the works at the CFW."

"She was memorable," he said. "There's no doubt that the President knows how to pick them."

"Perhaps," she replied. "It depends on his selection criteria," she laughed.

Simon Mallington nodded in appreciation of his guest's perspicacity.

*

Paradise Hotel, Vathi, the municipality of Samos
Tuesday/Wednesday: twenty-four hours

Sarah knew from the moment she spotted the man that he was a threat to their safety. He was trying to blend in with the groups of holiday guests at the Paradise Hotel but he was unshaven and ill at ease. That, by itself, would not have been sufficient to alert Sarah, as the area was populated by out-of-work islanders, immigrants, refugees and gypsies. The first of the giveaways was his skin which was unaffected by the sun. He could have come from the Russian tundra – which was not too far away from the truth. Was he a hitman who had been trained in the badlands of the Baltic countries? The second clue Sarah noted was that some of his beach clothing was new; there was still a packaging label attached to the back of his shorts. Add to these factors his steely, alert eyes, and Sarah was on her guard.

She assessed the situation. Najwa was at a swimming gala for the day and she had collected Max from the general hospital at Kallistratou earlier in the morning. He was now in their room sleeping soundly. They were scheduled to fly out of Samos, and back to England, on Thursday. The remaining outstanding document had been delivered and they were ready to depart for London. The only possible interference to their plans was that a terrorist had arrived and Sarah's instinct was that he intended killing someone and, almost certainly, either her or Max.

She had several hours to undertake the first of her retaliatory actions. It would have been helpful if Najwa was around although Sarah was relieved that she was, temporarily, out of harm's way. It took her nearly twenty minutes to quietly circle around the table where the stranger was drinking a beer. She took off her blouse and made sure her bikini top was as revealing as she could muster. She strolled past him and turned back after twenty paces. If he had noticed her, he concealed the fact rather carefully. Sarah decided that his target was more probably Max.

She moved to her next action point by settling down in the vicinity and, as naturally as possible, taking a photograph on her phone of two children playing in a sand pit. In the background she captured the stranger who seemed unaware of her actions. Sarah returned to her own table and sent the photograph to London. Within fifteen minutes she received a personal text message from Norman Delamount urging great caution. She had photographed Spartak Grankin's personal bodyguard, a man known as Eugene Sokolov. She responded to London asking for details of his last three killings. When these came through, she recognised a pattern that she hoped would be repeated the following day, assuming her fears were realised.

Sarah visited the swimming gala, watched Najwa playing with her friends and was pleased to see that slowly she was regaining her correct weight. She would be there in the pool for a further two hours. Sarah used the time to go for a long walk and plan tomorrow's retaliation knowing there was one advantage in her favour and it had to be used correctly. It so much depended on Max's body language and she had now worked out the optimum moment to pounce.

That night, sleep became secondary as Sarah tossed and turned as she planned the next day's ambush. She was certain that Sokolov would pounce as soon as he could and she had no time to bring in help. Max was vulnerable and he was the target. She went over her strategy again and again; she knew that one mistake would be fatal. She found herself bending double as she rehearsed her defence.

The following morning Najwa, after receiving a liberal coating of suntan lotion, skipped happily away to re-join her friends in the swimming pool. Sarah had spoken to the main lifeguard and paid her some euros in return for taking care of her little girl for the next two hours. Even as the tension inside her was rising, Sarah could not prevent herself from watching Najwa display a strong swimming stroke as she reached the far side of the pool.

She returned to the hotel gardens and found Max who was playing around with his sunglasses. She hugged him and noticed that he had redressed his leg wound himself. She poured a drink and served some bread in a bowl which she placed in front of him.

"Max…" she said.

Instinctively, he knew it was trouble. He pushed the dish away and looked at his partner.

"You are going to do something for me and you are not going to ask any questions."

"What?"

Sarah placed her fingers over his lips. "You are going to go for a walk," she said and then gave him directions which would take him out of the hotel and, after about a mile, onto the hills overlooking the Aegean Sea.

"You will follow the directions to the east and you will come across a notice which will have this written on it." She handed him a slip of paper that read:

Epikindyno vracho me ta podia

"It means, roughly translated, that the path indicated is a dangerous cliff walk."

He managed to remain silent although his willingness to follow instructions was being sorely tested.

"You will take the path indicated," she said. "You will continue walking for a mile and then come back to the hotel." She again placed her fingers over his lips. "Max, no questions. Just do it." She smiled without any warmth. "I'm going to go back to the hotel," she said.

She reached underneath the table and brought out a backpack.

"I want you to put this on and leave for your walk in ten minutes time. I'm going to hug you as though I'm suggesting a period of absence."

263

Sarah completed the performance and departed the area, leaving Max sitting still and reflecting on what he had been told. He was bemused and concerned at the officiousness he had witnessed from Sarah. But he had two choices and he decided to see through the charade. He stood up, looked around him, put on the backpack and began the walk. His leg was throbbing but the rising temperatures made him feel more comfortable.

He reached the coastal walk, turned east along the hilltop path and found himself among a number of holiday makers who were walking off their breakfast and generally enjoying themselves. He reached the sign which Sarah had indicated and took out the piece of paper she had given him. He took the path which started a more adventurous route albeit the views of the bay were spectacular. There were small boulders on the way and he stumbled on several of them. He looked ahead and observed an increasing gradient down to the rocks on the shoreline. He stopped, rubbed his leg, and as he stood up, he knew that he was not alone.

Coming in from his right was Eugene Sokolov, pointing a pistol at Max. He needed the body to fall on the path because his instructions were to take a picture of the corpse. He therefore circled round to the front of Max so that he would fall backwards onto the ground. The whole area was deserted apart from the cormorants hunting breakfast in the still waters of the bay.

He raised his weapon and Max couldn't think what to do. He was unarmed, and he couldn't run on his damaged leg. As he watched Sokolov prepare to fire, he thought of the story he had read of the couple who had jumped off a mountain in the Pyrenees. That was how he felt – helpless and out of control. 'Mad Max' was gone and in his place was a man who simply wanted to go home.

He looked at his murderer, tensed and waited for the shot.

From the right-hand side came a momentary blur, a movement, a horizontal shadow that changed into a hurtling body. Sarah hit Sokolov on the upper thigh with a velocity which contained all her anger and rage. She made the mistake of wrapping her arms around his body and, as he headed for the cliffs, she was taken with him. Max screamed out as his wounded leg gave in underneath him but he managed to generate enough movement to grab her by her ankles. The killer was over the edge, fighting for traction on the rocks which simply crumbled away. He had managed to secure one of Sarah's arms and, as he fell, he began to take her with him.

Max was holding on to her legs, still yelling out with the effort. She struggled to release her left arm and then realised that Sokolov was wearing shorts. Once more she called upon her special knowledge and plunged her fingers into the flesh on the inside of his thigh. She dug as deep as she could and blocked out all the other pain she was experiencing. Sokolov finally gave in, cried out in pain and was gone, his body falling onto the rocks below where some crabs were soon investigating the visitor to their territory.

Sarah and Max lay side by side, panting. He took her into his arms and held her.

"Max, I'm so sorry," she cried out. "It was the only way I could think of defending you."

He raised himself up and gasped at her body. The

razor-sharp bushes had shredded her skin and there was blood everywhere.

He looked at her and smiled.

"Let's go home," he said.

Fortnum & Mason, Piccadilly, Mayfair, London
Wednesday: 3.00pm

Lady Christel Hemmingway-Brunton waved the waiter away.

"I really object when they try to refill my glass when I haven't finished. Perhaps they are on commission," she laughed. "Mind you, Issy, it will not take much to persuade me to have a second glass. This prosecco makes me feel a little…shall we say, content."

"And I'm paying for it," said Isobel.

Christel beamed as she swept the room at Fortnum & Mason with her eyes to ensure they were not being overheard.

"Naughty girl, tell me all," she said. "Actually, Issy, the wager stipulated Claridge's but I think the Diamond Jubilee Tea Salon will do just as well." She stared at her companion. "Was it magical, Issy?"

Isobel sighed and put her hand over the fingers of her friend.

"Chrissy, you are like a desert island in the midst of a tropical storm. You make me so relaxed," she said. "I've actually won the wager but I couldn't wait to tell you my news so here we are, with me paying the bill."

"I sense some intrigue on its way," said Christel.

Isobel proceeded to tell her the whole story including the involvement of Robin Pargetter, the discovery of where the list of bank accounts was concealed, the lunch with Roland and her demand which left the solicitor speechless. The information resulted in a second person almost lost for words. Christel stood up and left the room returning a few minutes later and collecting the waiter on her way back to ensure she was served another glass of prosecco. Isobel contented herself with the cream cakes which were being served with English tea.

"Right," announced Christel. "I think we need to have a serious chat." She paused and sipped her wine. "You want Graham's name cleared – which leads to several questions: why, how and what for?"

"He's my husband and he's the father of our two children."

"Issy," snapped her friend. "He's a fraudster and a sexual pervert."

"He's my husband, and Nick and Emily have a right to make their own decisions," replied Isobel. "Let's deal with your comments."

Christel held on to her hand.

"Issy, I'm on your side. Everything I am saying is in your best interests."

"You've made three accusations, Chrissy. I have the right to ask you to allow me to answer them."

"I think I'll have a scone," she said. "That jam looks wonderful."

"Graham is a very astute businessman. I have it on good authority that the banking scheme was both brilliant and legal. It went wrong because some second-rate bankers got the taste of money and were corrupted by it. Graham took his eye off the ball and, for that, he showed weakness and was punished."

"Oh? How was he punished?" asked Christel.

"In his world, reputation is everything. He was

267

protected by his Elite associates but within their system he was damaged." She paused. "Lord Mallington told me that in the City, in other words, the money men, there's a code. Many of them manage to do something a bit naughty. Providing it's not too serious there is an unwritten rule that the person goes away for two years and keeps their nose clean. They will then be allowed back."

"Sounds like a group of boy scouts to me," she suggested.

"It's a jungle and Graham made a mistake. I am asking that he be allowed back."

"We'll discuss that in a minute. I will admit that you've expressed your position rather persuasively. Now for Hope House. I doubt that you can convince yourself on that one, let alone me."

"I can forgive him," said Isobel. "We gave over twenty refugees a new start in life and, had events turned out differently, we would have cared for many more. Graham was wrong to do what he did and he was very wrong that he did it with a child." She paused and signalled that the waiter should attend their table. When he arrived, she ordered a further glass of wine for her guest and a vodka and tonic for herself. "He was able to do it because of the involvement of a corrupt doctor and several of the care staff at the home."

"But he did it," said Christel.

"Perhaps it was partly my fault," Isobel replied.

"You, Isobel!" cried Christel. "Are you saying he did it because you didn't give him enough sex?"

"I'm saying that perhaps I allowed the children and my parents to dominate my attention and I neglected to ensure that my husband was satisfied."

"Tosh," she said, "utter twaddle."

"I think Graham should be charged with having underage sex, serve his sentence and then return to a life with his family."

"Glory be," said Christel. "That will never happen." She paused. "You'll need to have him castrated as well. He's a sex maniac."

"I was at a Conservative cocktail party last year and there had been another scandal involving a junior minister and a researcher. The minister was there trying to convince everyone he loved his wife. This slightly drunken politician came up to me and said that the reason there are so many relationship issues in Parliament is simply because of the opportunity. He said many more men would stray but simply never get the chance."

Christel remembered the ending of her own marriage. She was helped by the reality that the family wealth was in her name.

"Do you think, Chrissy," continued Isobel, "after all Graham has gone through that he'll be the same in the future? I think he'll want his family back. I'm still his wife and I know him better than anyone."

"What about Roland?" asked Christel.

"He has to clear Graham's name," she said.

"And then he gets the banking details."

"If he can convince me, first." She gazed around the room. "I want my husband home again and I will nurse him back to health, as best I can." She laughed rather politely. "I can at least thank Roland Shaw for updating me on the modern Lothario. Donna Summer singing 'MacArthur Park', I ask you!"

"And nothing stirred inside you, Issy?"

"Perhaps, just a little, Chrissy."

Christel looked at her friend.

"It will never happen," she said to herself. "Roland Shaw will never get your husband back home."

+ + +

CHAPTER THIRTEEN

Mayfair, London
Wednesday: evening
Lord Mallington was not himself and the waiter sensed his angst as he snapped his fingers. He was struggling to remain in control and exude his usual self-confidence; he was reacting to events. Just before leaving the office to meet Roland Shaw at his club he was told, in a telephone call with Spartak Grankin, that the attempt on the life of Max Hemmings had failed and the assassin himself was dead. What the Russian oligarch did not know was that the peer had received a confidential briefing that Spartak himself was facing a criminal investigation in Moscow over the alleged bribing of defence contract procurement officials.

"Roland," said Simon Mallington, "this is getting messy and I do not like it when this happens." He sipped his glass of whisky. "I was entitled to rely on your undertaking that, according to you, Isobel de Lille Rutherford was wrapped around your little finger. That is what you boasted to me."

"That is what I believed," he replied.

"We also have a situation where Graham thinks he knows where the list of banks is hidden when, in truth, Isobel now has that information. She, for her part, wants her husband back home and his name cleared."

Roland stared down at his drink.

"I've had a chat with Norman," continued the peer. "He knows his way round the judiciary and we think we may have a way of meeting her demand."

"That's a huge step forward," responded Roland.

"You will have to see her again because nothing further can happen until we have that list of bank accounts." He stared at the lawyer. "We will not accept anything less," he said. "We've misjudged Isobel from the beginning. We all jumped to the assumption that she was a loving mother and housewife. Graham was such a powerful character that it was as if there was no public role for her except to look the part which, Roland, as you have discovered, she does rather well."

"Perhaps," replied the bruised lawyer, as the reference to his failure to carry conviction with Isobel began to hurt him. "Can you please develop your theory?" he asked.

"Because of events at Hope House, we all jumped to the assumption that she'd want to separate her life from him." He called for their glasses to be refilled. His club was surprisingly quiet for a midweek evening. "We were wrong," he said. "She wants to clear his name." The peer paused and sighed. "In a way it's unhelpful that the President has written a letter to her."

Roland agreed that added a further hurdle.

"We can't tell her about the President's demand to hasten a united Ireland?" he said.

"No, we can't." Lord Mallington paused. "We wish he'd stay out of it but he has been got at by the Washington group." He accepted his refilled glass and savoured the scotch. "We might be able to find a way round that but what we can't do is to reveal the name of our inside person. That would be catastrophic."

"For all of us," added Roland.

"We must have those bank details, Roland. It's the

least the President is expecting."

As he left the club, Roland began to feel more positive. He decided that perhaps he had stirred Isobel's amorous feelings and that was the way to secure the answer to where she was hiding the details of the bank accounts. He decided to risk everything and send her a text message.

'Lunch tomorrow. Car at 11.45am. I've good news'

Her response was almost immediate. He groaned as he read her reply.

'Yes. Is the good news for me or you?'

Samos International Airport, Greece
Thursday: morning/afternoon

They were on their way home. Sarah, Najwa and Max were sitting in the reception of the Paradise Hotel from lunchtime onwards, awaiting the arrival of their taxi to the airport. A black luxury car arrived and out jumped a man who represented SC Group in the Greek Isles. He shook hands with Max and ordered the porters to load their small amount of luggage into the vehicle. He then produced coats for all three of them, explaining that London was experiencing an early spring cold spell. He sat down and went through the paperwork. Their scheduled flight was leaving at four-thirty and they would change planes at Athens and fly on to Heathrow, London, where they were expected to arrive at nine-thirty. He would accompany them on the first stage and they would be met at Heathrow by a London operative who both Sarah and Max knew well. He went through their travel documents with them and reassured the travellers that everything had been vetted personally by Norman Delamount.

For the first time in several months everything proceeded as planned. The flight changeover went without a hitch and, about an hour out of Athens, Sarah found herself peering out of the window at the Mediterranean landscape beneath the half full plane. She watched Najwa who was sleeping in Max's arms; her partner had his eyes closed. Her thoughts went on to the situation at home. She had been hurt by the email she had received from her soon-to-be former husband, Nick. He was lashing out at the settlement, which he had agreed through his solicitor, but was one that he now considered to be morally wrong. He listed her crimes including adultery, desertion of her children and disgusting selfishness.

She indicated to the stewardess that she did not want either of her party disturbed but she accepted the proffered glass of wine and bowl of vegetarian crisps which she proceeded to eat, one by one. She reflected on the moment that she decided to travel to the Middle East and find Najwa. Apart from the fact that it was a hopeless cause, and had no substance in reality, it had been quite absurd to expect other people to understand her reasoning. She put the glass and bowl on the tray and began to slumber as the cabin crew had now turned off the main lights.

She winced as she reflected on the total rejection by her teenage son, Marcus. He had reached a point where the only communication between them was the tales told by Susie when she visited Kensington. He was prospering both at school and with his sport including reaching almost international level at judo. It was clear that a wall had been erected with her on the one side and Marcus long gone on the other.

Najwa stirred. She seemed content and secure and

her rescuer was thankful for that.

Sarah realised she was following her checklist thought process, reflecting her training as a police officer. The particular skill that she had brought to her career was the ability to know when to break the rules. Her medal-winning passage to promotion had been accelerated by feats of extraordinary bravery. She reflected on the saving of the lives of the Royal Couple in The Mall but it was the stopping of the passenger train at Bridego Bridge in Buckinghamshire, the scene of the Great Train Robbery, and the prevention of death and injury amongst four hundred commuters, that had given her the most personal satisfaction – unless she recalled saving the life of her daughter Susie from a deranged former lover called Dr Martin Redding.

She checked her watch. There was an hour to go before landing at Heathrow airport and beginning the process of rebuilding her life. Her employment with SC Group was now contracted and a special relationship guaranteed with Norman Delamount as she had been part of the revenge team that extracted a vicious retaliation against the man he blamed for the death of his secret daughter, Gabrielle. The ticks in the box continued as she thought about her daughter who was going to love Najwa and their new home in Fulham. Her boss had even had all her belongings transferred from her flat to the new address.

She reflected on Max and watched him sleep. They would be living together, which is what he so desperately wanted to happen. She recalled the moment when he had killed Michael Duggan, just as Duggan was about to murder her.

The plane landed in heavy rain at London

Heathrow and the arrangements continued to proceed without any delay. The SC Group operative soon had them through customs and in the car on their way to a new home; fortunately, the rain in West London was abating. Sarah wrapped the coat around her but, as soon as she stepped into the hall of their London terraced property and sensed the warmth of the central heating, she felt comfortable. By midnight Najwa was asleep in her room and Max had gone to bed. Sarah sipped a coffee and read a personal note from her boss. His comments were warm and generous and why wouldn't Najwa quickly adapt to life in London?

She looked out into the street at the rows of parked cars. There was a stray dog on the other side of the road trying to get into one the wheelie bins that the residents had put out for early morning collection.

It was then that she began to sense that something was wrong. She again read Norman's letter and searched for a clue. It was there but Sarah was looking in the wrong direction.

The offices of Hannings & Richards, Lincoln's Inn Fields, London
Thursday: 12.30pm

Isobel de Lille Rutherford was puzzled by the arrival of her chauffeur-driven car which had pulled up outside the offices of Hannings & Richards in New Square on the south side of Lincoln's Inn Fields. She was even more surprised when her door was opened by Roland Shaw. He shook her hand and led her up the steps and into the reception area.

"I've booked a room for us," he said as he took

her coat.

She followed him into the same room where they had first met many weeks ago. She sat down and he poured some coffee. In the centre of the table were sandwiches and a selection of cheeses.

"I want to start today," he said, "by asking you a question."

Isobel had rehearsed several possible scenarios including a gushing charm offensive or perhaps tickets for the theatre. She held her nerve and realised that she was enjoying the formality of his approach.

"Today, Isobel, is about outcomes."

"What does that mean?" she asked.

He pushed the plate of sandwiches towards her and she pushed them back again. She checked that her bag was safely attached to the chair.

"If we approach the situation we face with restraint and vision we can arrive at a sensible place."

Isobel smiled and decided to wipe her face with an embroidered handkerchief.

"Roland," she said, "several baffling statements delivered in your usual patronising style is getting us absolutely nowhere!"

"What do you want, Isobel?" he snapped.

She decided not to repeat their last conversation and re-state her condition because it was obvious that Roland Shaw was decidedly nervous. The clue, as far as she could assess, was that he had changed the anticipated location from the Bunghole Cellars to the formality of these offices. As she was tiring of steak and mixed salad, she had no problem with that.

"Make me an offer, Roland," she smiled.

"We can arrange for Graham to come back to the United Kingdom and we'll do our best to rebuild his

277

reputation. In two years, he may be able to return to Rutherford Finance House as a director."

She stood up and walked round the room.

"Just like that," she said as she looked out of the window and spotted the daffodil bulbs pushing up from underneath the lawns.

"I cannot make any sense of this meeting unless you decide what it is you want in your life at this moment," he said.

"I think Lord Mallington has been coaching you," she suggested.

Roland also rose to his feet but initially made no attempt to approach Isobel. He then started to follow her but she sat down again; he followed suit.

"It's pointless asking you to trust me," he said.

"We are in complete agreement on that moment of enlightenment," she said.

"Please, Isobel, what do you want the most?" he asked.

"I want my husband back home, I want him to be with Nick and Emily and I want to nurse him back to full health," she said. She then banged her fist on the table. "What are your wretched conditions, Roland?" she shouted.

"There is just one," he said.

"A piece of paper?" she quizzed.

"The details of the bank accounts," he replied.

"Now we are getting there, aren't we Roland?" she said. "You have told Graham that I have found the piece of paper."

"Yes, he knows."

Isobel looked at the man with whom she once thought she might begin a relationship.

"You want the piece of paper before you'll

organise for Graham to come home," she said.

"Yes," he said.

"And you expect me to roll over and accept your offer," she said.

"I also have a piece of paper, Isobel," replied Roland. "We realised that you would have great difficulty with the decision we are asking you to make."

He reached into a file on the table which Isobel had spotted the moment she had entered the room. He took out a plain white sheet of what appeared to be a hotel letterhead.

"It's from Graham to you," he said. "His handwriting is rather shaky but we hope you can read it."

Isobel took it from him and quickly scanned the three paragraphs. Her mind went back to her afternoon tea with Lady Christel and her incorrect prediction. She breathed a sigh of relief as she knew that they had all arrived at the same solution.

"Lord Mallington at work," she said.

"He's played an important part," said Roland.

"And they've agreed," she said.

"There's a process and, to some extent, we are not totally in control of that process but you must trust me on this point. I think it will happen as we have negotiated."

"If I give you the details, when will Graham arrive back in the UK?" she asked.

"He's twenty minutes away in a small hotel in Berkeley Square. He was seen by a doctor this morning."

Isobel stared at the solicitor. She was preparing to take a risk but she felt she was on solid ground.

"You know, Roland, if you can carry on being a professional, sensible human being you might be able to find the third Mrs Shaw," she said.

She opened her handbag and took out a piece of paper, which she handed over. He quickly scanned the list of bank accounts and breathed a sigh of relief.

"There's a car outside waiting to take us to the hotel," he said.

She stood up, reached over and brushed his face with her hand.

As she began anticipating meeting her husband, she asked herself how she would handle an explanation to Nick and Emily. She also knew that it was just the first of a series of challenges which lay ahead of her.

As the car moved away, and headed for Mayfair, Roland put his hand on hers.

"He's not in good shape, Isobel," he said.

"Yes, I know that," she said. "But he's home and I can work from there."

The rest of the journey was conducted in a tense silence.

The Cabinet Room, 10 Downing Street, London
Thursday: 4.00pm

Eight people gathered together in the Cabinet Room at the request of the Prime Minister. Terence Barrington looked around and decided that this was a better way to plunge the governmental knife into the back of a colleague. He was still smarting from the working over he had received from the former Minister for Defence, Melvyn, now Lord Donaldson.

It was no longer a secret that the Prime Minister's possible successor was Heather Cousins who seemed to be growing in stature as her colleagues, one by one, were being derailed, partly by personal circumstances and in part due to the complexity of the post-Brexit negotiations. The only outsider was Elizabeth Shaw and her hard work in Northern Ireland was cementing a growing respect for her abilities. She managed to maintain cordial relationships with many of her colleagues and negotiated the almost inevitable tensions between the Prime Minister and the Chancellor by ignoring them.

The Chancellor never relished meetings where he did not know the agenda and, once more, he felt he was being thrown to the lions following the adverse publicity for further cuts in departmental budgets in order to fund the vast overspend on the NHS. He had his retaliation ready and, in his case, had photocopies of confidential departmental accounts which would allow him to deflect the NHS crisis, which was bleeding dry the Government purse, on to the Health minister.

The last and most vulnerable member of the meeting was the Foreign Secretary who appeared to be in another world which, as he had just returned from Japan, was not surprising. He had spent part of his time at the Embassy negotiating with the British ambassador his allocation of tickets for the 2020 Olympic Games.

Terence Barrington tapped the table and immediately secured the full attention of his colleagues. He reviewed the latest opinion polls and noted a downturn in the party's ratings. He then went into a rather detailed analysis of the latest European negotiations and avoided answering the question as to why the Brexit minister was not present at the meeting.

"I've invited you here today," said Terence Barrington, "because the one remaining challenge we have is the question of the Irish border. I will, of course, update you but first, Elizabeth, we all value your hard work on this matter."

"Thank you, Prime Minister," said the Secretary of State for Northern Ireland. "The talking goes on in the Parliament Buildings at Stormont albeit there is now an operating executive. However, the tensions between the DUP and Sinn Fein are continuing." She paused. "Frankly, the issue is never the actual matter being discussed. They are going to disagree as a matter of principle. Whatever solution is proposed for the control of the border is immediately opposed by the other side."

"You've been saying that the only real answer is reunification," said Maurice Henson.

"Yes, Foreign Secretary," she replied. "That is the only solution, in my opinion."

"But," said the Prime Minister, "you've never actually said that publicly."

"Obviously not," she replied. "That would create an immediate polarisation."

"You've also told us that there is someone on the inside," he said.

"That was confidential," she snapped. "I'm not happy with the way this discussion is proceeding, Prime Minister."

"I'm sure you're not," said Terence Barrington, "because the insider is, of course, you."

A sudden silence descended on the meeting and several ministers looked down at their papers. One realised that the Prime Minister was banishing any chance of an attempt to replace him. Another pondered as to why this hatchet job was not being completed in his private office. Elizabeth Shaw remained completely calm, on the outside.

"I think you need to justify that statement," she said, "before I call for a vote of no confidence in your leadership."

The Prime Minister reached into his case and took out a tape machine which he placed on the table.

"This is a conversation you had with a senior member of the Democratic Unionist Party. You were not aware he was recording the event which was in his office. My colleagues also need to know that you handed him the minutes of a meeting between the Taoiseach and a senior European negotiator who I do not propose identifying."

He pressed the start button and the eight politicians listened as Elizabeth Shaw discussed Ireland's position on the post-Brexit situation and her plan that the DUP would win all the arguments. The discussion became convoluted as each proposal she presented was questioned. However, it was clear that there was a cordial atmosphere. The Prime Minister ended the recording.

"Prime Minister," said Elizabeth Shaw. "I have been meaning to inform you that I have decided to leave politics and take up an offer I have received from the private sector."

"Why?" said William Davidson. "Why have you betrayed us?"

The Secretary of State for Northern Ireland picked up her papers and started to leave the room.

"Have you any idea what it's like listening to those morons go on, hour after hour, milking the

Government of as much money as they can and earning ludicrous fees?"

Terence Barrington also stood up.

"Nobody pretends it's easy and the job of Secretary of State for Northern Ireland is as difficult a Cabinet position as can be imagined," he said. "But that's not the real reason. My long experience does not stand for much but one thing I do know. When a Minister resigns it's usually about power." He put his hand to his mouth and coughed. "In your case, it's been about loss of power. If Ireland does re-unite, your job is over. What you've been doing is to ensure that the DUP and Sinn Fein make no progress whatsoever."

"Is that what you think?" said Elizabeth.

But she did not wait for the answer. Three hours later the requisite letters were exchanged; she visited her constituency, avoided her department and the civil servants who had tried so very hard to support her, and returned to civilian life leaving the media scratching its head. This was to be one of the rare occasions when there would be no Cabinet leaks.

Later that day, it was announced from Downing Street that the National Health Service was in crisis, the Health Minister had been sacked, the Chancellor of the Exchequer was imposing new departmental cuts to finance an emergency funding of staff recruitment and everybody would be able to book a doctor's appointment within forty-eight hours.

In Belfast, Willie watched the news programme while supping his glass of Guinness. His admiration for the British Prime Minister was at an all-time high.

*

Terence Barrington ignored his doctor's orders and poured himself a large scotch. He had finished the first of two personal letters. His message to the DUP Member of Parliament William Jarvis expressed gratitude and briefly explained the afternoon's events. He suggested a name to replace the ex-minister and asked if Willie could give an opinion. He added a postscript saying the machine and recording had been destroyed.

His second communication was to a member of the House of Lords. The Prime Minister had been surprised at the ease with which he had managed to offload the Secretary of State for Northern Ireland. He had one piece of information which he had kept to himself and for which he now thanked the peer. Spartak Grankin was gone and Russian funding to Ireland was drying up. He expressed his sincere appreciation to Lord Mallington for this rather useful intelligence.

The Offices of SC Group, Knightsbridge, London
Friday: 11.00am

The boardroom on the fourth floor of the building from where Norman Delamount ran his security company was always slightly forbidding. Sarah could not understand why, after all that had happened, they were not being received in his private office. An assistant had arrived, following an early morning telephone call, and reassured them that Najwa would be safe in her care. As Sarah and Max left their new home in Fulham, the carer had already begun to play with Najwa. Sarah and Max had arrived at the offices of SC Group and went immediately upstairs to the fourth floor. There was a tension in the air and Sarah was on her guard.

"There are times," began Norman, "when events move in a mysterious way." He waited while a member of staff poured them all coffee and was then waved away. Max wondered why Daisy had not attended to the formalities.

"There is much to discuss and I have still not yet decided how to recognise your courage and bravery. We are all proud of you both." He paused but held up his hand to stop Sarah begin to ask her first question.

"You may find what is about to happen rather confusing," he continued, "but I would ask that you both trust me and allow me to handle this in the way I think best."

Again, Sarah started to speak and once more was deterred from doing so by her boss. She looked at Max who simply shrugged his shoulders.

"I have taken a course of action which you may disagree with and you will certainly want explaining. But," he hesitated, "you must give yourselves time to try to understand."

"Norman," said Sarah. "I simply do not understand what you are saying."

He picked up the telephone and delivered a brief instruction. Within a few seconds there was a knock on the door and Daisy Maitland brought in an elegant woman. Both Sarah and Max stood up and gazed at the newcomer who they instantly recognised.

"I think you will know, if only from photographs, Mrs Isobel de Lille Rutherford," said Norman. He asked everyone to sit down.

"I'm going to ask Isobel to explain to you why we are here," he said.

Isobel looked and seemed her confident self.

"I'm going to say two things first," she began. She paused as she checked whether she had them all listening to her. She was not to know that, out of the corner of his eye, Max was watching the Paradise fish. "I must thank Norman for his assistance. Perhaps more importantly, I understand that you may have difficulty in accepting what we have caused to happen." She then stood up and started to walk round the room. "Even last night I lay in bed arguing with myself why a certain course of action is to take place." She smiled at Sarah. "We are both mothers," she said. "You know the extraordinary love that you feel for your offspring. For that reason alone, I am sure that what Norman is making happen is right."

"Why don't you tell us what you're talking about," said Max whose disappointment that the male fish were not fighting each other was being matched by the events taking place which were baffling him.

Isobel walked over to an adjoining door and opened it. A few moments later, in limped a man who looked exhausted. It was Max who was the first to react.

"You're fucking Graham de Lille Rutherford," he shouted.

"Sit down, Max," ordered Norman.

"You put a contract on me," yelled Sarah.

"And *you* nearly killed my husband by putting flesh-eating crabs on his body," said Isobel, staring at Max.

There was a moment's silence in the room. Isobel grabbed at her husband's hand.

"Graham has agreed to compensate every single business which was damaged by the banking fraud," said Norman.

"He killed Gabrielle," said Sarah.

"The bankers in prison killed my daughter," said Norman, "but, yes, I've been through agonies trying to rationalise the decision I have reached."

"Which is what?" asked Sarah.

"I have used my connections to enable Graham to return to his home here in England."

It was clear that de Lille Rutherford was becoming restive. When he tried to speak, the sound that came out of his mouth was a guttural wheeze. The reason for this was that the transfer from a warm Mediterranean climate to the chilly winds in London had proved too much for this weakened man. His audience was just able to understand what he was trying to say.

"I'm finished as a businessman," he said. "I'll use my wealth to right some wrongs and I'll try my best to make things up with my wife and my children," he said.

"What about what happened at Hope House?" asked Sarah.

"We are re-establishing the home," said Isobel. "I'll run it this time. We've agreed that some of Graham's money will be used to fund it."

"Who agreed that, Norman?" asked Max.

"It's the way these things work," he replied.

"Graham will never go near Hope House again," said Isobel.

"I should expect not," said Sarah.

"We have to forgive him," said Isobel.

"*You* forgive him," said Sarah. "I'll concentrate on protecting young girls from sexual perverts like your husband."

"Thanks to the crabs Max put on my husband,

Graham is no longer a threat to anyone," she sighed.

"I'm sorry. This just does not feel right to me," said Sarah, looking at Max.

"You're right," said Norman. "That is why we have demanded that the events at Hope House are answered."

"I'll get some more crabs," suggested Max.

He had not noticed that Norman had pressed a bell and the entrance door had been opened. Into the room came three police officers. The one in charge walked up to Graham de Lille Rutherford who stood erect.

"I am Detective Inspector Georgina Morris," said the senior police officer, "and I have with me Police Constable Jordan and Detective Constable Benson. Graham de Lille Rutherford, I am arresting you for the offences of having sex with a child and filming lewd acts with children at Hope House in Ealing during the last two years. You do not have to say anything but it may harm your defence if you do not mention when questioned something you later rely on in court. Anything you do say may be given in evidence."

As he moved towards the police officers, the prisoner turned to Sarah.

"Now you have the justice you wanted," he said.

As the police party left the room, DI Morris looked at Isobel and nodded.

Norman invited Sarah and Max into his office and went over to the drinks cabinet. He handed Max a scotch and Sarah a vodka and tonic.

"You've pulled some strings, Norman," said Sarah.

"Graham de Lille Rutherford and I have

something in common," he said. "A love of Churchill and all he achieved." He drank his scotch and refilled his glass. "Perhaps my favourite Winston saying is one that might apply now," he said.

"Try me," said Sarah. "I doubt if Churchill could help me understand what you've been up to," she gasped.

"He said:

'Success is not final; failure is not fatal: it is the courage to continue that counts'."

"And that makes everything right, does it?" she replied.

"Life must go on, Sarah," he said.

"If I'd had a gun in that room," said Max, "I would have shot him dead."

Norman stood up and refilled his glass.

"That, Max, is the difference between you and I," he said.

"You've been seduced by Isobel, have you Norman?" asked Sarah.

"Perhaps the word 'charmed' might be a better choice," he said, "but, yes, I have found her to be a rather impressive and determined woman."

"They can all live happily ever after," said Sarah.

"Do you really think that?" said Norman.

"No, of course not," she replied. "It just feels, I don't know, shall we say, unfinished."

"There is something else I need to tell you," he said.

"Must you?" said Max.

Norman ignored the sarcasm and looked at Sarah.

"De Lille will probably receive a suspended sentence," he said.

She stared at him in utter bewilderment.

"I know: you are offended," he said as he registered her anger.

"You are pushing the boundaries," said Sarah.

"The crabs you placed on his body, Max. He is physically ruined as a man. The defence will focus on that and I suspect the CPS will accept a plea bargain."

"I want to be with Najwa," said Sarah. "I'm going home."

"I need to discuss some business with you, Max," said Norman.

Sarah stood up and walked out of his office.

+ + +

CHAPTER FOURTEEN

Mayfair, London
Friday: 9.00pm

The waiter served brandy and port to the four diners and was then waved away.

"I'm enjoying being a peer, Simon," laughed Melvyn Donaldson.

"It does sound rather grand," commented Elizabeth Shaw.

Lord Mallington sat back and looked around the lounge area of his club, which was half empty. He commented that this came as no surprise as many members were already back on their estates, preparing for the weekend activities.

"Tally-ho," laughed Elizabeth.

"Tally-ho, indeed," confirmed the peer. "The quarry has been sighted." He paused. "Graham de Lille Rutherford is back in England!" He raised his glass. "Well done, Roland Shaw," he proposed.

The Lincoln's Inn Fields-based lawyer grimaced.

"While you landed gents retire to your country homes, there's me with a London flat and my run round the Docklands. I should probably sue for allowing the estate agent to convince me it has two bedrooms." He sighed. "It's a strange thing, the law. My two ex-wives both have luxurious suburban homes and all I have are debts and a flat."

"We can help there," said Simon. "We'll know the total amount in the de Lille Rutherford accounts by the middle of next week. You'll be receiving a rather generous dividend which, Roland, and I know I speak for all of us, you deserve. You did a great job with

Isobel de Lille Rutherford."

Roland allowed his thoughts to wander. Isobel had been in a different class to his two wives. For a brief period of time he wondered if he had found the person who would bring out the best in him. He thought that her dedication to her husband was almost unbelievable. He puzzled over what Graham de Lille Rutherford had that he didn't? Was it just their shared children?

"So, Elizabeth, are you ready for your long flight out East?" asked Melvyn.

"You have to hand it to Terence Barrington," she said. "Downing Street managed to bury my resignation in the NHS crisis."

"Are you travelling together?"

"We are," replied Elizabeth. "We are spending three days at SC Group next week with Norman and Mad Max. I must say, he sounds dishy. Then we'll go to South Korea from Heathrow."

"You're covering South East Asia," said Lord Mallington.

"That's what Norman has said, but it's obvious that his focus is on North Korea. He's told us he's sending his best operative out there."

"Can you two work together?" asked Melvyn.

Elizabeth leaned over and kissed Roland on the cheek.

"We spent the first sixteen years of our lives together," she said. "We're actually twins, although I'm the senior."

"By less than ninety minutes," laughed Roland.

"It's a smart move by our friend, Norman," said Lord Mallington. "You, Elizabeth, have great political connections and Roland is a bright lawyer who has

293

demonstrated an aptitude for the dark side."

"As the Korean ladies will be queuing up to seduce my brother, I'll also be on protective duties," laughed Elizabeth.

"Norman will demand results," warned the peer.

"He'll get them," said Elizabeth. "We're a winning team."

"What's the news about Spartak Grankin?" asked Roland.

Their host ordered a further round of drinks and waited until they had been served.

"He's almost certainly in Lubyanka Prison," he said. "He was taken back to Moscow several days ago." He was enjoying his glass of brandy. "There will be a trial but that will be stage-managed. He's crossed Vladimir Vladimirovich Putin and offending the Russian president usually has one outcome."

"What did he do, Simon?" asked Melvyn Donaldson.

"He was greedy. It's nearly always about money. He was initially really smart. The presidents of both the United States and Russia wanted Brexit to succeed and the UK to leave Europe. A key player has been the Irish Taoiseach because he is a member of the council of the twenty-seven member states. Spartak was funding the Continuity IRA and the Dublin Government." He paused and wiped his lips. "He then fell into the trap of believing his own hype. He was offered a fortune by a group of dissidents in Russia who were building up a network of sleepers in the UK. Moscow found out and was keen to keep it quiet, so they cut off his funding. He therefore needed Graham de Lille's money. In the end he was outsmarted by Isobel de Lille Rutherford."

"And I played her 'MacArthur Park'," thought Roland. "It should have been 'Gorky Park'," he chuckled to himself.

"Where does Mr President of the US of A fit into all of this?" asked Elizabeth.

"From what I gather through our contacts in the CFW, the President will be re-elected," said Lord Mallington. "His interest in a united Ireland will evaporate along with most of his other policies."

"The President does not get the credit he deserves. He's much more aware of detail than any of his predecessors," suggested Elizabeth Shaw.

"Let's be disgraceful," said the peer. He waved at the waiter, who was looking at his watch.

"I've been told that he keeps a transcript in his desk of the speech that the Secretary of State for Homeland Security gave at the CFW dinner. When he's had a row with his wife he sits in the Oval Office and reads it."

The waiter came and took the order.

"I've heard a rumour that he's going to promote Martine Newcross."

*

A House in Fulham, West London. Sunday: morning

Sarah put her shopping bags and overnight case down in the hall and gave Max an affectionate hug. Her decision to leave Najwa with Max and spend the previous day and night in London with Susie, had been a good one. She felt refreshed and was looking forward to the day ahead. She was close to closing down her flat.

Max broke away and asked her to join him in the

lounge. He fussed around the room, straightening the curtains and tidying the cushions. He turned a light on, then off. He stared at Sarah.

"Najwa is not here," he said.

"Why?" asked Sarah. "Where is she?"

"She's on a plane back to the Lebanon," said Max.

"Who has allowed that to happen?" she shouted. "I'm her guardian."

"She's the daughter of a Lebanese couple who were fleeing to Turkey," explained Max. "Najwa was separated from them about a year before you found her. They were searching for her when they came across the doctor who you ambushed at the camp at Bab al-Salameh. He recalled you all too well and from there they traced their daughter to the Mother Mary's House in Turkey. They managed to track down the officials who had organised her papers to allow her to fly to London. They contacted Norman."

"You and Norman decided her fate? Without consulting me?" snapped Sarah.

"Norman told me on Friday that they were in London waiting to be reunited with Najwa. You decided you wanted to see Susie yesterday, and it seemed to me that the best solution was to let Najwa see her parents. When they met, she let out a huge cry and immediately ran to her mother. They hugged each other, Sarah, and Najwa would not let her go."

Max sighed because he was sharing the hurt that Sarah was feeling.

"It was clear that I had to let Najwa go with them. Norman checked – there was no doubt that they are her real parents."

"But why didn't you tell me?" said Sarah.

"We had to make a decision," said Max. "We did

what was best for Najwa."

"Without asking me," she said.

"She was never your daughter," he said.

"But I found her, Max," she said, and tears flowed down her face. She stood up and moved back into the hall where she picked up her case.

"I need to be alone," she said. "I'll be back next week."

"You know I'll be waiting for you," said Max.

"Yes, I know that," she said. She opened the front door as she wiped her face with her handkerchief.

"Max, did Najwa say anything about me? Did she give you a message for me?" she asked.

"She was speaking in French," he said. He watched her begin to leave the house.

"Sarah," he said.

"What?" she replied.

"Norman wants to see us both tomorrow morning."

"I've had my fill of Graham de Lille Rutherford, Max," she said.

"He's sending you to South Korea at the end of the month."

"Why?" she asked.

"He's established a link inside the North Korean inner circle. In early May you're seeing a woman in Seoul who is in contact with Kim Yo Jong."

Sarah came back inside the house and put down her case.

"Is there a file?" she asked.

"It's on the dining room table," said Max.

She went up to her partner and ruffled his hair.

"I better prepare for the meeting," she said. "Will you do me a favour, Max?" She held up a bunch of keys and an envelope. "I've closed down my flat. Can you take these to the letting agent?"

Max looked at the address on the envelope and complained that it was a mile walk. Sarah suggested it would test out his leg and had he remembered to book in for a blood test with the doctor? He left and went straight to the nearest pub. As he enjoyed a pint of real ale, he breathed a sigh of relief. It had been the only way to settle the Najwa situation. He had agonised about telling Sarah that the refugee child had literally flown into the arms of her mother. Max had questioned the father closely, helped by his fluent English. There was no other decision to consider. Najwa had to have the priority she deserved and now she was on her way home.

Mad Max reflected on the last few weeks. His mother was ill and he felt he should go and see her. He had a career secured by a five-year contract with SC Group and a home in Fulham. He needed to sort out Daisy Maitland and ensure she finally rid herself of the poison: he wondered how her relationship with Thelma was progressing.

He knew he shouldn't but he went back to the bar. As he sipped a second pint, he thought about Sarah. Her exploits had been extraordinary; she was different, amazing, and capable of emotional roller-coasters. Max yearned for her complete commitment. It would come, of that he was certain.

*

Sarah settled back into the house and went into the dining room where a green file was laid out on the table. By its side were two pictures in new frames.

One was of Najwa and the other showed the three of them by the poolside at the Paradise Hotel in Samos. Between the two was a red orchid. She sat down and put her head in her hands as she pondered the gesture, which was most unlike Max. It was a close call whether her soon-to-be former husband Nick or Max managed to avoid the romance of giving flowers more often. She then realised that beneath the plant pot was a printed note produced by the florist. It read:

Orchids are a symbol of love, beauty and strength. The word comes from the Greek word 'orchis' meaning 'testicle'. This was because the ancient civilisation thought that the fleshy, underground tubers of the orchid resembled testicles. The red orchid emphasises passion and desire.

Sarah sighed deeply, scanned the contents of the file, stood up and brushed her hair off her face. She wiped her eyes and, before returning to the lounge, tidied her skirt and took another deep breath.

She listened as Max came through the front door. She waited until he joined her in the lounge.

A house in Mayfair, Central London
Sunday: early evening

The ringing of the bell and the simultaneous knocking on the door alerted Isobel de Lille Rutherford that someone was demanding her attention. The children were upstairs preparing for school the next morning. She went to the entrance and viewed the security camera. It was Lady Christel Hemmingway-Brunton who was preparing to knock on the door once more. She was pre-empted by Isobel operating the lock and allowing her visitor to enter.

"Chrissy, what a lovely surprise!" she exclaimed.

"Don't call me that!" she exclaimed. "My name is Lady Christel."

Isobel strode into the lounge, knowing that the irate arrival would follow her. She suggested that Christel sat down and poured a glass of sherry which she handed to her.

"You're angry," she said.

"I thought that you were exaggerating," she exploded. "I never believed you'd manage to get him back here and I am told he'll get a suspended sentence."

Emily put her head round the door and was asked to return upstairs.

"I have done what I believe to be right," explained Isobel. "He is in a poor state of health and the rule of law has taken its course." She paused and looked at the sherry bottle. "My family is together and we will rebuild. Graham will never go near Hope House. We are paying off all his debts." She slammed her fist on the table. "That is what I believe should happen and I make no apology for that." She paused. "Lady Christel," she added.

Her companion stood up.

"But what about our standards?" she exclaimed. "We are born to lead. My husband and I set levels of personal behaviour in our community. Until his premature death, he and I were respected members of society. Your husband is a fraudster and a paedophile."

"What did Alexander die of?" asked Isobel.

Christel put her hand to her eyes in an attempt to conceal her emotion.

"Issy, you know that. He had a heart attack at the age of fifty-two years old. I was widowed and our children lost their father."

"Except that is not true, is it, Chrissy or bloody Lady Christel, if it means that much to you?"

"How dare you, Isobel; how dare you impugn the memory of my husband!"

"He died of a heart attack brought on by syphilis, didn't he?"

Christel seemed bemused and appeared to panic.

She slumped back into the chair as the memories flooded back. The discovery that her husband had been using prostitutes to satisfy his extreme desires. It had started with a visit to her doctor to ask why she had sores in her mouth. Whatever she was given was too late because a week later a blotchy rash appeared on her feet; back to the doctor, and the discovery that she had syphilis. She had screamed with the humiliation and shame. That was before she discovered the genital warts.

Her husband had taken what later seemed to be a rather weak leave of absence from the family wealth management company to accommodate a mid-life crisis by walking the river Nile in Africa. He never came back alive and his illness was covered up by the family at some considerable expense.

"How?" posed Christel, "How did you know?"

Isobel explained that researching the Elite and finding pieces of paper in her husband's study had taught her several new skills.

"I never understood why you went so long without contacting me," she explained, "and then, in recent times, when we met to talk about Graham, something told me you were acting a part. I decided to investigate you."

The two came together and locked in an embrace.

301

As Isobel tried to reassure her friend with a hug that they would have a future together, she felt Christel shake with emotional wreckage. She gently pushed her away and wiped the tears from her face.

"Life's a bugger, isn't it, Chrissy," she smiled.

A House in Fulham, West London
A few days later

Sarah was tired, frustrated and fed up of studying Korea, north and south. Their departure had been delayed by visa difficulties and she was angry that Max was seemingly spending time with Daisy trying to ascertain their progress. Daisy had fallen out with Thelma and was distraught. Sarah was not interested that she was continuing to fight off her Valium habit.

She had taken an instant dislike to Roland and thought that Elizabeth was so enticing that Max would last perhaps two weeks before things developed.

It was not her bloody fault that she was in her middle forties and she was desperately cutting down on the carbohydrates; the luggage around her waist was increasing. She was now running around Hyde Park once a day and all that happened was that she ate more food. Susie had cancelled her visit the coming weekend and the divorce from Nick was now complete. She knew she shouldn't but she telephoned Marcus who put the phone down on her.

The package dropped through the letter box.

Sarah picked it up, tore off the brown paper and discovered a plain cover and a CD. She switched on the television in the lounge and inserted the disc. It started with a mosaic of flowers circulating around the clouds. The camera came down to ground level and there was a children's play-pool and cascading waters. Through the spray came a beautiful young fair-haired girl who swam to the side, lifted herself out of the pool and held up a placard.

"We love you, Sarah," it said and there were her parents beaming, waving and smiling.

Najwa held up a second board.

"We love Hax," it proclaimed.

The scene changed and there was Najwa with three other youngsters all of whom were waving to the camera.

"My brother and sisters," said the notice that was being held up.

Finally, there was Najwa with the smile that Sarah had come to adore.

And that was that.

Sarah Rudd, fortyish, divorced, thickening at the waist and easily jealous, sank to her knees. All she had were the memories. She and Max would stay together: they were a pair. She had a house; a five-year contract; her professional relationship with Norman Delamount, despite his part-pending retirement; Susie; and, a partner.

Within a week she would board an aeroplane which would carry her to one of the most dangerous places in the world. When in North Korea she would infiltrate the inner sanctum. She was just at the start of trying to rescue Elizabeth Shaw from the infamous Kaechon concentration camp, known as Camp 14.

Sarah heard the front door opening. Perhaps Max would help her with her self-defence techniques. She undid the top two buttons of her blouse.

303

Chequers, Buckinghamshire
Sunday: late morning

The church bells were ringing somewhere near to Butler's Cross and reached the hearing of the two walkers, so adding to their joyous reunion. The Prime Minister of the United Kingdom, Terence Barrington, relished these infrequent opportunities when he could enjoy the company of his younger daughter. Corrin Barrington's athletic stride was so reminiscent of her mother and she relished strolling in the grounds of the occasional home of the country's leader, listening to her father.

"I spoke to your sister in South Africa; she seems in good form," he suggested.

"Peach, hell, she's got everything she ever wanted, Dad." She laughed in the same way as his wife. "Hulk of a husband, three kids, a nanny and a home in Cape Town beneath Table Mountain."

They walked on, savouring the early spring air coming off the Chiltern Hills.

"Why did you and Mum call her Peach?" asked Corrin.

"It was your mother's idea," defended Terence Barrington.

"You still miss Mum, don't you, Dad?"

They carried on because neither of them was in any doubt as to the answer to Corrin's question. She kicked over a pile of freshly cut grass.

"You seem to be getting good press, Dad, but did you have to sack the Health Minister?"

Her father laughed and put his arm around her shoulders.

"You make it sound as though I'm in charge of the

country," he chuckled.

"Seriously, Dad. You seem have the European issues under control, the economy is strong, we have full employment, what can go wrong?"

Terence Barrington stopped and turned to face his daughter.

"In the early sixties there was a Conservative Prime Minister called Harold Macmillan," he said. "He was asked by a journalist what was most likely to blow his Government off course. He replied, "Events, dear boy, events"."

They walked on towards the front of Chequers.

"Are you watching events in China, Dad? My fellow doctors in A&E are wondering if the Government are taking them seriously enough."

"You mean the flu epidemic in, er…"

"Wuhan, Dad, in Hubei province. The World Health Organisation is watching it carefully."

"I've read a report prepared by the Minister of Health's senior officials," he said. "I've been to China and seen their 'wet' livestock markets, and they certainly have a different diet to us with their love of snakes and bats."

"Not forgetting the pangolin," laughed Dr Corrin Barrington.

"What is a pangolin?" asked her father.

"It's a small mammal which looks like a scaly anteater. The Chinese eat its meat and the scales are used in their medicines."

The Prime Minister stopped and turned to face his daughter.

"I respect your amazing knowledge, Corrin, and I'll look up the pangolin." He paused and then put his hand underneath her arm. "The advice I have is that

305

it's a flu epidemic and it's a long way from here: in fact, nearly seven thousand miles."

"It's not a flu epidemic, Dad. It is potentially much more serious." She hesitated. "Wuhan is five and half thousand miles from here and the virus almost certainly started with the pangolin which eats bats."

Terence Barrington watched his daughter, who grabbed his hand.

"Please, Dad, now, this minute, instruct your officials that you want a full report on the coronavirus by eight o'clock tomorrow morning."

Terence Barrington stared at his daughter. He would never have believed that a slipped disc could have taken the life of his wife.

He took out of his pocket a mobile phone and called a number. His words could be heard across the Chiltern Hills.

"When I say 'now', I mean 'now', do you understand."

It was not a question.

THE END

ABOUT THE AUTHOR

Tony Drury

Tony is the author of five DCI Sarah Rudd City thrillers. In each, he draws upon his career as a London financier to expose the underworld of dark practices and shadowy characters. None, however, are able to withstand the bravery and incisive detective methods of one of the police force's bravest officers. Her juggling of career demands, husband, children and her own demons, make riveting reading.

He has now written two more novels which trace the early career of probationary police constable Sarah Whitson. In 'On Scene and Dealing' she meets her future husband Nick. In 'Journey to the Crown' she has a devastating affair with Dr Martin Redding. The final chapter jumps ahead to sample her future life as a private detective.

Tony has created an innovative series as a novella writer. Reflecting iconic cinema classics, his first was 'Lunch with Harry', which is inspired by 'Breakfast at Tiffany's' followed by four more. City Fiction (www.cityfiction.co.uk) has attracted new authors and the series now has ten titles.

Aged seventy-three, Tony is a follower of the wisdom of Albert Einstein: "When a man stops learning, he starts dying." He lives in Bedford with his wife Judy. They value every trip down the M1 to Watford to be with Grandson Henry.

Email: tonydrury39@btinternet.com
Website: www.tonydrury.com
Twitter: @mrtonydrury